DEAD MAN'S CUT

ROSS CROTHERS

Disclaimer: All characters appearing in this work are fictitious. Any resemblance to real persons, living or dead is purely coincidental.

Acknowledgements:
My thanks to the following wonderfully talented people, who have helped, professionally and otherwise, bring this book into the physical and online world.....

Alexandra Nahlous – Editor
Graham Toseland – A Fading Street – Proofreading
Ginger Marks – DocUmeant Publishing and Design – Cover Design
Jason and Marina Anderson – Polgarus Studio – Formatting
And to my wife and daughter for their (sometimes solicited) advice, in keeping the whole work moving forward.

For more information on Ross Crothers and his books, visit
www.rosscrothers.com
www.facebook.com/rosscrothersauthor
www.twitter.com/RossCrothers

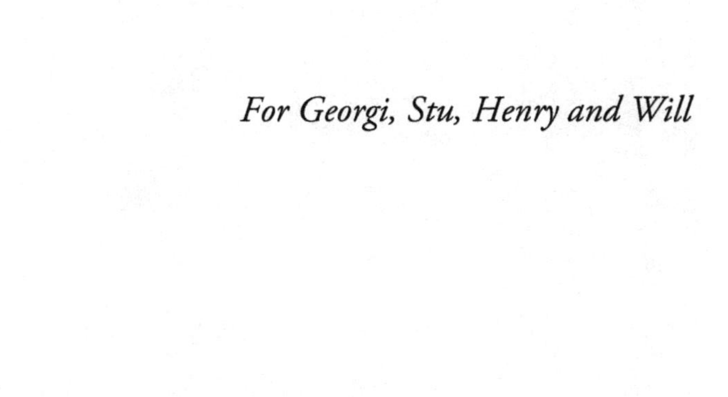

For Georgi, Stu, Henry and Will

1

The explosion in my left ear was the first clue that all was not right. The furious sound and burning smell of metal searing across asphalt, was the second. When we stopped on a steep slope, maybe forty-five degrees, well that was the clincher.

I was at the bottom.

Trapped.

Silence.

Metallic dust filled the air.

I coughed.

Couldn't move. Knees pinned by the collapsed dash.

"You okay, Sal?" I said.

More silence. Black silence.

I coughed again.

A sharp light flashed through the windscreen. Blinded me for a second. A male voice called out, "Shit, mate, are you alright?"

"Can you roll us the right way up? Gotta get to the hospital," I said. "Wife's having a baby."

"Hold on, buddy," said the voice.

Sirens started. Getting closer.

The dust, thick from the heavy, humid air, settled in my eyes and mouth. The acidic taste was bitter, stinging.

The siren wailed right on top of me. Then it stopped.

Somebody pulled Sally out, and a paramedic stuck his head in.

"Take her to Prince of Wales, fast," I said. "Baby's name is Jack."

He said, "You hang in there, mate. Okay?"

Time passed. Quickly? Slowly? I don't know. Maybe both.

A machine started—loud in my left ear again. Someone said, "This'll be noisy, but we'll have you out in a jiffy." It was like a giant can opener, and they cut the car out around me. Lights swirled. Another car lay flipped on its roof about thirty yards away. I wondered what it was doing there. A paramedic led me to an ambulance, and they took me to St. Vincent's hospital.

A nurse from Accident and Emergency ushered me aside and I caught a glimpse—my headshot—in a mirror. Blood streaked across my face, onto my shirt. Under the fluorescent light it looked gruesome, but strangely it didn't hurt. She cleaned me up for twenty minutes. When she was done, there wasn't a scratch. Sally's blood, I guess.

In a narrow hospital room, under a harsh ceiling light, I sat alone on a small bed against a wall, legs dangling, trying to make sense of what had happened. A mid-twenties policeman came in.

He took off his cap. "Are you Commander Ash Todd from the Australian Federal Police?"

I nodded. He handed me my wallet and badge. "Found these in your car."

Another slightly older cop arrived. Similar age as me. They both stood mute for a moment, heads down. Not a good look.

The older one shook his head. "Commander, I'm very sorry, but your wife didn't make it."

My mind whirred…confused. Sally…didn't make it where? Here? This guy's got it wrong. She's at Prince of Wales—the maternity hospital. I was in St. Vincent's because it was the closest emergency ward to the accident.

"My wife?" I said. "No, no…my wife is…different hospital… she's in Prince of Wales. Having our baby."

"I'm sorry, sir. They had to bring her here. No time…you see…"

This couldn't be. We've only been married a little while. This is not what happens. Not when you're having a baby. That was it…they had the wrong woman.

"It's the surnames. I'm Todd, she's Sinclair…that's the problem." I felt my spirits lift a little. But the cop just looked away.

A doctor appeared, dressed in a blue operating gown, a mask hanging loosely around his neck.

"I'm sorry, Commander." He placed a hand on my shoulder. "There was just nothing we could do."

Nothing they could do? The words echoed in my head. *Nothing they could do?* At that moment, I felt a pain. Middle of my stomach, and it felt like I'd been whacked with a sledgehammer. A hard belt of reality, which didn't feel real. My thoughts raced to a dozen different, muddled places in succession. None of them made sense. I gasped a breath. I felt empty. All these fuzzy, churning ideas raced through me, with no beginning and no end, yet my mind and body felt completely vacant. Come on, I told myself...*focus*.

"What about the baby?" I rasped. The doctor shook his head. Another nurse came in with Sally's hospital bag and a teddy bear.

"So...you mean...they're dead. Both of them?" I barely choked the words out. The policemen, the nurse, and the doctor stood almost to attention. None spoke. After an awkward silence, the doctor merely nodded and said again, "I'm sorry."

Somehow, I managed to shuffle from the hospital to a waiting police vehicle, though I don't remember a single step. The two officers drove me home in silence. I couldn't bring myself to look at the bear.

The older cop looked back at me, as they pulled up outside my apartment block.

"Have you got family we can call?"

"No. They were my family. That's it."

"Is there anything you'd like us to do?"

In the heavy, suffocating blackness that had enveloped the street, the police car, the two cops, and me, I could only think of one thing.

"Bring them back."

2

For four months, I was married to Sally Sinclair. A lawyer. Tall, long legs, very pretty, very smart. We lived in an apartment in Elizabeth Bay, in Sydney, overlooking the harbour. Two bedrooms, the second one very small, and a balcony covered in brown tiles and surrounded by a glass railing. Ugly things those tiles, from the 1970s I think. But the balcony looked out onto that blue water through the glass, so I didn't notice the tiles.

We'd been together for about a year. Ten months ago, Sally fell pregnant. I don't know if we were in love when we kicked off, but I do know that by three months in, we were. Head over heels, as they say. Pregnancy can do that to a man. The mother glows. Sally glowed. Every day she looked more beautiful. Every day I was busting just to feel her belly. We took long walks. I liked that—so I could show her to the world. Look—this is my woman. Look—she's having a baby. My baby.

We married five months into the pregnancy, in a little, old, brown-brick church up the hill in Kings Cross. The druggies used to camp in the entry vestibule, until they put big metal gates across it. Now they just piss against the church wall, so it always seems to stink a bit. No big deal wedding, her parents are dead, as are mine. So, we invited a few friends, maybe ten or so.

All twelve of us piled into the church, which left plenty of vacant space if anyone else was interested in witnessing the nuptials. No-one was. My best mate, Dick Mayvers, was my best man. He's an Australian Federal Policeman, like me. We started together, and are in the same unit. Have been since day one. I've got a few other mates…mostly from the Feds…but it's pretty much Dick and me who are the closest. It's funny, but I don't keep a lot of friends. Never did. One or two up in Queensland…from my days in the force up there…but I haven't seen them for half-a-decade, or more. Guess I just like my own company…and in this career, solo is less complicated.

Anyway, Dick got a new girlfriend about the same time I hitched up with Sally, and our lives seem to run in parallel. The only small difference is he's a Superintendent, and I'm a Commander. And a detective too. On the job, we're all Field Officers, or FO's, but it means I'm winning. Or so I tell him.

Julie Fotheringham-Smythe was the best girl, or matron-of-honour, or whatever. We call her Fothers—it's just easier. She and Sally were best friends from school, and now she's a mother of three and lives across the harbour at Mosman. Married to an investment banker called Simon. Shitloads of money, nice big house, two BMWs. I'm six-five, and on tiptoes I can just about see their big house from our little, brown-tiled balcony.

The marriage service was quick, and we gave the nice minister a decent wad of cash for his effort, which made him happy. Then all twelve of us walked down the hill in the warm autumn sunshine, and squeezed into our little apartment for the wedding breakfast. Actually, it was about ten hours of booze and food. I made a speech no-one can remember, which is a good thing. Everyone knew about the baby—they all wanted to pat Sally's stomach too. The tests showed it was a boy.

The labour pains began. They were quite some time apart, maybe a few times a day at first, then several hours. Late one evening, they got much closer together. Five minutes or so. Sally was booked into hospital—Prince of Wales—a fifteen-minute drive. Ten if I used my badge. Now, they were four minutes apart. I said, "What's a minute or so?" Wrong attitude apparently. At three minutes apart, and at eight minutes to one in the morning, Sally said, "Time to go."

I got her to the car, hospital bag in tow. In it was a small teddy bear for our soon-to-be, Jack Todd. Two minutes apart. I took off—up through Kings Cross, past the strip joints, across the William Street overpass, and hurtled though Darlinghurst. Made a set of lights, just. I'm sure it wasn't red. Empty streets, no traffic, eighty kilometres an hour…twenty, no…thirty, over the limit. Another set of lights, staying green. We made these, easy.

Someone else made them at the same time.

3

There was a funeral, and it was held at the little old brown-brick church with a grey slate roof, up the hill in Kings Cross. The one where we were married.

This time it was full, but I'm not sure who was there. A hearse took mother and baby away, as one, for the cremation. Nobody seemed to know what to say, and frankly, I didn't want anyone to say anything. I walked down the hill, alone, to our little apartment and stared at the harbour. All that was one month ago.

I went back to work a few days later. I took to the gym—twice daily workouts. I had to do something, and sitting on my butt staring at nought was doing my head in. Nobody at the office seemed to know what to say, and I still didn't want them to. They'd shake my hand, or pat me on the back, but they couldn't look at me.

And then came the booze. Bourbon mostly, but sometimes whisky. A bottle a night and maybe more. After a while I stopped counting…it didn't seem important, so I drank until the pain went away. The mental pain, mostly, but also the physical. The thump in the gut.

Sally would appear in my alcohol fuelled dreams, in the middle of the night, with the same question. *"What were you doing…?"* I had no answer, and anyway, she was gone again before I could find one. When I woke, anytime from four o'clock on, my mind played out that drive to the hospital over and over. It was too fast…I was going too fast. Somehow, I had to find a way to do it again, but with a different result.

Sometimes, mid-dream, an answer would arrive. Cindy. My thoughts would race to our affair on the Riviera, the year before. I could feel the sweat from our bodies, pressed together in the little hotel room above the harbour. The affair I had when Sally had fallen pregnant. The pregnancy I didn't know about…but that was no excuse. And it threw up another question. *Was this a payback for the fling with Cindy…?*

The office gave me no new cases. Maybe they thought I couldn't handle them. I pored over old files—some approaching cold-case status. First a drug shipment from Asia, which we'd been watching nineteen months earlier. The cargo was jettisoned off the coast north of Broome for a local pickup and promptly sank. Its caretakers fled the scene before anyone in authority realised what had happened.

The second involved an investment banker, one Brendan O'Hara, who had misplaced some funds from the boutique institution he headed in Perth. Apparently eleven million dollars had vanished out of a total of thirty-five million. His backers were not pleased, it seems. Then Brendan vanished. No word of him for over two years. Nothing of interest in either of those.

Despite my nightly dose of bourbon, sleep became increasingly difficult. Sometimes, after untold re-runs of the hospital trip and just as I was deciding I should crawl from bed and get to work, I'd fall asleep. Then I'd wake mid-morning, and in a panic, drag some clothes on…any clothes…and dash to the office. Often, I turned up unwashed, unshaved, and reeking of last night's stale booze. My immediate superior, Andrew McPherson, ignored the first few slip-ups.

Mac, an Assistant Commissioner usually based in Canberra, was the most senior person in the Sydney office. He held the title of National Manager Serious and Organised Crime and officially was on secondment to Sydney. It had been so long, it seemed the move was permanent. On the third…or fourth…occasion, he pulled me aside and said, "Ash, I know it's a tough time, but you've got to get a grip on yourself."

I stepped back, hands on hips and stared him down. "Get a grip? Who are you kidding, buddy? Have you ever tried this shit?" I could feel the booze doing the talking, taking over my mind to the point that it seemed the words came from a totally different person. Mac simply looked away and moved off. I don't think he knew how to handle it…me, the situation, grief, or any other part of the whole mess. Not part of the Fed's training.

At other times, with my head banging and too tired to bother dressing, I'd simply ring in sick and crawl back to bed, curled into a sort of semi-foetal position. How long I stayed there was anybody's guess. I became increasingly difficult, and I knew it…but I didn't care. Caring had long since deserted me. Someone running a red light, just like I had done only moments before the smash, had changed my world forever. They told me he was dead too. Care-factor? Zero.

Two weeks later, on an otherwise perfectly agreeable spring

day, I snapped. I couldn't concentrate. The crap on my desk bored me. Letitia, our plumpish, bubbly PA popped her head in my door. She smiled her angelic smile. "You want to come down for coffee?"

I looked up at Letitia and gave her a hard stare. Just like the one I'd given McPherson. Her being so upbeat irritated me. Why should she be so happy? Was she trying to make me feel sorry? I said, "No. I don't want to go anywhere for fucking coffee." Letitia's gentle face began to crumple, and she scurried off in tears. I usually don't swear…at least not at women. And certainly not at soft, placid Letitia. I felt bad already, and now I felt worse.

I sat at my desk, head buried in my hands, and felt the sting of my own tears rise. In the six weeks since Sally and Jack's death, I hadn't cried. When my parents died, I didn't cry. But then, they were pretty old, so maybe they didn't need crying over. No, I didn't cry. This was all my damn fault, and crying wouldn't fix it. Wouldn't bring them back. I blinked the tears away, and bashed both fists down on the desk.

After some moments frozen in a mixture of anger, frustration, and grief, I looked up to see McPherson staring at me. A big, burly man, with wavy brown hair and dark eyes…his frame overfilled the doorway. He fixed me with a gaze of concern and sympathy. At least, that is the way I like to think of it. Otherwise it was a look of horror.

"Ash," he said, "this is no good. You're a mess, and it pains me to say this, but you're also a potential risk to this office. And to yourself."

I stared at him. "You want my resignation?"

He shook his head. "Take time out—whatever you need. Get

away, get professional help. Your office will be here when you get back."

I fixed my gaze on my desk, seeing nothing. All I could think was that I was now unwanted. Of no use…to anyone.

"Sure, sure, you're the boss…so what do you suggest? I've already got too much free time. Middle of the night, and all that." My smart-arse tone wouldn't have gone unnoticed, but he didn't flinch.

"You take a break—I'll see what I can do to help."

"Right. Help, eh? And how are *you* going to help? I'm out of here. I know when the odds are stacked against me." I stood, and with a sweeping right-arm motion, made an exaggerated bow at McPherson and said, "Sayonara, old pal."

I shoved my chair in hard against the desk, and grabbed my coat. McPherson stepped from the doorway to let me pass. My phone rang. I snapped it up.

"Yeah, what?"

"Ash, darling!" The gentle, sweet voice stopped me mid-stride. A voice I hadn't heard for weeks.

"Fothers?"

"Thought I'd check-in…see how you are getting by. How about lunch?"

4

The view through the huge picture window was sublime. Across the Macau waterfront and Nam Van Lake, across the bridges linking Macau to its islands of Taipa and Coloane, and out to sea. An infinite mass of water, all the way to the bottom of the earth. All was quiet. Bullet-proof glass cancelled traffic noise from the streets below. The only sound…the faintest 'shhh'…came from the air-conditioning system.

Sebastian Lam stood at the window, taking it all in. Arms crossed, he lightly fingered the lapel of his suit coat. The delicate texture of the cloth was soothing. Just knowing the cost of it made him feel powerful. It reinforced his feeling of command. He turned his attention slightly to the left, taking in the sweep of casinos. The two monoliths of MGM and Wynn. Their high-roller rooms were nothing compared to *his*. His *whole* operation was high-roller.

Minimum bet, five hundred thousand US dollars. Minimum daily wager per member, two million US dollars. Can't find two mill? Don't bother showing. The place was booked solid for the next six months. Four hundred of the wealthiest men and women on the planet, desperate to do business with Sebastian Lam. He smiled inwardly at the thought, and resumed his gaze over the lake.

Lam's vast suite took up a little over three thousand square feet. Two thousand of that was office…plush, deep-red, down-filled sofas, and a gently curved, jade-coloured, marble-topped desk, all carefully arranged on a striking herringbone parquetry floor of Purpleheart. To the far left-hand-side, taking in a full view of the Bank of China, sat a board table. Black marble, with ten black, high-backed leather chairs each side and one at each end. The chair at the end closest to the entrance door had a slightly higher back than the others. Lam's chair.

Spanning twenty-feet either side of the corner behind his desk, were forty-eight closed-circuit television screens. Six per row, four rows deep. Two banks of each. The left bank covered the basement, the discreet, street-level lobby with twenty-four-hour concierge, and the first three levels of the Lam operation. Reception, office, housekeeping, and security on the first…and five one-bedroom suites on each of the second and third. Six-star naturally.

The right bank covered the next five levels. A further five suites on each of the fourth and fifth and three exquisite private dining rooms and two bars, on the sixth. But it was the seventh and eighth levels which were the driving force of this enterprise. Five private gaming rooms per floor, ten in total. Four of baccarat, and three each of blackjack and roulette.

On his desk sat a further five screens. One large screen which was connected to the house computer, showed a continuous state of house profits from each of the tables in the five gaming rooms.

The other was Lam's personal computer. Three smaller screens were connected to cameras covering Mr Lam's floor—one each for his lobby, his office, and his bedroom suite. These five screens were for Lam's eyes only.

Sebastian Lam could slink in his oversize office chair, and survey his little kingdom in a matter of seconds. It occupied the nine uppermost levels of one of the most prominent buildings on the Macau waterfront. The most circumspect gambling operation in Macau. Totally under the radar. No phone listing, no website. Members only. And membership by invitation only. Bigger than high-rollers. Whales, the lot of them.

A bespoke casino…made to measure punting. What a genius idea. Founded by his father, and now controlled by Sebastian. Yes, sir, he did enjoy being top-dog of The Golden Mountain Club.

5

I pulled my apartment door closed behind me, and let my breath slide out with a small hiss, as I made my way down the fire escape and out into the street. Even the simple act of stepping out in public seemed to require a concerted effort to relax. And I'd taken to using the fire stairs so I didn't have to stand close to someone in the lift. That awkward silence…and then they'd ask me something…just to appear friendly. But I didn't want to have to answer anything…to anyone. Checked my watch—midday. On time at least.

At 11:00 a.m. it had been raining hard. The day was windless, so the rain sheeted straight down, turning the harbour into steel-grey froth. The whole view from my apartment had looked like a one dimensional, charcoal-coloured canvas. Now the clouds hung low, but the rain had stopped.

My head still hurt a touch. The whisky from last night was obviously more than the recommended quantity for one sitting. Same as yesterday. Only that I put down to bourbon. Hell, I'd even put ice in it. They say water is good for you…but it's not that good. My head was proof. I'd gulped a couple of painkillers, stood motionless under a steamy shower for what seemed like half-an-hour, and pulled on clean jeans, t-shirt, and a waterproof jacket.

I had plenty of time to walk the few blocks up the hill to my date. Lunch with Julie Fotheringham-Smyth. Fothers. I was touched that she'd rung in the first place, but then I rationalised it all away, as usual. After all, she was Sally's best friend. She probably just wanted to give me space to get my head right. And that didn't work. Of all the things that were wrong, the most wrong was my head.

I reached the end of the block and on a whim, decided to take a quick detour. On the opposite side of the street, at the back-end of a dark, narrow laneway flanked by a couple of cream-painted 1920s walk-up apartment blocks, sat the workshop of my motor mechanic, Vince Lombardi. Cars tandem-parked four deep, and jammed door-to-door so tight an anorexic jockey would have had trouble gaining access. All this on a lightly greased cement floor. Grease seemed to feature prominently in his world—everything had a fine film covering it. Except the cars. They were kept pristine. I had no idea how he knew what car needed to be where, but somehow it worked.

I liked Vince. He had a client base that read like a who's who of Sydney's Eastern Suburbs colourful characters—SP bookmakers, drug dealers, pimps, hookers, and bagmen of all kinds. And the odd politician. I knew this because I'd seen many of them over the years, as they collected their cars. And I had file pictures of more than a few on my office computer. Or did, before I began my enforced holiday. If you asked Vince what work any of them did, he had absolutely no idea. "Not a clue, mate," he would say in his Australian-Italian accent. "So long they pay, I no care."

He had an opinion on nearly everything, mostly negative. As in, "I don't know what the country is coming to. Young people, you know, have no respect." He knew gossip on nearly everybody of note in the city, except of course his clients. Vince was only in his early fifties, but was going to retire soon. Or so he said. Had been for the last ten years, and I reckoned one day he'd be right. "There's no money in fixing cars anymore, mate," he'd say, shaking his head as he handed over the invoice. When I read the bottom line, I wondered if we were talking about the same piece of paper.

"Heyyy, Ash," Vince called out as I approached. "How you doin', eh?"

"Great mate, just great. Listen, I'm thinking of getting a convertible. Gotta get a new car, so what do you think?"

Vince appeared to give the idea serious thought, frowning, rubbing his chin. Then he turned his black eyes up to me and said, "What you want a bloody convertible for? You too big. And they leak, some of 'em, so she'll be all the time in here for fixin'…not that I mind of course, and you know my rates are reasonable…too bloody reasonable and that's why I'm gonna give it all away, see…"

I held my hands up in mock surrender. "Okay mate, I got it. Just a thought. Catch you later." I turned on my heel, and headed back down the laneway.

I strolled on up the hill and into the small café I'd suggested for a bite. Fothers was already seated at a window table, her red raincoat and matching umbrella neatly stashed in the corner behind her chair. She stood, gave me a kiss on each cheek, clasped my arms and leant back to get a proper fix on my face.

"You look good," she said, "better than I expected."

"So do you." And she did. But she always did. Immaculately groomed, her shoulder-length blonde hair flopped gently onto a camel-coloured waistcoat over a red and white striped blouse. Black, tight leggings hugged her firm bottom, and for this coolish day at least, black knee-boots completed the outfit. As far as I could tell, Fothers' daily ritual consisted of getting her children off to school…coffee, lunch, and shopping with friends somewhere…and being home for the kids after school. In between she went to the gym, played tennis, and practised yoga. Otherwise she co-ordinated an army of home help—cleaner, gardener, grocery delivery, and the occasional tradesman.

She pushed back again and her deep-blue eyes gave me a harder, piercing stare. "Now I look again, maybe not," she said. "Your eyes are shot, Ash. And what's that smell? Are you drinking?"

"Well…maybe a little." I looked away. I felt like a pimple-faced schoolboy who'd been sprung dissecting a porn magazine. She dipped her head and screwed her nose, giving me a stern look of disapproval as we sat down.

"Sorry I'm late," a familiar voice mumbled behind me, breaking the silence. I looked around to see Dick Mayvers.

"Don't get up—I'll get my own chair," he said. He winked at Fothers, pulled one in from a neighbouring table, and shook my hand.

I shot him a startled, open-mouthed look. "What are you doing here?"

"Yeah…very well…thanks for asking. And you?" His gentle

mocking caused me to snort out a short laugh. It was a strange feeling, that small release, and I suddenly realised it was the first happy sound I'd made in weeks.

"I'm...okay." Had I said anything else, Mayvers would have called me on it straight away. He knew 'okay' was a stretch, but anything better than that would have resulted in a resounding "*Bullshit!*"

"Ash," Fothers cut in, "I hope you don't mind me asking Dick to come along, because there are a couple of things I wanted to talk to you about."

"A couple of things? You only rang a few days ago...just to see how I was...the list is building pretty fast."

She ignored my poor attempt at humour. "Well, I really did want to see you...to check in...I figured it had been long enough, and I was neglecting you. I was always there for Sal, and she was there for me, and I realised I hadn't been there for you. Then...after I called the other day, you sounded so...I don't know..."

"Agitated?"

"No...awful, I think. Distressed, was what I told Simon. Anyway, we decided I should ring Dick, and see if, collectively, we could do something to help. So that's why he's here."

I nodded, but I was wary of anyone offering assistance. It always seemed to end up with them thinking you owed them, no matter how strong the friendship. "Very kind, but I don't see what you can do. Or Tricky, here..." I said, putting my arm across Mayvers' shoulders, and giving him a shake. "I've got to get through this myself."

"No, you don't," said Mayvers, trying to brighten the mood a little. "I've been chatting to McPherson, and I've got a little proposition for you."

A waitress, dressed entirely in black, with powerful black eye makeup and a couple of kilos of metallic adornment covering every visible orifice, poured water for each of us, placed the bottle in the middle of the table, and handed out menus. I waited for her to disappear.

I looked at them both. Chatting, were they? About me? I leant in and whispered, "How many people are in on my case? Can't a bloke grieve privately?"

"Grieve, yes," Mayvers said, "but self-destruct? Not while we're here. Anyway, I want you to think back to your early days with the Feds…soon after you left Brisbane and came down to Sydney."

"Yeah, right. What about it?" My mind began to flick back a decade.

"Who was the best field officer…who helped you the most… took you under his wing?"

"Ahh…that would be Bynow. Bruce Bynow," I said, "he really showed me the ropes. Good guy, Bruce, but he's long gone."

"Yeah," Mayvers said, "so have you heard from him since?"

"Not for years. Went to Asia, or somewhere, didn't he?"

"He did. Mac knows all about him, and suggested I give him a call and go over your situation. I hope that's cool with you, because it's too late anyhow…I've done it."

"What have you done?"

"Bynow is a PI in Hong Kong. And from what I understand, has a bloody good business up there. So, I called him and told him your story. Or the more recent bits of it."

"You mean the boozing?"

Mayvers' eyes crinkled as he fixed me with a sideways grin. "Not specifically…I thought I'd leave that to you. Anyway, the long and short of it is he wants you to get in touch. He might have some work you can help him with. Be a good break from here, I reckon, and give you something useful to do without the pressure from the office."

I looked down at the table and fiddled with the cutlery. "I…don't know…maybe…I just don't know what to do…"

Fothers put her hands over mine, her eyes earnest, almost pleading. "Ash, no matter what, Sally wouldn't want you to be like this. Maybe you feel like the accident was your fault. Well it wasn't, and you've got to believe it. Dick tells me even the investigating police confirmed it. Isn't that right Dick?"

I cast Mayvers a glance. "Sure is," he said, "and you'll hear no more of it from them."

"But I was thrashing it…way too fast. If I'd just been…you know…taking it easy…?"

Fothers cut in, "Ash…that's a '*what if?*' We all have those, and there are just some things we'll never know. Somehow you have to find a way to let it go…so you can function again. This would be such a good break for you…just for a while…"

I took all this in slowly. These two were ganging up on me, and that was a feeling I didn't like. Maybe they thought it was for my own good, but I didn't like being crowded into a corner. Maybe if I humoured them…go along with their little game…they might leave me alone.

"A private investigator, eh? In steamy Asia? Maybe…maybe." I nodded at the thought. "Bynow got a number?"

Mayvers pulled a piece of paper from his coat pocket, and slid it across. "He says call him anytime."

"Okay…maybe…okay." My head was down, peering intently at the paper but not really registering what was written.

The metallic waitress reappeared without a sound and opened her pad. "Ready to order?" We gave her our selections, and she looked up and said, "Any drinks?"I turned to scan the shelves up high, behind the register. Bottles of booze lined the two top rows. My trained eye spotted what looked like bourbon, and a whisky, side-by-side, but I didn't recognise the maker.

"Is that bourbon?" I pointed to a blue-labelled bottle.

"You got it, honey," replied our waitress, "want one?" I glanced back, and realised both my dining companions were holding me in a steady, very serious gaze. My face flushed at the attention…the sheer scrutiny…and I looked up at Ms Metal.

"Just coffee for me thanks. Black. No sugar."

6

The grey phone on Sebastian Lam's desk blooped quietly. There were three phones in a neat line—one grey, one black, and one red. Deep-red, just like his sofas, and his chair. The grey phone blooped again.

Lam diverted his attention from the view over the water, moved quietly to the chair behind his desk, and pressed the 'Talk' button.

A sweet-voiced receptionist came on the line. "Mr Lam, you have a visitor arriving in about six minutes," she said. Perfect English, with a soft Chinese accent.

"Thank you, Lily, and who would that be?"

"Mr Zhou, from Shanghai. Our driver just called."

Lam stiffened at Zhou's name, swallowed hard, drew a long breath, and let it out so Lily couldn't hear. He clenched his teeth and smiled. "Excellent. The usual fingerprint identification of course. He may complain, but if so tell him we are fully booked."

"Yes, Mr Lam."

Lam swivelled in his chair to take in the screens showing the gaming rooms. Blackjack 2 would be ideal. Only one other client currently playing. Zhou disliked crowded games. Lam pressed line number two on the black phone.

He could see the room manager pick up his call. "Yes, Mr Lam?"

"Zhou Wei Li, in fifteen minutes. I'll advise details shortly. A bottle of Laphroaig 40 Year Old, and two glasses. Do we still have some 1966 Cohibas?"

"I believe so, sir."

"Then three of those. I will return."

Lam glanced at the screen covering the street entrance. The club's courtesy limo, a black Rolls Phantom was parked outside, the driver retrieving a suitcase from the trunk. Mr Zhou stood inside the street reception vestibule, being greeted by security and receptionist. Both appeared to be making an appropriate fuss of him. The driver deposited the case, and the receptionist accompanied Zhou to the lift, and up to check-in.

Lam followed the progress of his client on the screens. Once he arrived at check-in, Lam flicked on the sound button on his remote. He could hear Zhou say, "This is outrageous, checking my fingerprints. You must know who I am? I won't agree to it."

Right on cue Lily said, "Of course, Mr Zhou, but we are fully booked, and we have clients waiting for a cancellation. Do you wish to...?"

"No, here," said Zhou, thrusting his hand out for scanning.

Lam smirked as he watched on. He loved the idea of shoving a big stick up the arse of someone important...show them who was in charge in this place. But reality returned, and he stiffened again. He moved to check his own presentation in a mirror by the board table. Brushed off the shoulders of his coat and pulled it straight, swept back his hair, and at the sound of a sharp rap on his office door, flicked the remote. All forty-eight screens went black.

Lam opened the giant door and beamed. Zhou, slightly taller than Lam but equally as thin, stepped inside. He moved with ease. He was dressed in a light-grey three-piece suit, royal blue shirt, and a bold red and yellow floral silk tie. Black brogues gleamed against the parquetry floor. A mother-of-pearl tipped cane dangled from his left hand, and a gold fob chain snaked across his waistcoat. At sixty-eight he didn't need the cane yet, but liked the effect. Lam noticed these things. Quality always impressed him, and Zhou looked as though he had flown in direct from his tailor.

"Ah, Mr Zhou, welcome. How was your flight?"

Zhou eyed Lam up and down. No emotion, no smile. Maybe the slightest hint of a frown. "Just so-so. Much turbulence over Guangzhou."

Lam indicated for Zhou to sit on a sofa, taking in the view. "Thank you, Lam, I'll stand. Been sitting all day." He did take in the view however, and stood with his back to the whole office. He leaned forward slightly, both hands clasped lightly on his cane.

"So, how's the petrochemical industry? Still booming, I trust?" Lam liked to make light chat initially, but he also desired to keep abreast of his client's interests. After all, they were also his interests. And it might deflect Zhou's thoughts from anything else.

"Ah, we always live in interesting times." Zhou's response seemed half-hearted…almost automatic. He remained staring out to sea.

Lam sensed he needed to keep things moving. "We certainly do. I believe your luggage has transferred to your room. I've taken the opportunity to place you at a discreet blackjack table, with one other. I hope you find the whisky and cigars to your liking. Any issues, please just ask the room manager, and he will attend to it. Now, do you have an investment in mind?"

Zhou spun on his heel to face Lam, his face all business. "I've given it some thought, and I don't have much time. I need to be on my way by mid-tomorrow. Four hundred million Yuan—can you handle it?"

For a moment Lam feigned serious contemplation, crossing his arms, and resting his chin on an index finger. Fifty million US? In two sittings? He beamed his dazzling white smile, extended his right hand for Zhou's, and placed his left on Zhou's back to direct him to the door. Zhou ignored the attempted handshake.

"Of course, Mr Zhou. Whatever you require, The Golden Mountain Club can accommodate."

"Good." Zhou stared at Lam. "And my other money? You found it yet?"

The question Lam hoped wouldn't surface. He stiffened again. This time he faltered…on defence. "No…n-no…unfortunately, not yet."

"Then you'd better damn well try harder."

At that precise moment, Sebastian Lam did not feel in charge.

7

I turned on my iPad and clicked on the email tab. It was showing eight unread messages. Three were from survey companies or something similar. They wanted to know what I thought of things. I didn't give a shit about their things. Hit delete. I looked out on the harbour.

It had finally stopped raining, after two solid days. Still grey, though. My head hurt again. I made a firm decision to change brand of bourbon. The ice I put in it still wasn't working. Damn it, I'd even been to the gym to punch some blood round the system. That should've stopped the bourbon from attacking me. I didn't have much energy, though. Normally I can press three hundred, or more. Flat out at two yesterday.

Two emails from car salesmen. I'd been looking at a convertible, despite Vince's dire warning, and now they had my details they were like terrier dogs with their deals. Vince was probably right, and anyway these guys were becoming too pushy. Hit delete.

I wandered into the kitchen, and made some coffee. Somewhere in a nearby street there was a loud screech, and a thump. The sound gave me a start, and I felt a wave of nausea hit. I don't even know if nausea is the right word—it's a punch in the gut and it's not just a thought. It's a real physical sensation in the pit of my stomach. I guess it is from my trip to the hospital, and I carry the sound, smell, and feel of it in my system, everywhere. I peered out a side window, but couldn't see any action. Must be blocked out by the next-door buildings. Bad start for a Sunday for someone. I shuffled back to the computer.

An email from my gym, offering a super deal for the next six months. The last six-month one I took up was supposed to be the best deal in the country, but apparently not. They now had one even better. Nope, forget that. Hit delete.

Another email from Veronica. I opened the attachment. Her blonde-haired snap smiled tantalisingly at me. Big boobs. She wanted to begin correspondence. Maybe even get married. I'd received emails from her before, as well as from Natalie, and Natasha and a host of others. Russians supposedly, but they could be anybody. They always looked very appealing, but what hell would unleash if I were silly enough to respond, I wondered? Took a sip of coffee, as I considered her attractive offer. Sorry, not today. Hit delete.

I headed for the kitchen again, made some toast and another coffee, and gazed out over the water. The day seemed to be brightening a bit, and I hoped that my own fog would start to lift soon, too. It seemed to go on forever. On the far side of the harbour a huge passenger ship made it's slow, elegant departure from Sydney toward the Heads. It let off a couple of short, mighty horn blasts, which gave me a start. As I picked up my coffee, I realised Bruce Bynow's number was sitting beside it, staring up at me from the bench. Nearly forty-eight hours since my little lunch with Fothers and Dick, and I still hadn't made the call.

I sat back on my sofa, sipped at the coffee, and fiddled with the small piece of paper, finding reason after reason not to pick up the phone. What good would it do? Why would Bynow be interested in helping me, after all this time? Surely it was better to do this myself, to get over things, at home, where I wouldn't bother anyone else? At some point during this internal self-evasion, my phone rang. I just managed to answer it before the voicemail kicked in.

"Ash Todd?" A male voice, and it seemed vaguely familiar.

I hadn't spotted the caller's number, so I kept my response frugal. "Possibly."

"Bruce Bynow here. Mate, I'm sorry to hear your news. Dick Mayvers called me…maybe he told you…and I had no idea. So, how you doin'?"

"Bruce…good to hear from you. Yeah, he mentioned you'd been talking. Thanks for your concern, but I'm okay."

"Ash…I realise this may seem pretty quick, particularly as we haven't spoken in a long time, but Dick said you might be interested in getting away for a bit. Believe me, I understand. Been through it a bit, myself. Anyway…"

An angry flash shot through my head, and I could feel my face redden with it. What would he understand? I've killed my wife and baby…all my fault…and now I have nothing. How would he know what it was like?

"How do you know…?" My question trailed off as Bynow read my mind.

"I know, I know…it's not the same. It can never be the same. Ash, many years ago I lost my wife. Not long before you joined us in Sydney, in fact. I nursed her for months. Cancer, you know? We didn't have kids…not yet…she was only in her early-thirties…but we were planning to. Then she got sick, and the rest, I suppose, you can guess. So, as I was saying…"

"I-I'm sorry Bruce. I had no idea…"

"No, a lot of people didn't. I didn't publicise it, and in your case, you weren't even on the scene, so you couldn't know. But I bottled it all up inside me for months. That's not a good move, but it's bloody easy to do. Easier than dealing with it publicly. So, when Mayvers called with your news, I thought, why not? Do you good…that's my diagnosis…and for what that's worth—it's free."

Bynow's offhand comment caused me to laugh out loud, and I caught myself again realising how little I found anything at all funny lately. And that little chuckle released a wave of warm relief right through my body.

"So," I said, "you want me up there? To do what?"

"Well, when Dick rang, I didn't have anything specific, naturally. I just sort of thought you could help me out—with my usual private stuff—disappearing people, cheating spouses—you know the drill. But this morning I got a call from a client—an old bloke down in Macau. He's loaded—in the gambling game—and he *will* pay. Anyway, he wants a job done for a few days on the company cruiser. Big boat apparently. And I thought to myself…Brucey, this is tailor made for Commander Todd. Minus the title, of course. So, how about it?"

"Ahhh, Bruce, I don't know. Mate, it's good of you to think of me like this, but…"

"Look, how about you let it swirl in the subconscious. Like I said, I know it's quick. But like I also said, I reckon it'll do you good. I've gotta go back to him in the next day or so, so sleep on it and let me know, eh?"

"Sure, sure…I'll do that…thanks Bruce."

I closed the call, put my head back and let my eyelids slowly droop. A heavy sigh leaked from my lips. I tried to picture a big boat in Macau, but I'd never been there, and the vision wouldn't come. Nothing but a dark, blank mind. So, I decided I'd do as he asked, and think on it overnight.

But the worry was, how was I going to tell Bruce Bynow '*no*', without totally pissing off my two best friends?

8

Three boats cruised silently across Nam Van Lake, two heading out, and one in. A couple of thirty-footers, and one about fifty. Sebastian Lam stood at his office window, watching their leisurely progress. From his vantage point, they looked small. A thought crossed his mind, "*Ha, fishing craft...wait until you see mine.*"

It was ten in the morning, and he was already tired. He had stayed at the office until 4:15 that same morning, taken a cab home for about three hours sleep, and was back on duty at 8:30. He wore a new outfit...a black Irish-linen suit, a striped shirt in candy pink and white, matching pink pocket square and a black woven silk tie. All delivered direct from his Savile Row tailor yesterday. The only accessory missing was his monocle, but his eyesight was not so good. He'd need two, and that would make him look stupid. So black tortoise-shell spectacles it was. He looked just dandy, and loved it.

His grey phone blooped, and he moved to his desk to answer.

"Yes?"

It was the receptionist, Lily. "Your father on the line, Mr Lam, and Miss Jay-Dee is here also."

Lam was a little annoyed at all this simultaneous activity. "Mmmhh...alright, send her up."

Ah, Lam Chao Heng. Sebastian always hesitated for a bit before taking a call from Lam senior. His father was nearing eighty, and ill health had caused him to retire from active involvement in The Club. That was why Sebastian was now in charge. But it was father's baby, and a payoff after years of grind in the casino business.

Sebastian's mind raced through the old man's story...a story drummed in to him relentlessly. His father, known as CH, was born into a poor Macau family. As World War II ended, and he was still just a kid, he found a job on fishing boats. He should have been at school...but the family needed money. He scrubbed decks and hauled nets for almost twenty years. But he was too smart for that line of work forever, and eventually landed a stint in the casino industry. He worked for those who controlled the game, the Fu and the Ho families, for forty-three years. He knew how they worked, what games worked, and who the players were. The players who mattered. He became friends with those same players. Not best-buddy type, more a professional friendship. He arranged things for them, things they would prefer no-one else knew about. And he kept confidences.

At an age when most other employees had been well and truly terminated, he had been kept on for his knowledge of the operation. He was still sharp, but retirement was now staring him down. That would be at best, modest. Then fate intervened. A whale, one of Macau's biggest punters, wanted a word. Privately.

The whale was establishing his own casino, a small exclusive operation. He could get the licence, had the connections. Lam didn't doubt it—he knew the whale's background almost as well as he knew his own. The whale would fund it, he wanted CH to run it, and the payoff? A forty-nine percent partnership. At sixty-nine, Lam Chao Heng was finally on his way.

The operation was a hit from day one. Money flowed through. CH and the whale were like kids in a lolly-shop. Then suddenly the whale died and it shook CH to the core. He was sure that would end the party, but to his amazement the whale was unswervingly faithful. The whale's share, the controlling fifty-one percent, he had reduced to fifty and left it in the hands of another business associate. The extra one percent he handed over to CH to go with his forty-nine.

'*He will help you carry on the wonderful business we have created,*' the whale said in his will. The will also read, '*to my partner CH Lam, and the only honest man in the casino business. You're now fifty-fifty. I'm proud to call you my friend. You deserved this break a long time ago.*' Apparently, such an emotional tribute from someone as important as the whale, made CH cry.

But father had quickly brushed away his tears, and continued. The cash piled in, and up. Eventually he fell ill, but now retirement would be anything but modest. He handed the reins to his son, but Sebastian always felt it was with some reluctance. Sure, CH had taught him the industry…got him jobs with the big outfits. And in return, he showed up, kept out of major trouble, and worked hard. But he knew CH thought there was something missing, which he couldn't nail. To his father, Sebastian seemed distant at times, and kept weird hours. He was awake too much. He was also aware CH just wished his son would marry, and have a family. Then he might settle into a more regular lifestyle. Sebastian knew it chewed away at CH, quietly, but he was never going to calm the old man's fears.

Sebastian picked up the receiver. "Hello, Father, keeping well?"

"Just fine. How's the business?"

"Excellent. We almost have a full house, and most are staying in." Sebastian's attention was interrupted for a moment from a tap on his door. Miss Jay-Dee's finely featured face appeared around it, smiling. She was, as usual, heavily made-up. Sebastian gestured for her to enter.

"Good to hear, my son," said CH, "now I have a couple of old clients I haven't heard from for some time. They want to come in this afternoon. Mr Ma and Mr Grekov. Can you look after them?"

Miss Jay-Dee was dressed in a short, black satin dress. The hemline finished about a foot above the knee. Light brown, sheer stockings finished at her red, high-heel platform stilettos. Thick mascara curled impossibly long eyelashes heavenwards, and her lips were coated with a red gloss matching her shoes. Her breasts were modest, but firm, and pointed straight ahead, seemingly unaffected by gravity. She moved silently behind Sebastian's chair, brushed the top of his head with a kiss, and slid her hand down inside his new, black, Irish-linen suit trousers. Her touch made him gasp.

"Did you hear me? You alright?" CH sounded concerned, the momentary silence, and Sebastian's sharp breath, punctuating the conversation.

"S…sorry," Sebastian said, "my assistant just popped in with something. Distracted me for a moment. Their names again?"

"Ma and Grekov." The reply from CH was sharp.

Another silence. Sebastian's mind raced. This was not good. "You did say G-Gre…?"

"Grekov. G.R.E.K.O.V." CH spelt out the letters, his voice rising with each for added emphasis. "A problem? What is wrong with you?"

Miss Jay-Dee massaged Sebastian's groin firmly, then moved in front of him, knelt down, and swiftly unzipped the fly of his new, black, Irish-linen suit trousers. Sebastian slid a little lower in his chair.

"No…Father…nothing wrong. We will look after them." But this was one task he would prefer not to have.

"Please do that," said CH. "They are good clients to have, and will be a great addition to the business. They know the score."

"Thank you, Father. Was there anything else?"

"No, not for now. Keep well, son." CH closed off the call, and Sebastian could picture him screwing his face in disgust. But, as he slowly replaced the handset, something else demanded his attention.

Miss Jay-Dee now held his fully fledged erection in both hands, stroking, stroking. "Mr Sebastian, what a big surprise you have for me today," she breathed, peering up through her giant eyelashes. Sebastian hauled her up until she was standing over him. He ran his hand up her smooth inner thigh, and found the rapidly expanding piece of flesh he was seeking. He cast her a wicked grin.

"Yes," he said, "but not as big as yours."

9

Despite my determination to ditch any idea of joining Bruce Bynow in Hong Kong, it appeared I'd failed. I'd even dialled him back three times within the few hours following his call, each time with the intention of telling him, "Thanks, but no." On the final call, Bynow said, "Ash, if you weren't even remotely interested, you wouldn't keep calling. Forget the excuses, just get your arse up here. This gig might even be fun."

So now, barely twenty-four-hours later, my Qantas flight dropped into Chek Lap Kok Airport around 7:00 p.m. The new airport was all hustle, bustle, and extreme efficiency. Not that it was new exactly, but it had been some time since I'd flown into Hong Kong, so it was new to me. Acres of white tiles and white domed ceilings, and thousands of people scurrying in every direction. People always seemed in such a hurry. Reminded me of an ant colony.

I thought back to my first trip here, maybe twenty-odd years ago. I was young, at university studying law, and on my first big overseas adventure. We seemed to land amongst the apartment towers. People going about their daily lives, cooking, watching television, exercising, and we had a birds-eye view of them as we touched down. That was at the old Kai Tak airport, where we didn't even warrant the luxury of a terminal for our arrival. Dropped on a distant tarmac, and bussed in.

I can still recall the taste as I exited the plane that evening. The all-enveloping warm humidity after a brief storm, the pungent smell of aviation gas, and the whine of jet engines as aircraft taxied about. All surrounded by a mesmerising display of glowing skyscrapers. It had seemed like another planet.

A fellow traveller, a Hong Kong businessman I'd befriended on the flight, noticed my wonder. "Can you smell that?" He took a deep breath as we stood at the top of the air-stairs. I, too, breathed in deeply.

"Yes, I think so," I said, but I was not exactly sure what particular smell he was referring to.

"That's the smell of money, my friend." He laughed and slapped my back. In time, I found he was right. Hong Kong did indeed smell of money.

I snapped back to the present. Now I just had to find my way out of this vast terminal. I collected my luggage—a big, navy, duffel bag—and joined the queue for a cab. By the time I'd been dropped, it was 8:30 p.m…thirteen hours after leaving my apartment in Sydney…and I was now ensconced in a room at the Hotel Benito in Tsimshatsui. And opposite me, kicking back in a faded-blue tub chair, sat Bruce Bynow. He took a long swig at a cold beer, and I copied his move.

Bynow had aged well. He was, as I recall, about ten years older than me, so either side of fifty, but he could have passed off for five years younger, or more. He was pretty much average height and build, but in good shape, and tanned. I guessed he worked out a bit. His blue-green eyes were friendly, and crinkled at the sides when he smiled, which was a lot. He had a full head of gun-barrel-straight brown hair, but it troubled me that it looked a bit too brown. And too straight. That was the one thing out of place—at his age almost nobody has hair of one, solid colour. Oh, and the second thing—was it a toupee? I shook my head to clear the thought. Bynow pulled again on his beer.

"So, Ash, you want to tell me what happened?"

I gave him a confused look. "What…happened…oh, you mean the accident?"

"Only if you want to…"

I didn't really want to relive the events again, but figured I owed him a bit of an explanation. I guess he needed to know just how wounded I was, and they say if you talk about things, it gets a little easier. I could leave out the bits that were just too hard, so I gave him a summary of our life together, the pregnancy and the wedding, and the crash. Bynow listened in silence, nodding his head left and right as I talked on, and by the time I'd finished, he wore the expression of a man whose dog had just died.

He shook his head. "Life throws some daggers, at times, eh?"

I just nodded, hoping to change the subject. "So, now I've got myself here in record time and at vast expense…this job…what's the deal?"

Bynow laughed. "Well, where do I start? I've built up a pretty good business here…and I've put together a few clients in the gambling arena over time. I've got a client, like I told you, and he runs this casino in Macau. A private operation…exclusive client list…and he tells me they own a big cruiser. They've got some clients going out for a trip on it over the next few days, and it seems the old guy…name's Lam…CH Lam, but everyone calls him CH…has handed the running of the operation over to his son. With me?"

"All good so far."

"Well," Bynow continued, "it also seems that CH is not too sure what his son is getting up to, so he wants someone to go on this cruiser for the trip, and keep an eye on things."

"What sort of things?"

"Anything strange. How the son treats the clients, the staff…anything at all I guess, and then CH wants us to report back to him. You'll have a title…head of security. And the pay is good—you can have the lot—ten grand for the job. So, how we doin' now?"

"Who else is on board?"

"Clients…big gamblers…but there will be others," Bynow said, winking at me, "always are in that industry. If you get my drift? Then he has a captain…some bloke he's known for a bit…and a first-mate, plus other staff to feed everyone. Look, I reckon this'll be a piece of piss. Yeah…they're business clients…and knowing his business they'll be loaded…but these trips are not about that. Shaggin' and boozin', mostly. Keep your eye on the son…but stay out of the way…give the usual 'yes, sir, no, sir' to the captain, because CH seems to rate him…and report in at the end of the trip. Cruisey, eh?"

I nodded, but my mind wondered if it could really be that easy. It rarely was. "So, who do I report to on the boat?"

"The captain, and first-mate…and other than that, to CH Lam. He's the one paying the bills."

“This captain and mate got names?”

“Patrick Hogan and Wil Wallis. Here…” Bynow slid his business card upside-down across the table, with two numbers scrawled on the back. “Top one is Wallis. Call him for directions. The other is for CH, for when you’ve finished the job.”

I looked down at the numbers for a long moment. When I lifted my gaze Bynow was giving me a quizzical look. “Well?”

“Well…” I said, “looks like we’re a go.”

10

Ding Jei De, Miss Jay-Dee to most, checked her face in the elevator mirror. It looked a mess. Smudged lip gloss, a loose eyelash, hair dishevelled. She could not continue in this state for the rest of the day. Must get home, she thought, and clean up. She rummaged through her tote bag and found a soft hat. Pulled it down firmly over her head, covering most of her face. Checked in the mirror again, straightened her dress, and stepped out onto the busy pavement.

Of course, Ding Jei De was no ordinary woman. For a start her given names, Jei De, were male names. Her face, from a distance, was feminine. Pretty even. But up close it was a little rough. Maybe not like a westerner, but still she showed unmistakable evidence of stubble. The laser treatment was a slow process. She had breasts, but they were not real. The implant program was proceeding nicely, but there was a way to go. She was a B-cup now, and D was the target.

Her voice was still too deep. She practised her pitch every day, and she was sure it was getting higher, but not enough. More work required there. But she was happy with her deportment.

She had perfected the art of the swinging hip, the elegantly held elbow with chin resting on hand, and when sitting, the leg-cross with show of thigh. Yes, these were good. People noticed. She was a work in progress, and she *was* progressing.

Right now, though, she felt less than lovely. On foot, she set off for her apartment. It was only ten minutes away even through the lunchtime crowds. The platform stilettos were difficult over any distance, and the perfect hip-swing became jilted. She took the shoes off, shoved them in her tote, and continued barefoot. As she neared her apartment, she stopped by a take-away, bought some steamed chicken and rice, and coffee, and pressed on.

Her apartment was on a low floor in an eight-storey block built in the sixties. Renovated twenty years ago, it needed a freshen-up. The paint in the lobby was yellowing a bit, a good match for the mustard-brown floor tiles. Cooking smells wafted freely through the building. Still, it was comfortable enough for Miss Jay-Dee with one main living area, an open kitchen, a bathroom, and upstairs, a loft bedroom—and only a few blocks from all the action.

She lived alone, but with pleasant neighbours she never really felt alone. Old Mrs Wu next door was like everyone's favourite grandmother, and Angel lived above. She liked Angel, and they often caught a quick dinner together. Her parents didn't like it much, though. Ah yes, her parents. Father was a doctor in Hong Kong. In fact, she very nearly became a doctor too. Back then she was just Ding Jei De, third year medical student at Li Ka Shing. She was He, and doing nicely…good grades…comfortable home life.

But somewhere that year he had an epiphany. What did they

call it? Yes, an 'ah-ha' moment. He decided he was no longer attracted to women. Never had much luck with them anyway. He fell in love with another med student, the son of a wealthy property developer. Jei De moved out of his home and in with his lover, into a high-rise apartment twenty-six floors up, in a tower block built by his lover's father.

At the urging of his new boyfriend, Winston, Jei De decided he would rather live as a woman, and began to dress and act as such. He started the hair removal process, then the boob implants. The relationship blossomed. They even discussed vaginoplasty, to make the transformation complete. Then without warning, Winston left. No reason. One day they were living together, the next he received a text from Winston saying he was in the US. Forever. Oh, and *sorry*, but Jei De had to move out within a week.

He was shattered, and confused. And too ashamed to go back to his parents. He needed to make a break. Macau was easy, just across the water, and totally embraced transsexuals. That was two years ago, and now, as Miss Jay-Dee, she was a successful part of the lady-boy industry in the gambling capital of Asia.

Miss Jay-Dee finished her lunch and coffee, and took herself to the bathroom. Her eye with the dislodged lash was a little swollen, and darkening. Her backside ached. She hadn't noticed it as she scurried home, but it was just part of the deal in this business. She carefully peeled her tight dress up and off. Genitals all intact, but her balls hurt a touch. Stomach and boobs okay. She slipped the dress over her head, and stared at her naked body. Her martial-arts training was paying off. Aside from sharpening her self-defence skills it kept her in good shape. All looked good, except her neck.

She looked closer in the mirror, gently running her fingers along the large, dark bruise marks. She pushed, and they each hurt a bit. She winced. The pain was one thing, but the look was what bothered her. How could she work with other clients in this state? One sighting of these and they'd drop her instantly. And in less than twelve hours she had a job booked. A high-paying job.

Damn Sebastian Lam, she thought. He paid well, and was as regular as clockwork, but this price was too high. Every time with him was like this and seemed to be getting worse. The choking seemed to last longer. As she carefully removed her wig, and readied for the shower, a fleeting thought crossed her mind. A thought that made her shudder.

What if, in his orgasmic frenzy, with his hands squeezing hard around her neck, Sebastian Lam forgot to let go?

11

Sebastian Lam carefully folded his trousers, and placed them in a white, plastic laundry bag. His new, black, Irish-linen suit trousers. They had become collateral damage during his fast and furious sexual encounter with Miss Jay-Dee. He carefully tied the top of the bag, and placed it in the lobby outside his bedroom suite. A staff member would collect it, and take them for cleaning.

He had farewelled Miss Jay-Dee twenty minutes earlier, pressing three, crisp, one-hundred US dollar bills into her hand. She smiled and kissed him goodbye, but there was no doubt, she did not look nearly as attractive as when she arrived. Her bright-red lip gloss had smudged onto her cheeks, and her red-tinted hair seemed to have moved sideways for some reason. Sebastian wondered if she might be able to find a better wig-maker. And one of her eyelashes had dislodged slightly. It had been a torrid, messy seventeen minutes.

Sebastian had showered, and selected a new outfit. This time a navy suit with a fine red pin stripe, a sky-blue shirt, and a silk and cashmere tie in blue and red checks. He slid a red silk square into the breast pocket of his coat, and carefully adjusted his navy, buffalo-horn spectacles. Excellent. He quickly made his way back across the lobby to his office.

A light flashed on the grey phone. He pressed the button, cancelling the light, and Lily's message replayed. "A reminder, Mr Lam, Mr Zhou will be here at twelve." He glanced at the wall clock. Eleven minutes. He scrolled through a list of numbers on the grey phone, found the one he needed, and pressed the automatic dial.

The call rang six or seven times, but no answer. The voicemail message said simply, "I'm obviously busy—leave a message." *Ignorant*, thought Sebastian, but he left a message anyway. "Sebastian Lam here. I need to talk. Please call. Thank you."

He glanced at the clock. Seven minutes. He scrolled through the numbers again and found the marina in Hong Kong. Direct line to the manager.

"Ah, Mr Lam, how are you today?"

He didn't need small talk. Not now. "Fine, fine, thank you…tell me, is the boat ready?"

"I'll check. Please hold."

Sebastian drummed his fingers on the desk. He scanned the screens behind him, and noted a few clients playing. That would change, and so would his afternoon. Soon. He stood and checked his clothes in the mirror, smoothed his hair. Where was this manager? He sat down, and resumed drumming.

The manager finally returned. "Mr Lam, the boat is right to travel."

"Thank you, and tell me, is she booked to go out tomorrow?"

"One minute *please*." The manager appeared agitated at the separate questions.

Sebastian glanced at the clock again. Two minutes. He began drumming.

The line clicked. "Mr Lam," said the manager, "I believe your skipper has indicated he will be taking her out sometime tomorrow. Exact time to be advised, though."

"Good. Good. Thank you for that." Lam hung up the phone, stood quickly, took a deep breath, and exhaled loudly. There was a rap at the door. He shut down the screen bank behind him, glanced at the one on his desk covering his lobby, took another deep breath, and swiftly moved to the door greet his guest.

"Mr Zhou, welcome back. Please sit. A whisky perhaps?"

"Thank you," said Zhou, nodding, and slumping into a comfortable sofa. He looked tired, a little crumpled and the cane had gone. Sebastian handed him a sizable crystal glass, half-filled with spirit.

"Well, tell me, how was your stay, Mr Zhou. Any luck?"

"No. Four hundred and seven million Yuan I have put through. All into your coffers. Does that sound like luck?"

"Depends how you view it, Mr Zhou. You've had some enjoyment I assume?"

"Oh, yes. And of course, a not entirely unexpected outcome."

"Good," said Sebastian, "now perhaps we could ease the burden a little. How about a short cruise on our company boat? First class food and accommodation, limited guests, and of course additional pleasurable activities to soothe the soul? Interested?"

Zhou brightened at the offer. "Definitely. My doctor advises to take *additional pleasurable activities*, but when would you have in mind? I'm heading now to Hong Kong, for a meeting this evening."

"How about Wednesday? She's leaving from the HK marina so you can board there. I'll let you know the time, later."

"And where are we heading?"

"South China Sea…well out…so if there is any business to attend to we are in international waters…away from prying eyes and control…"

"Fine." Zhou stood and moved to the door, "I'll await your call. And speaking of business…the other money—have *you* had any luck?"

Lam felt a shudder at the mention of it. He shook his head. "No…still no luck."

Zhou gave him a long, hard look. "Let me remind you—time is not on your side. Your father would not delay like this." He opened the door and almost as an afterthought, turned back slightly. "However, in other ways, you are more like your father all the time."

Sebastian nodded, lips parting in a weak smile and closed his office door. His mind flipped to Miss Jay-Dee. No, Mr Zhou, he thought, I don't think my father would agree.

12

"Welcome back, Mr Hogan." The young bar-manager's face broke into a wide smile. "How was your trip? Sydney, Australia, right?" On a low table, he carefully placed a bottle of beer on a coaster, and set an empty glass on another coaster beside it.

"Good enough," Hogan mumbled. He always told people he'd been to Sydney, even if he hadn't. Need to know basis only, and the bar manager sure as hell didn't need to know. "You sure you don't have any dark and stormy?"

"What is dark and stormy?" The manager looked concerned. "It not stormy, Mr Hogan. You look outside. It beautiful day."

"I've already been through this with the other barman. For God's sake can't you get some in? Aaah…never mind." He slipped him a US ten dollar bill. One thing Patrick Hogan had learnt over time was how positively staff responded when paid in US currency. Keeping some on hand had become his usual practice. "And keep the change."

The duty manager slid the cash into his pocket and beamed. "Thank you, Mr Hogan." He beat a hasty retreat, just in case Hogan changed his mind.

Hogan glanced at his phone. It showed four new messages. He checked the missed call display. Four or five from the same number. He knew who it was, but shut the phone off anyway. He didn't need to speak to anyone but Wil Wallis right now, and Wallis was late. He poured his beer, and took a big guzzle.

He surveyed the bar to his right. No sign of Wallis. The Gold Coast Hotel in Hong Kong had become like a second home to him. The big, orange-pink building sat right on the beach, overlooking the marina and only minutes from the boat he skippered. When he was in town, which had been most of the time lately, this was his base. He liked the place. A refuge far from his irritating ex-wife and useless son, and paid for by his boss. Cost effective. He took another swig of his beer.

He surveyed the bar to his left. No sign of Wallis. He had a room on a high floor. Pink walls and light grey carpet. Always the same room, with a king size bed, two sofas, a table and two chairs, and a balcony from which he looked down on the marina. And his boat.

He and Wallis had flown in the previous night, and arrived at the hotel a little after ten. Wallis had a similar room overlooking the marina, though slightly smaller, and two floors below in the smoking section. He had despatched Wallis into Wan Chai earlier that day, to arrange some boat staff for the next few days.

They had their regulars...a chef, an assistant chef, and three waitresses who also doubled as cleaners. And security. But this security was new, and untested. As usual, CH Lam had arranged him, and CH reckoned he should be faultless. But if Hogan had one rule, learnt from bitter experience...it was that no-one was faultless. Indeed, his own performance over half-a-century was proof enough of that.

They also needed one more waitress, and three or four entertainers, depending on the guest list. No singing required, no comedy. Maybe some dancing. Vertical or horizontal. Maybe both. Again, it depended on the guests. Hogan liked them dancing, especially pole dancing. Especially when they were all oiled up. But he was getting ahead of himself here. He finished his beer.

There was an order required in these things. Exact number of entertainers to be determined once guest numbers were confirmed. That's what the missed calls on his phone were about, Hogan guessed. Confirming the guests. And then match up the girls against the guest desires. It was far too important to leave to Wallis alone, and Wallis should have been here with them. No sign of him.

Hogan signalled to the barman for another beer. He swiftly delivered it, and Hogan rustled about in his wallet and produced another tenner. "Don't forget, get some dark and stormy, that's what I want. Got it?"

"Certainly, Mr Hogan." The barman nodded and moved off. He couldn't care less, Hogan thought. I'll have to see management. He fumbled about replacing his wallet in his hip pocket and became aware of someone approaching quickly. He looked up, as Wallis pulled up.

"Where have you been? Sampling the merchandise?" Hogan sounded agitated. "I've got to get to the boat and check her out, and I've got these interviews with the girls. And that you-know-who is ringing me every half an hour…"

"Who…Sebastian?"

Hogan nodded. "Yeah…little prick…"

"Well, why don't you take his call? Put him out of his misery."

"Ahh, stuff him," said Hogan, "it's his old man I work for. He's the one who put me…us…on, and he's the one I answer to. Always have. And while he pays, that's the way it stays. That little bastard has taken over, and thinks the centre of the universe emanates from his arsehole. He can wait. As long as we look after CH, we'll be right. So, what'd you get?"

"Keep your panties on," Wallis said. "I have some candidates, one waitress and a few for amusement. Sorry, entertainment. I think they'll be acceptable. Would you like to see them?"

"Well I'm not waiting here for a bus, am I? Of course I want to see them. My room in ten minutes?"

"Go and prepare yourself," said Wallis. He reached down and hauled Hogan up from his chair, "But let's make it fifteen so you can take a shower. You stink."

*

Wil Wallis stood outside the entrance to the Gold Coast Hotel, checking his watch. He drew hard on his cigarette, inhaled, and slowly blew a cloud of smoke up at the sky. Hogan would be ready in about five, and they should be here soon. He took another puff, as a white minivan with blackened windows drew up.

Wallis slid open the door, and the first of his selected entertainers stepped on to the forecourt. Two more slid out carefully, followed by his waitress. Wallis poked his head in the van. "No Belle?"

"No, she had another job. Decided to take it," said the small brunette, Mae, who was the first out.

Wallis ground his teeth, his lips parting. "Is she coming?"

Mae shrugged. "I think so—later."

"I bloody hope so."

Wallis surveyed the troupe. Cherry was tallish, five-eight, blonde and said she was from Brazil. Venus was a similar height, with brown-blonde hair and green eyes. From her accent Wallis guessed she was European. Little Mae was Asian, and the no-show, Belle, was a leggy redhead. At least six feet. Pity, thought Wallace. He liked redheads, and she would have rounded out the group nicely. Something for everyone.

He cast an eye at Gina, the waitress. Not bad—a little older than the others. Probably late-twenties, thirty max. Dark hair, good body. At a pinch she might be okay, if they needed more entertainment. If she was prepared to entertain. Time would tell.

Wallis walked round the van, peeled off a bunch of notes and paid the driver. As the van slowly moved off, he took a final draw on his cigarette and stubbed it out with his boot. "Now, ladies, follow me." The girls, all stilettos, legs, and short skirts, hoisted their overnight bags and wobbled along behind.

He led them through the vast marble-tiled lobby. An elderly American couple at check-in was distracted by the entourage. The husband stood open-mouthed, his eyes following the jiggling bits as they approached the lifts. His wife gave him a swift elbow to the belly, about right above the spleen. "Stop dreamin', and give the man here your credit card."

A quick-stepping duty-manager approached Wallis from an adjoining office, and pulled him aside. He whispered close in Wallis' ear. "Sir, where are you taking these, umm—ahh, ladies?

You know we don't allow umm—ahh certain, ahh ladies to umm openly…aah…"

Wallis took the duty-manager around a corner, away from the lifts and the gaze of guests. He put his arm around his shoulder, pulled a one-hundred bill from his pocket, folded it, and slipped it into the duty-manager's breast pocket.

"Understood," said Wallis. He pushed his most charming smile through his beard. "But we'll cause no trouble. And these are not certain ladies. These are entertainers, and they are just here for an audition."

He walked back to the lift, pressed the button and the door opened.

"Right, ladies, up we go."

13

Wallis gave a couple of quick raps on Hogan's hotel room door, and poked his head in. "You right, Pat?"

"Yeah, yeah, hurry up." The response came from deep in the room.

Wallis pushed the door open, and ushered the girls in. Hogan lay back, legs up, on one of the sofas. He'd changed into a dark blue kimono, and, Wallis noted, nothing else. At least he appeared to have showered.

Wallis introduced each of the girls. "This is Cherry, Venus, and Mae. Our entertainers. And this is Gina, our waitress." The girls smiled and each said "hello" in turn.

Hogan looked them up and down. "We're one short." The look he gave Wallis was more a question, than an observation.

Wallis cast a glance at Mae, and rolled his eyes to the ceiling. "That's Belle. She's on another job…be here later."

Hogan nodded a few times. "Well, girls, show us your wares."

The girls looked at Wallis, frowning. Mae spoke up. "What he mean wares?"

Wallis said, "Your gear…clothes…he wants to look at your

body. Time to get it off." The girls looked at each other, shrugged and began undressing.

"But I'm not a…a…you know…performer," protested Gina, "just a waitress."

Wallis gave Hogan another questioning look. Hogan shrugged.

"Okay," said Wallis, "stay as you are. For now." Gina sat on the other sofa.

Hogan watched the undressing, his lips parting slightly forming a crooked smile. The naked girls stood before him. Looking awkward. Nobody knew what the next move should be.

Hogan looked back and forward, at each girl. "Can you dance? Anything?"

The girls began twirling slowly, still unsure exactly what type of dance was required. Without music, it was disconcerting. Wallis watched on from a far corner, noting the near perfect bodies. Interesting, he thought, how they each had identical pubic hair. A short strip about an inch or so wide. He guessed it must be the fashion.

"Now some pole dancing," commanded Hogan. The girls wrapped themselves around imaginary poles, one leg crooked up, and began sliding up and down. Wallis took himself to the balcony door and gazed over the marina.

"Now, show me you love me," Hogan croaked. The girls moved onto the sofa with him, alternately stroking his head and chest. His kimono fell open, exposing genitalia for the room to view. Mae began to massage it gently. Hogan moaned. "That's it." His voice had almost disappeared. The girls swapped positions and Cherry took over at his groin. "Ohhh, baby…" he said.

Wallis looked down at him and shook his head. He said, "Jesus, I need a smoke."

Hogan craned his head around the girls. "You can't smoke here. You'll have to wait."

"Well hurry up," said Wallis. The girls continued stroking and fondling, but Hogan was not responding. His head was moaning appropriately, but nothing else moved.

Mae looked concerned. "What wrong? You not like?"

Hogan looked down at his shrunken member. "No, no, don't worry. Not your fault. Damn thing doesn't want to work it seems."

"Too many dark and stormys," said Wallis. He glanced across the room at Hogan, and grinned. The girls looked puzzled.

Hogan scowled, and hauled himself off the sofa. "Get dressed," he said. The girls quickly covered up, each pulling on a light top and short skirt. Nothing else.

Hogan collected himself, finding a pair of shorts to slip on under the kimono. He stood at the balcony door, and turned to the assembled group. Venus stood, brushing her hair vigorously, and Cherry had hold of a small mirror, touching up her lipstick. Mae and Gina sat waiting for the next command. Wallis took up his position next to Hogan.

"Here's the deal," said Hogan. "You already know Wil, and my name's Pat. We have a boat trip to take for the next couple of days. On the boat, you call me Skip. We leave from here tomorrow, after lunch. Don't know our destination yet, maybe not until morning. Probably just motor about. But we'll deliver you back here. With me?"

The girls all said "yes."

"You three, the entertainers, will share cabins on the main deck. And the other one…what's her name?

"Belle," said Wallis.

"Right…Belle too. Gina will live in the crew quarters. There's three more waitresses, the chef, and his assistant, also down there. Right?" Gina nodded.

"We'll have a number of guests. Maybe three or four. Just men, all VIPs. You won't need their names. All our guests are called Mike. You will be assigned to look after one Mike for the trip. Food is top of the range, as is booze. All supplied. Rule is…don't drink too much. You are there to look after your Mike. Okay?"

The girls all said "okay."

"You're on full daily pay rate, starting from when you left the city. The usual your agency pays. If your Mike tells me you've done a top job, I'll toss in another two hundred US a day. Each. Cash. We have two rooms booked here at the hotel for tonight, so you can choose who you bunk with. Don't go out—use room service for everything. Any questions?"

The girls looked at each other. "Any special service we have to perform for our Mike?" said Cherry.

"Whatever he wants. If he gives you trouble, though, you let me know. Or security. We have a security officer. New." Hogan cast a glance at Wallis. Wallis eyes screwed closed as he nodded agreement, and forced a smile through his closed mouth.

Venus looked up. "What is the boat like? Is it big enough for all these people?"

Hogan scanned the group, then slid open the balcony door. "Step out here, ladies." All six stood on the balcony, looking down over the marina. The sun was setting, and a yellowish-brown haze cloaked the scene.

Hogan pointed down to a group of three mega-yachts. "See the one closest, at the front? The girls stared at the vast vessel, gleaming white despite the lengthening evening shadow, three decks towering above the water. "That's her, your home for the next few days. The *Golden Empress*. Now, you in?"

The girls looked at each other, and started giggling, then laughing. They jumped up and down in turn and kissed first Hogan, then Wallis.

"Oh, yes," said Mae, "we in, Skip."

14

Sebastian was becoming agitated. Five more times he had rung this number, and still no answer. Only the same dreary voicemail, "I'm obviously busy—leave a message." He had left a message—*five more* messages. He paced his office trying to decide how to approach his next meeting. 4:00 p.m. had just ticked over, and his new clients would soon be arriving. Not his idea of a pleasant afternoon. The longer he could avoid Grekov, the better.

The clients had, in fact, arrived at The Club much earlier in the day. He should have been there to greet them, if only to appease his father. But it was inconvenient. At that precise moment of their arrival, he lay stark naked on the bed in his private suite, staring up at his body in the mirrored ceiling. Miss Jay-Dee had just brought him to the point of ultimate ecstasy for the third time, only to back off. He was in mental and physical agony. What he needed was to get his rocks off, now. Lily's call regarding his clients only served to fuel his frustration.

He shoved the responsibility on to the house manager. He hoped the clients would understand his being unavoidably detained. He'd soon find out. They didn't have far to travel—a mere two floors up from their gaming room—and Mr Ma and Mr Grekov had certainly made their presence felt. They had only been playing since lunch, and according to the screen on Sebastian's desk, had invested in excess of sixty million Yuan—over eight million US. Each. And that was up until three o'clock. They would be expecting service.

Sebastian moved back to his chair, and surveyed the bank of screens. Ma and Grekov had left the room. Not long now. He picked up the grey phone and tried the number again. Same voicemail. "Ah, shit," he spat, and hung up without leaving a message.

Lily buzzed him. "Mr Ma and Mr Grekov, sir, they will be with you in two minutes."

"Yes, yes, thank you, Lily." He drummed his fingers on the desk, faster and faster.

Sebastian noted the final tally from the two men and shut off the screens. Give or take, one hundred million Yuan each. Twenty-five million, US, altogether. He checked himself in the mirror, his usual pre-meeting grooming, and stood staring over the lake. Dark clouds had formed, interrupted by occasional bolts of lightning. They hung low and heavy, seemingly at his face level. He guessed there must be thunder too, but cocooned in here he could hear nothing. It looked like a sizable afternoon storm was about to hit.

There was rap at the door. Sebastian swung round and moved swiftly to open it. Two men stood facing him—a tall, thin Asian, who looked him squarely in the eye, and a short, obese European who stared at the floor. The two new clients Sebastian had observed in the gambling room. The Asian in an ill-fitting black suit and white shirt. No tie. The European bedecked in a loud, floral, short-sleeve shirt tucked tightly over his belly into beige trousers. And mauve sneakers. Ma and Grekov. He'd never seen Ma before, but that was definitely Grekov. He'd had no idea Grekov was a client of his father. His heart skipped a beat or two at the sight of him.

"Come in, please," he said, with a sweep of his arm.

The two men sauntered in to his office. Ma appeared a little over fifty perhaps, and was completely bald. Unusual for an Asian. Grekov was at least sixty-five, and had a full head of hair, wavy and grey. He smelt bad. Cigarettes. And he needed a shower. They were the most unlikely looking heavy-hitting gamblers he had seen in quite a while—at least in his club.

"Gentlemen, a drink perhaps?"

"Sure," said Grekov, in a thickish accent. He still hadn't looked up. "Vodka. Do you have a bathroom?"

"Yes, straight across the lobby," said Sebastian. The Russian turned and waddled off.

"Mr Ma?"

"No, thank you. I don't drink. Grekov does that for both of us. Maybe some tea?"

"As you wish." Sebastian buzzed Lily with the order.

"Mr Lam," said Ma, "your father is an old acquaintance of mine. He assured us we would be well catered for here. The club is certainly an outstanding facility."

"Yes, we are proud of it…"

"But we expected you would greet us, not some house-manager. Is this your normal practise?" Ma was staring, expressionless and hard-eyed at Sebastian. The question was not just a complaint, it was a test.

Sebastian shoved his ego aside. "I'm sorry, did my secretary not tell you? I was unexpectedly caught up with another client. I felt it best you were attended to immediately."

"Who was this other client?" Ma's tone was sharp.

"I'm sorry, Mr Ma—we never discuss our clients with anyone. I'm sure you could understand that."

Ma fell silent for a moment, and nodded a couple of times. "Do you know how much we have put through here?" His face was still determined, unsmiling.

Grekov waddled back in, his shirt now hanging outside his trousers. Sebastian noticed his fly was unzipped. He wondered for a moment what had transpired in the bathroom, but decided to let the thought go.

"Ah, Mr Grekov, your drink," said Sebastian handing him the vodka. Grekov, head still down, took it without a word, and settled into a sofa.

Lily knocked and entered with Ma's tea. Ma nodded at Lily, but also said nothing, then joined Grekov at the other end of the sofa.

"Back to your question," continued Sebastian, "I'm not sure exactly yet, but..."

Ma cut in, looking sideways at Grekov. "I was just telling Mr Lam how disappointed we were he was not here to greet us. Don't you agree?"

"Yes, very..." Grekov slurred. He seemed to be falling asleep, then suddenly snapped. "We don't like to be treated like shit! Do you treat all your clients like shit?"

The outburst caught Sebastian off-guard. "Well…no…of course we don't. We…we value our clients…"

"Twenty-five million US dollars," said Ma, "that's how much we have invested here. Did you know that, Mr Lam?"

"Well, I knew it was substantial…"

"Twenty-five million hard-earned dollars from construction, Mr Lam. Building China. Creating a glorious future for our country, Mr Lam."

"Please, call me Sebastian."

"A glorious future, Mr Lam, and now you have the money. And we are disappointed," said Ma, now looking a touch sad.

"And you treat us like shit," chimed in Grekov, taking a gulp of vodka.

"Construction, you say," said Sebastian. He rubbed his chin as though in deep contemplation. "Construction is an area of great interest to our company. Perhaps I could ease your pain a little with a proposal?"

Ma looked at him and raised an eyebrow. "A proposal?"

Grekov's head was slumped forward, almost resting on his bloated stomach.

"Yes, I have a few thoughts in that area," said Sebastian. "One involves property, and the other leisure. I'll leave the property thought until a later time. However, our company boat will be here Wednesday, fully staffed. Name your desire, it's probably on board. Would a little cruise, just for a couple of days, be of interest?"

Ma peered up at Sebastian. He smiled. Or maybe sneered. Sebastian couldn't be sure, but it was better than the death stare he had so far displayed.

"Your company boat, you say," said Ma, "is she big?"

"Oh yes, but lightly occupied. You won't be disturbed, unless you wish to be, of course."

"Then we are definitely interested, aren't we, Grekov?"

Grekov didn't answer. Ma gave him a gentle shove, which appeared to rouse him. "The company boat—a cruise, Grekov—we are interested, aren't we?"

"I won't be treated like shit." Grekov said.

"No, no you won't, Mr Grekov," said Sebastian, "give me a moment, please." He moved to his desk and buzzed Lily. "Please send the house-manager up to show our guests to their rooms. They will be cruising with us for a few days."

He strode back to the sofas, where Ma was helping Grekov to his feet. Grekov stood, wobbling, and finally looked up to take in his surroundings. At the sight of Sebastian, he flinched, taken aback.

Grekov's voice became a low growl. "You…what are *you* doing here?"

"It's…m…my…my club," Sebastian said.

"It's not your fucking club. It is CH Lam's club."

"Yes…well…he's my father."

Grekov turned, and looked out over Macau. Processing. He turned back to Sebastian.

"Then where's my money?"

"I…I don't have it."

Grekov scanned the view again. Unseeing. He turned to Ma. "Come—we go." Then he looked back at Sebastian.

"And you—no more time." Grekov wagged his finger in Lam's face. "You give me the money, *on the boat.*"

15

Patrick Hogan looked to be in a hurry. Dressed in a t-shirt, navy shorts and boat shoes, he strode quickly, or as quickly as his short, stumpy legs would carry him, along the timber-decked pontoon to which his boat was moored. Past the line-up of jet-skis, onto the marina foreshore, and straight toward his hotel.

He had just left the marina manager, and his boat. His inspection of the *Empress* had to be brief, because everything this day had run late. It was now after 8:30 and dark. He was hungry, and thirsty, and he still had calls to make. His phone was full of messages. Some, from boat staff mostly, he had handed on to Wallis to take care of. But there was still the boss' son, little Mr Important, and he would not be pleased that Hogan had dodged him all afternoon. At least the *Empress* was right to travel.

He strode in to the bar, and spotted Wallis at a small table in a far corner. "I'll have a beer, thanks," he said to his first-mate, plonking himself in an armchair beside. "Boat's good to go—what about the staff?"

Wallis shook his head at Hogan's lack of grace, and motioned for the barman to deliver another drink. "Chef's right, he'll be there about eight in the morning. Food and booze will be delivered about nine. The girls are tucked up tight in their rooms." He pulled his buzzing phone from his trouser pocket and answered a call.

"Wallis," he said.

"Mr Wallis, Ash Todd here. I believe CH Lam has mentioned me?"

"He has—where are you?"

"In Hong Kong. Just arrived. Where do you want me?"

Wallis looked across at Hogan, winked and gave him a thumbs-up sign. Hogan took a swig of beer.

"The boat's at The Gold Coast Marina—in the New Territories. Take a cab in the morning, about forty-five minutes. She's called *Golden Empress*. Be here about nine. Got it?"

"Nine tomorrow. Right."

Wallis hung up the call and looked at Hogan. "And security is in place," said Wallis, his beard twitching from his crooked grin.

Hogan took another pull on his beer. Now he checked his phone. "This'll be good," he said, and took a deep breath as he dialled a number.

"Sebastian Lam," the clipped voice answered.

"Patrick here…"

"Where in the hell have you been? I've been trying you all afternoon. I have left many, many messages. Again, I ask…where have you been?"

"Sorry, I've been very busy…"

"So busy you cannot take even one call from me? I pay you big money. Have you forgotten?"

Hogan looked across at Wallis and winced. Wallis could hear

the blurred screech from Hogan's phone. He grinned back and made a slow clapping motion. "No, no, I haven't forgotten..." said Hogan.

"I have some very important clients for you to look after, and they are waiting to hear from me, you understand?"

"Yes, of course..."

"Perhaps you would like me to terminate your captaincy. Maybe the job is just too much for you. All this money I pay you, but you cannot return the courtesy by taking my call. It is a manner of operating which I simply will not tolerate...am I making myself clear?"

There was a silence in which the only sound to be heard was that of clinking glasses at the bar. Hogan's mind raced between a dozen different thoughts, chief among them that his well-paid job might be about to be pulled by the weasel, Sebastian. And running a close second, was that his dislike for Sebastian had just doubled in intensity as a result.

But Hogan wouldn't back away. "You can't sack me, because I don't work for you," he said. "You seem to forget I work for your father, and we go way back, so if you like we'll give him a call together and discuss my termination."

Sebastian flipped gears, in an instant becoming warm and fuzzy. "Look, Skip, I don't want to worry my father about this. Tell me, is the boat ready? What time can you leave?"

Hogan allowed himself a small smirk, the corners of his mouth twitching slightly as he registered his little victory. He knew damn well Sebastian wouldn't risk dragging their differences to the old man. Hogan had witnessed enough of Sebastian's outside interests on previous cruises, and he always felt sure that if CH knew of any of it, it would be Sebastian's job, not his, that would suffer.

"Boat's ready, and we'll be right to cast off any time after one o'clock," Hogan said.

"You have entertainment?"

"All organised. Security too—from your father."

There was a short silence on the other end. "Very well. I will have Mr Z join you on board in Hong Kong. Mr Mike Z—midday tomorrow. OK?"

"Sure," said Hogan.

"Then you will come here, to Macau. You should be here by four o'clock, right?"

"Should be."

"Here you will receive Mr M and Mr G. Mr Mike M and Mr Mike G. Got that?"

"Got it. Mike M and Mike G."

"And, of course, our usual guest, Mr W. Mr Mike W."

"Right, so four guests? Is that it?"

More silence on the other end. "No, this time I will join you, so please make sure my cabin is prepared."

Hogan's stomach was beginning to knot. Five guests, including the boss. He needed this Belle to show, otherwise it would mean a mercy dash into the city for Wallis first thing in the morning. And she had to be right!

"So, for your guests…any special orders?"

"Only two…Mr G likes redheads. And we have a redhead, yes? We always have a redhead, don't we?"

Hogan looked at Wallis. He repeated Sebastian's question verbatim.

"We have a redhead, don't we?"

Wallis shrugged, then nodded 'yes' and kept on shrugging.

"Yes," said Hogan.

"Good...and of course Mr W, our regular, likes Asians. So, you can accommodate everyone then?"

"Sure can," Hogan said. He pulled in a long, slow breath.

"And I will bring my own entertainment, so you needn't worry."

Hogan pursed his lips and slowly blew out the same long breath, relieved that they had the guests covered, as long as Belle fronted.

"She will stay in my cabin," Sebastian said. "Her name is Miss Jay-Dee."

16

The red taxi dropped me at the marina a little after nine. After the cool air-con of the cab, the early-morning warmth hit me. Sticky…humid, with the sun trying to push through a heavy, yellow haze. My head was a little hazy as well, possibly from the half-a-dozen bourbons I'd stumbled onto the evening before, once Bynow had departed.

I hauled my duffel bag from the boot of the cab, wandered toward the pontoons, and cast a gaze over the flotilla. I guessed one hundred and fifty boats, maybe more, were moored. Most looked to be thirty to fifty-foot motorboats, and an occasional sailboat. I'd bought a few boating magazines for the flight. After nine hours of solid reading I was now a near expert in them.

I looked further right, toward the hotel. Right down the far end lay two big boats. One white, one blue. That looked promising, and I set off across the gangway. The pontoon vibrated under a hive of activity, people rushing in both directions, pushing trolleys, and carrying cartons. I reached the blue boat, which appeared to be locked up. I moved on to the white. That's where the carton carriers were headed.

The boat towered above the water, three levels up. A mid-thirties Asian man, dressed in black and white check trousers and a white coat, swept past and said "hello", without looking up. I nodded back. He was in hot pursuit of a trolley pusher, yelling something I couldn't understand. He did not sound happy.

I strolled along the side of the boat, toward the bow. Large gold lettering told me she was called *Golden Empress*. I guessed this was her. I pulled out my phone, dialled Wallis, and a few seconds later heard a phone ring somewhere on the boat.

"Glad you could make it," said a voice from above.

I glanced up and could make out the silhouette of a bearded head, with a hand held to its ear, peering down at me.

"Ash Todd?"

"Yep."

"Get aboard." He pointed back to the stern. "I'll meet you there."

I did as ordered, waiting while three men heaved a heavy trolley, loaded with cartons, across the boarding ramp. The trolley suddenly speared sideways, toward the water, as Wallis appeared. He grabbed the top cartons, steadying the load until the carriers got it under control.

"Whisky," he said, "our guests' favourite. Two grand a bottle and it doesn't float. Better not to drop it."

I ran my eye over the twin sets of steps curving up from the boarding platform to the main deck. "Impressive looking gin palace. So, CH Lam owns her?"

"Yeah…or his business does. Let's go up." We climbed the port side steps. "Dump your bag in there," he said, pointing to the bar occupying the back corner of the main deck, "and I'll show you around."

We stepped inside a salon furnished with deep-purple velvet sofas on cream carpet. The low cupboards along the walls were finished in high-gloss mahogany veneer, and striped roman blinds covered each window. The ceiling featured an impressive sculpture in the shape of a giant octopus, and recessed lighting.

In one corner was a grouping of armchairs, and behind that a giant flat-screen television. In another corner, carpeted stairs led to decks above and below. Beyond the living area, and shielded by a three-quarter height, ornate frosted-glass wall, sat a mahogany dining table, with seating for twelve.

"Casual living," said Wallis, waving his arm in big circular motion. "I'll show you downstairs first."

I followed him down the curved staircase to the lower deck. He opened a door and flicked the light at the stern end.

"The toy room," he said. I peered in at the collection. Two tenders, one about twenty-feet and the other about half that, three jet skis, a windsurfer, and an array of diving and snorkelling gear.

Turning toward the bow, we walked along a central corridor flanked by two enormous engines, and stepped through another door, ducking heads, and turning side-on to squeeze through. Beyond the door a small stairway on the left led straight up, and beyond that a collection of small rooms, maybe a dozen.

"Crew quarters." Wallis pointed to the cabins which were occupied. "Chef and his assistants sleep here...you can take your pick of the rest, but I'd suggest the end one. You might fit better. Three bathrooms—shared. Oh, and keep that door closed. It's soundproofed and sealed, so keeps the engine noise and diesel stink out. Okay?"

"Sure, looks cozy. But is that enough crew?"

"For our guests, it is. There's not much else to do, everything's computerised. I look after engines and ropes, Skip drives. We sleep upstairs. Come on...let's go."

I followed up to the main deck. Behind the dining area sat the galley and the small stairs from the crew quarters. A hall to the right led on to six queen staterooms and a couple of doubles...all different colour schemes, velvet sofas, huge pillows, and more roman blinds. Each en-suite had coordinating marble tops, gold fittings and white fluffy towels. A five-star hotel could offer no more.

We retraced our steps to the living area, and climbed the curved stairs to the upper deck, exiting to a blue carpeted, wood-panelled gaming room. The ceiling boasted another motif, this time in the shape of a jagged mountain. A roulette table occupied one corner, blackjack another, and a collection of light-grey armchairs and side tables were scattered between them and the centre of the room. A bar and spirit cabinet ran the length of the back wall. To the left a guest bathroom, and a small office adjoining.

Toward the bow, a hall, a replica of the one below, led to the captain and first-mate quarters, and the bridge. On the left of the hall was the owner's suite. I poked my head in.

Gold carpet, white walls and curtains, deep-red bed linen with matching armchairs and chaise. Gold cushions everywhere. Acres of silk and velvet. On one wall, a giant motif of the jagged mountain. In gold. To the left an en-suite. Black, white, and gold.

Full marble. Many years ago, I led a raid on a brothel, owned by one of Australia's wealthiest crooks. In newspaper-speak he was known as a 'colourful racing identity'. This had an eerily similar feel.

At the stern, adjoining the gaming room sat a private deck, half-covered, with a big round dining table, eight chairs covered in blue, and wrap-around sun lounge. We climbed some more stairs leading to the sundeck, housing yet another covered dining area and bar, fore and aft sun-beds, and a jacuzzi.

Wallis half-gazed out over the marina as he dipped his hand to test the jacuzzi temperature. "Beautiful, isn't she? So, any questions?"

I knew what Bynow had told me my task was, but I wondered if CH Lam passed the same message to everyone on board. Thought I'd send out a test query…

"Just one—what's my job?"

17

I followed Wallis back down to the upper deck, and sat in one of the blue chairs at the big round table.

Wallis pulled a cigarette from his pack, and glanced at me. "Coffee?"

"Black, no sugar. Thanks."

Wallis pressed an intercom above the buffet to one side. "Hey, Cookie, can we have two coffees, one black no sugar, and mine you know? We're on the gaming deck."

The intercom sprang into life. "Certainly, Mister First Mate. Give me some minutes." I couldn't tell if Cookie was taking the piss out of Wallis, or being genuinely respectful.

Wallis turned back to me and sat on the opposite side of the table. "The chef," he said and nodded at the intercom, "he's always likes a little, shall we say, dig, especially before we get under way. Oh, and also at mealtimes, and sometimes in the morning too. I think he drinks that cheap rice wine or something, but it doesn't agree with him. But you know, he's a good guy. Been with CH Lam, in one way or another, for years."

I nodded.

"Now, your job." Wallis struck a match, lit his smoke, and flicked the match over the stern. "We have four, no five, important guests arriving today. One is the head of the company which owns this boat…"

"CH Lam?"

"No, his son…Sebastian. The others are clients. We also have some entertainment for them. Should be four girls, but I'm still waiting on one to show. The boss camps in there," he said, pointing toward the owner's cabin, "and he is bringing his amusement with him."

"Where are the entertainers now?"

"With the skipper, in their quarters. You'll meet them shortly but for now he's giving them final instructions. Now, these guests are all very important. We are never told their identities, though a sealed list with their names is always given to Skip…for emergency use only. They are all addressed as Mike with an initial. The first one, Mike Z, will be joining us here in about an hour."

"Mike Z. Right."

"Your job will be to greet Mike Z as he comes aboard. One of the entertainers will be with you. She will show him to his cabin. You will carry any luggage, and make sure he's settled in. Then leave Mike and his lady alone. You do that for each of them."

"Is that it—I'm a boat porter?"

"No, of course that's not it. From then on, you're responsible for their security. These guys are heavy hitters, and we don't know what other baggage they bring with them…if you get my drift. They have meetings on board—they might play a little blackjack, or spin the wheel. They drink booze—shitloads of that whisky we nearly lost. And play with the girls. We…you…have to get them back to land in one piece."

"Are they friendly…to one another I mean?"

"Who knows? We don't know who they really are. We've had the odd argument between them in the past…different clients to these…but you never know. And then there are the entertainers. Some blokes are rough…treat 'em like shit. I don't want 'em hurt. If they have a problem with a client, your job is step between them. Protect the girl first. Unless she's the one causing trouble. Then you protect the client."

"You've had trouble before?"

Wallis gazed off into the distance. An assistant chef arrived with the two coffees, carefully set them down on the table, and disappeared. "Thanks, mate," I said. Wallis said nothing. He slowly turned to his coffee and took a sip.

"Once only. Poor girl was knocked about, bruising, black eye, busted lip. Client must have given her some. Security stepped in to look after the girl, and the client took exception."

"What happened…to security, I mean?"

Wallis went silent again. He nodded towards the ocean. "Back home…across there I guess. States, I think."

"You don't know?"

"I don't ask. He was, shall we say, relieved of his position immediately, and they took him away with the girls when we reached shore."

"So, what about the client…what happened to him…after he's belted the girl?"

Wallis shrugged. "Delivered back to shore in one piece, as per instructions. Like I say, these guys are heavy. They make the rules. The boss says jump left, we don't jump right. Know what I'm sayin'?"

I slowly let this news sink in. The job seemed more suited to a UN peace mission, not a single security guy. But Wallis obviously knew nothing of my real task—watching Sebastian. I thought I'd not bother to mention it.

"Hey," Wallis said, changing the subject, "can you handle a gun?"

The question startled me. "Why? Will I need to?"

"Don't know…let's all cross our fingers, eh?" Wallis looked a little irritated. "But just in case…I've got five FNP 45s on board. You know 'em?"

I nodded. "Heard of them."

"We've got one hidden per deck…I'll show you where…and a spare for you. Only to be used in dire circumstances. Protect the boss, or the skipper, that sort of thing." He passed me a handset. "And this pager…keep it with you. Works from the intercom system. So, you clear on the task?"

I didn't believe there were only five guns on board. No way would Wallis leave himself unprotected, and he seemed to be a specialist in revealing information as it suited him. Given the experience of the former security personnel, the ten grand for the week was now looking a bit light on. What I needed was bourbon, not coffee.

"Perfectly clear."

A clatter started behind me, from somewhere in the gaming salon. Voices chattering. Females giggling. I stood up and turned to face it. Wallis stood too. The three entertainers, dressed in skimpy see-through yoga tops and short, tight skirts, made their way up the stairs. Following behind was a small, dark-haired woman…late-twenties I guessed…dressed in a striped t-shirt and white jeans, and behind her a shortish man with a jiggling beer-belly, sporting a white captain's cap. He was blowing a bit from the climb.

"Ah," said Wallis, "Ash meet Venus, Mae, and Cherry. Our entertainers. And Gina, one of our waitresses. Girls, this is Ash, our security man. He'll look after you."

"Ladies." I nodded at each in turn.

"Oooh, he's big," said Venus. She walked behind me, and smacked me lightly on the backside. "Very strong."

"Hey," said the short man in the captain's hat, "don't touch."

"And this," said Wallis, "is our captain. Skip, meet Ash Todd."

I held out my hand and gave him a solid shake. "Glad to have you on board," he said, withdrawing his hand as soon as he could. But he didn't look at me when he spoke. He looked sideways, at Wallis. Very odd.

Familiar, and odd.

18

I decided a further reconnaissance of the boat was required. There was obviously little regard for anyone's safety, except perhaps for the owner. He pays the wages, therefore he must survive. If I was responsible for the protection of everyone, even if there was a pecking order, I needed to know this ship backwards.

First, though, I had to unpack. I grabbed my duffel, and headed to the crew cabins. Wallis' advice was good…the middle at the bow was definitely the biggest available. It was tight, but I could live with it.

Second, communications. I checked my phone. Full signal. At sea, I wasn't so sure. I made a mental note to ask. I opened my iPad. All working. Opened my emails. More junk with internet deals. The car salesman with the convertible was very persistent. If I would care to drop by today, he could do an even better deal. Today? Not sure I could make it. Hit delete.

Another from Veronica, the gorgeous Russian. She seemed to be chasing me across the world. For all I knew she could really be Mae or Cherry or Venus upstairs. Or even Wil Wallis. That was a scary thought. Sorry Veronica. Hit delete.

One caught my eye. From Dick Mayvers. *Hey, mate,* it read, *all good back here. Pretty quiet, just another little drug bust. Nothin' I can't handle. Hope u r holding up. Cheers.* Imagine that, Mayvers was one-upping me. Nothing he can't handle, eh?

I typed a reply. *Just heading out for a cruise. This is the life…wall to wall luxury. Booze and broads…but it wouldn't suit you!*

But as I pressed *Send,* I suddenly wanted to be home. Not back at work, just in my pad. Looking over the harbour. I thought of the car smash I'd heard a few days ago. Wondered what had happened to them. In my mind, I heard the crunch again, and the smell, of my own smash. The feel of Sally's warm blood trickling onto my face. My baby and my wife…gone in a flash. I felt sick.

The intercom in my cabin buzzed. I pressed to speak. "Yep?"

"Ash," said Wallis, "don't spend too much time there. Do whatever you've got to do, but we've got Mike Z here in twenty, and I still have to show you the armoury."

"See you on the boarding deck in ten."

I set off to the back of the boat, and checked out the toy room again. There wasn't much there I'd have a problem with. Sure, I'd told Wallis I had no boat experience, but that was just to keep his scent away from my real job. Power boat training, sailing, jet skis…they were all part of my life for years. A few minutes brush-up and I'd be good to go. The big tender looked the most cumbersome, but everything was craned in through a door on the starboard side. Should be a snip.

I headed up to the main deck and scanned the salon and dining, then the galley. I peered down the small stairs to the crew cabins—the chef's access. More like a ladder really. Next to these was a small, half-door I hadn't noticed before. I slid it up—a dumb waiter.

I moved on to the staterooms. I noticed each had the motif for a card suit on the door. First on the left, a heart. I looked in. Purple décor. Opposite, a diamond. Pink. Second on the left, a spade. It seemed a black and grey combination. Opposite this, a club. It was blue. At the end were the twin rooms for the entertainers. The left hand door was red, the right hand black. They might be in. I knocked on the red door.

Cherry opened it. She stood smack in the middle of the doorway. Naked. Well, her top half I was sure of. Quite impressive. I guessed the bottom half was similarly attired. She was directly below me and I thought it best to appear cool. Don't stare. Her blonde hair was tied up into a kind of bun arrangement behind, and the small wisps not caught up, hung loosely. She gazed up at me with her big, brown Brazilian eyes.

"Oh, you were quick to come, big boy. Couldn't wait, eh?"

"Sorry to disappoint," I said, "just a security check."

She bounced back into the cabin, and flopped on her bed. Venus lay on the other, topless but still with her skirt intact, reading a magazine. She waved her pinkie finger at me, and smiled. I gave the room a quick once-over.

"Thanks, just getting the lie of the land. If you need any help, buzz me. Crew cabin C4, or the security button, both on your intercom. See you in a bit."

"I hope so," she said, "hurry back any time."

I pulled Cherry's door shut and knocked on the black door adjacent. Mae opened it, holding an emery board and a bottle of nail polish in her spare hand.

"Can I take a quick look?"

She nodded. Identical layout to the red door, but both were furnished in neutral tones. I supposed the eyes needed a rest somewhere, and this was it.

Mae followed me in. "Ash…you know these men, Skip and Wil, for long time?"

"Only just met them. Why?"

"Oh, no reason. Funny man, that Skip." She shrugged.

"Well, if he gets too funny, call me. Buzz C4 or security."

She smiled, but looked kind of sad I thought. I retreated to the salon, and climbed the stairs to the upper deck. I took a quick look around the gaming room, the bathroom, and the small office. Another look at the owner's suite, just to make sure I hadn't dreamt it earlier. It was even gaudier this visit.

I moved along to the captain's quarters, past a small opening for the goods lift from the galley. I knocked. No answer. I looked in. Navy blue and white décor, timber panelled cupboards, a queen bed to the right, and bathroom to the left. Clothing was scattered about, and a small handgun lay on the bedside table. That would be number six. Must be seven on board, then. I shut the door quietly, and moved to the first mate's room opposite. Similar, but smaller. Straight ahead lay the bridge. I stepped in.

Impressive…like a sci-fi set. A huge, sharply angled windscreen spanned more than the width of the bridge—over one-eighty degrees. Mega-sized wipers lay at different angles across it. Two, grey-leather, high-back pilot chairs sat in front of the dark blue console. One at the wheel for the captain, the other for the first mate. A bank of computer screens stretched across the console, with an array of switches between each. Behind the pilot chairs, against a timber panelled wall, sat a high, matching grey-leather sofa, long enough for four.

I moved in closer to the computer screens. Some registered changing numbers, another appeared to be constructing graphs. A couple were switched off. I gave the wheel a shove. Heavy, hardly moved.

I heard a click behind me. A familiar click. I lifted my hands off the wheel and away from me, and began to turn slowly.

Skip stood in the doorway, shirtless, a towel wrapped about his waist. He was pointing a pistol at me. I guessed that pistol must have been the number six from the bed. I also guessed that pistol was now ready for firing.

He glared up at me. "What do you want?"

"Just checking out the operation. Got to know where everything is. That includes looking after you."

"Not in here. Not without me. Always ask first. Got it?" He gradually let the pistol drop.

"Yeah, I got it. And sorry I can't stay. Mike Z will be waiting."

19

I pushed past Skip, whose squint-eyed gaze never left me, and made my way back down to the boarding deck. Wil Wallis leant against the aft garage door, puffing on a cigarette and scanning the pontoons for approaching human activity. A few feet away Venus sat back in a blue deck chair, now more elegantly clad in a loose, white shirt and tight-fitting sky-blue pants. She was engrossed in a magazine, taking an occasional sip from a tumbler of water which sat at her feet.

"You took your time," said Wallis, "any trouble?"

"Just checking-out the whole show. Ran in to Skip on the bridge, but he didn't seem too pleased to see me."

"Likes to protect his territory. Probably warned you off, eh?"

"Something like that. Seems a bit trigger-happy."

"You'll get used to him. Speaking of triggers, better show you the on-board defence system." Wallis glanced at Venus. "You wait here. We'll be back in five." Venus gave a small wave of her hand, without looking up.

Wallis pressed a button to the side, and the garage door slowly rose, exposing the contents of the toy room. The door silently closed behind us as we entered, and made our way into the hallway which led to the engine room. To one side, next to the stairs which led up to the salon, was a small cupboard. Wallis unlocked it, and pulled out a belt-slide holster and handgun. Another identical weapon sat loose, inside. He handed me the holster.

"This is for you. Pull the slide and she's good to go. Magazine has fourteen rounds. Might pay to get yourself familiar with it."

I pulled the pistol from the holster, gave it a cursory look-over, and replaced it—no point looking too knowledgeable—undid my belt and slipped it on. "Yeah, I'll spend some time with it later."

"Like I said, one of these per deck. Each with fourteen rounds. This one stays here," he said, locking the cupboard. "Come on, I'll show you the others."

We climbed to the other decks, inspecting small cupboards on each. One at the end of the dining area on the main, one behind the blackjack table on the upper, and one next to the bar on the sundeck. Each contained an identical handgun. The cupboard in the dining area held four additional magazine clips, each with fourteen rounds. The cupboard behind the blackjack table also contained a knife. I covered the handle with a handkerchief, and slid it from its sheath. Hunting knife—about a foot long with a partially serrated, seven-inch blade.

I held it up. "Expecting extra trouble?"

"Don't know why that's here—belongs to Skip." He dipped his head at the cover I'd put over the handle. "But why the precaution—you on the run from something?"

"Currently, no…but it pays to be careful."

"Ha, I guess…I'll get it moved later. Better get back down."

He locked the cupboard and we descended to the boarding platform. Venus was still sitting, nose in magazine. Wallis lit a cigarette, as an Asian man approached the boat. He moved quickly, despite his age, and was dressed in white trousers with a sky-blue polo shirt, navy blazer and matching lizard-print, tasselled loafers. A panama fedora, brim turned up at the back, sat atop his head shading his tortoise-shell framed sunglasses. His left hand lightly held a mother-of-pearl tipped cane, and in his right, a sizeable cigar. Following quickly behind was a young Asian man who wheeled a large suitcase with one hand, and carried an overnighter in the other.

He called out. "Is this the *Golden Empress*?"

"It is," replied Wallis, "and you would be Mike Z, if I am assuming correctly?"

"You are."

"Welcome aboard, Mike," said Wallis.

Mike's assistant deposited the bags onto the boarding platform, and was dismissed clutching a couple of sizable notes.

"Ash, here, is our head of security. He will take your bags for you."

"Mr Z," I said, nodding at him as I picked up the belongings.

"Please, call me Mike," he said, "everyone does."

"Very well, Mike."

"And this, Mike, is Venus," said Wallis. He waved his hand, motioning her to stand and join the group. Venus stood, smoothed out her clothes, flicked back her honey-coloured curls, and sauntered over. She moved straight to Mike, leant forward until her right breast just pressed onto his arm, and gave him a small kiss on the cheek.

"Hello, Mike," she said, "I've been waiting."

Mr Z was obviously startled for a moment by the husky European accent. He stared at her, his gaze fixed on the bridge of her nose. Or maybe it was on the divine green eyes.

Then he flashed a mile-wide grin, and placed his hand in the small of her back. "Venus…I'm so sorry to have kept you."

20

Patrick Hogan took a quick shower, towelled off and pulled on his captain's uniform…a short-sleeved, white shirt with shoulder epaulets of four bright-gold stripes and embroidered gold anchor and wreath, navy trousers and brown leather boat shoes. His white hat with black visor featured a gold chin strap, and above that a bullion wreath device surrounding the word, CAPTAIN. He placed the hat on carefully, making certain of the correct tilt. His favoured look.

Whether Hogan was entitled to wear an 'official' captain's uniform was the subject of some discussion. Mostly with Wil Wallis. Wallis had been a merchant seaman for ten years, in what was for him, a career path. He began as a rating and finished as a deck officer. Wallis felt he was genuinely qualified to consider himself a captain.

On the other hand, Hogan, according to Wallis, was nothing more than a show pony. A businessman with a boat licence, and a slick story. Sure, in the past Hogan had owned a couple of serious nautical pleasure palaces, and if Wallis was pushed, he would admit Hogan was a first-rate skipper. But to call himself a captain was a big stretch. Not that it concerned Hogan…he'd call himself whatever he damn well wanted. To him, that's what this boating was about. Business. Not merchant navies.

"And what precise business skills do you bring to the table?" Hogan would ask of Wallis. "Mere boating experience is not enough."

Wallis would bristle at the dismissive 'mere boating experience'.

"You should know my business skills," Wallis would reply, "I've kept you out of the slammer, against the odds, for years. Your business skills get you locked up. Mine free you. You got a fucking problem with that?" At this point the discussion usually terminated.

Each needed the skills of the other, and they knew it. Hogan was indeed lucky to have someone like Wallis onside. He had a total disdain for those in authority, and therefore a sharp sense of real trouble as opposed to grandstanding. He also possessed enough knowledge of the law to manoeuvre around an issue.

Hogan, on the other hand, knew people. He loved a deal. He was persuasive, master of the powerful pitch. And after explaining at length why he, Hogan, should hold the senior position, Wallis would respond in Latin. *"Plenus stercoris es,"* he would pronounce, and, for effect, flick his head up and repeat, *"plenus stecoris es."* This meant nought to Hogan, but roughly translated as *"you're full of shit."*

So, to keep the peace, Wallis was issued with his uniform. Same as Hogan, but with one less stripe on the epaulets, and his hat read, FIRST MATE.

Hogan's phone rang. He checked the number display, and pressed answer.

"Are you ready? Everything in order?" Sebastian Lam sounded impatient.

"Everything's just perfect," said Hogan. He could get mighty sick of Lam's shrill insistence, and a dull derision was his standard response. "We'll be ready to leave shortly. Just making up your room now."

Whether Lam picked up on the tone was not always clear, but he showed no interest in it. "We are in Macau, four of us. Three Mike's, and me."

"Yeah, I got it," said Hogan, "and don't forget your Miss Jay-Dee."

"Yes, of course," said Lam, "now I want you to come straight here. Ring me on approach."

"Will do. ETA about four o'clock, or a little after." Hogan ended the call.

Hogan gathered up his personal bits and pieces, locked his wallet and handgun in the cabin wall-safe, and moved to the intercom. He pressed the general call button. "First Mate Wallis, can you respond?"

About thirty seconds elapsed and the intercom sprang to life. "Wallis."

"Where are you?"

"On the boarding platform, taking delivery of chef's final order."

"Well move it along, we've got to get going—I'll be down in five."

Hogan made his way to the bridge, opened the door which led out onto the bridge deck, and scanned the marina. The day was hot, oppressively sticky, and the familiar pink-grey haze now cloaked everything. He retreated inside and settled in at his seat. He checked various screens, flicked a number of switches, turned two keys, and pressed two buttons. Far below, both engines sprang to life. He switched on the air-conditioning, and set off down to the boarding platform.

As he passed through the salon Gina and a chef's assistant carried a foam box, and a tray filled with glasses, in the direction of the galley. He nodded at them. "Ladies," he said.

"Lunch be ready soon," said the assistant.

"Good," said Hogan.

He noticed Mae and Cherry sitting at the bar off the salon, both immersed in their phones. He gave them a quick mock salute as they looked up at him. They half-smiled in return.

He moved to the back of the salon deck, and peered over, down at the boarding deck. Wallis stood below taking a final drag on his cigarette. "Well, are you ready?" Hogan called down.

"All good to go," said Wallis, flicking the butt into the water.

"What about Todd?"

"Yep, just doing his rounds. So, what are the instructions? Where to?"

"Macau. Four of them to pick up, plus his floozy. Then he'll let us know further. And the redhead?"

Wallis shrugged. "That's why I'm here…I called her…she said she'd make it. Fuck I hope she hurries. I'll get the lines."

"So do I," said Hogan, "otherwise we'll have to give Gina a gentle tap." He turned inside and headed back to the bridge, as Wallis stepped on to the boarding platform.

A shriek pierced the otherwise calm afternoon. "Wait, wait." Wallis snapped around to his left. A tall, leggy redhead, barefoot and clutching a small overnight bag in one hand, and a pair of sneakers in another, ran toward them along the pontoon.

Wallis grinned through his beard. "Belle! About time…what kept you?"

"Oh, darling…it was hell…the traffic." Belle glanced up. "Whoa, you didn't tell me you had such a big boat. Is everything on board this big?"

Wallis gave her a sideways glance, his mouth curling at the corners in a little smile, and he let out a small "ha-ha."

"C'mon," he said, "you'll miss the ride of your life."

21

Skip manoeuvred the *Golden Empress* from her mooring at the Gold Coast Marina at a little after 1:15 p.m. He slid past a couple of similar sized yachts, both securely locked. Nobody aboard. He eased out into the expanse of the South China Sea, and slowly made his way west around the tip of the peninsula. Just off a small bay he shut the yacht down, and dropped anchor. Time for lunch.

The cruise to Macau would take about two hours, which allowed the chef forty minutes to feed all on board. Plenty of time. He moved to the intercom and announced, "Attention ladies and gentlemen, lunch will be served in five minutes on the salon deck." He then dialled the phone in the Spade cabin.

A subdued voice answered. "Mike."

"Ah, Mike…Skip here. Will you require lunch in your cabin, or join the others?"

"In my cabin will be excellent, thank you."

"For how many—one or two?"

There was a short silence.

"For two, I think. Yes, two."

"Certainly, be there shortly."

Skip headed down to the salon deck, stopping in at the galley to relay the Mike Z instructions to the chef. Eventually this food organising would be handled by the staff, but Skip liked to be in control at the start. Just to ensure at the outset the guests were looked after properly. In the galley hall, he paused to allow Gina past. She was carrying a bottle of wine, and an ice bucket.

"For Mike," she said.

He retraced his steps through the dining area and salon. Two tables were arranged on the deck, with a waitress fussing about dispensing food. Wallis and Todd were seated at one and the entertainers at the other. He was surprised to see Venus sitting among them, sipping on a mineral water. He caught her eye, and motioned back toward the bow.

"Not hungry?"

"I've already eaten," she said.

*

Sebastian Lam sat at his desk and finished off his lunch—beef with egg-sauce rice noodles—and downed the last of his glass of white wine. It was later than usual, nearly 2:30, due to a particularly busy morning in the club. Half-a-dozen of his regular customers had arrived, and all had to be greeted personally. Each required an extended chat, lashings of false compliments, and organising into suitable gaming rooms.

Giant egos were a standard in this business, and pairing the wrong types in the same game could be a short-cut to financial disaster. He had learnt this some years prior, when he first took over at the Golden Mountain. Thankfully his father was around to sort out the problem. But Sebastian was not his father. CH was a humble man—he understood his clients, and never competed. Sebastian had no desire to compete with them, but he had no innate understanding of them either.

He understood money…and how to count it…but not so much people, or how to manage them. Getting the mix right was a time consuming, stressful affair for him. He was glad it was now done. He buzzed Lily to remove his dining implements, and quickly studied his bank of screens. All seemed in order, with each of the new arrivals actively pumping his hard-earned money Sebastian's way.

Lily appeared and removed the crockery. "Don't forget, Mr Ma, Mr Grekov and Mr Wang will be here at three," she reminded him.

Sebastian shuddered. He really didn't relish the thought of being around Grekov. "Yes, yes…now make sure Mr Wang comes in after the other two. I don't want them all arriving together. Give me a few minutes with them first."

Lily disappeared and Lam continued checking his screens. He then logged in to the company bank accounts, and scanned the balances. All good. He took himself off to his suite and changed into his casual attire. A yellow linen sports coat over a blue and white checked shirt, white chinos, and navy boat shoes. Nautical wear. He gathered up his pre-packed overnight bag, placed it at the suite door and resumed his place at his desk in the office.

A little after three Lily announced the arrival of Ma and Grekov. Sebastian greeted them at the door. "Enjoying your stay?"

"Not bad," mumbled Grekov, "but better if you pay." Sebastian thought he looked a little tired. Sweaty maybe.

"So," Sebastian said, "you have luggage?" They each pointed to their bags. "Excellent—the driver will be here shortly to collect them. Now, a drink before we depart?"

"Not for me," said Ma.

"A small vodka," said Grekov. Sebastian fetched it.

"Now," said Sebastian, "we have another guest who will be joining us. He will be here in a moment. You may have heard of him. Mr Wang—Mike Wang."

Ma and Grekov looked at each other, their faces expressionless.

Ma turned to Sebastian. "This Mike Wang...what does he do?"

"He's our dealer, for the cruise."

Grekov pursed his thick lips. "And where is he from? Beijing?"

There was a knock at the door.

"I believe so, but you can ask him yourself."

Sebastian opened the door, and an unremarkable looking man stood staring at the trio. Mid-forties, and dressed in grey trousers and a white shirt, he could have been any one of millions of office workers from China. Sebastian introduced each in turn. Wang shook hands, but showed no emotion. In fact, he appeared to not so much as blink. Just a cold stare.

"Tell me, Mike," said Grekov eyeing Wang up and down, "you from Beijing?"

Wang stared back. "Yes, just like my father and grandfather before me."

Grekov and Ma again exchanged their own expressionless glance. "Shit," said Grekov in his thickest Russian accent, "excellent shit."

The phone on Sebastian's desk blooped. He picked it up.

"Okay, okay." He turned to the assembled group. "Gentlemen, we have entertainment on board which I trust you find to your liking. I, however, will have my guest accompanying me."

Sebastian moved and opened the door. Miss Jay-Dee stood in all her colourful glory, a white blouse displaying ample cleavage, hot-pink shorts, and her inevitable platform shoes. She was freshly made up, with a new dark wig, hot-red lip gloss and nicely rouged cheeks.

Sebastian swept his arm in a big semi-circle, as she entered the room. "This is Miss Jay-Dee, my guest for the cruise. Jay-Dee…meet Mike M, Mike W and Mike G."

Miss Jay-Dee said "hello" and smiled at each in turn. When she reached Grekov, she dropped her gaze. Grekov stood motionless for a moment, dipped his head at her, and turned away. He took a solid gulp of vodka, swallowed hard and kept the glass to his lips. He puffed out a short, sharp sigh.

"Double shit," he said.

22

I sat on the salon deck with Wallis, working my way through lunch, which in this case consisted of a club ham sandwich about two inches thick. A mixture of sauce and mustard dripped from each end onto my plate as I grappled with the thing, trying to force it into my mouth.

I swallowed hard on some bread. “Skip won’t join us?”

Wallis shook his head. “Eats alone, mostly. Then when he’s ready, we’ll get moving. Mostly the guests and entertainers all retire about now…combination of food, booze, stinking humidity and the hum of the boat make them sleepy.”

At that moment, I felt the motors fire up again, and the *Empress* slowly turned toward Macau and gradually lifted to cruising speed.

Wallis said, “When we get there, your job is to pick up the guests from the wharf. We can’t get this boat in. Too big. So, we’ll anchor in the harbour.”

“How many people?”

“Three guests, plus the boss. And his handbag. So…five.”

“I’ll need the big tender?”

Wallis nodded.

"All called Mike, right?"

Wallis said, "Correct."

"What are they hiding?"

"Maybe nothing. Maybe something. I don't ask. Best you don't either. Just make sure they are looked after," Wallis said. He stood and flicked the butt of his post lunch cigarette into the water.

This was a funny mix, I thought. The hookers I could understand. And the expensive booze. But these four big-time businessmen, who don't want their names known, left in the care of a bloke whose father doesn't trust him? And Hogan and Wallis…now there were two blokes I would not have picked as front-runners to look after this show. Still, life can be strange… so, yeah…a very funny mix.

I made my way down to the garage. The big tender was a twenty-two-foot Novurania Chase 23. Plenty big enough, and with serious grunt. I checked the unloading system. A starboard side door lifted, which allowed a telescopic crane to simply drop an item onto the water. The crane had four straps, which connected to the tender at four anchor points. The tender was fuelled, key in ignition, ready to go. Seemed simple enough.

I climbed back up to the salon. The rear deck was empty, except for one. Venus sat at her lunch table, where she didn't eat, gazing back at Hong Kong as it rapidly disappeared in the haze.

"Mind if I sit?"

She seemed a bit startled. "Sure."

I settled in on the opposite side of the table, and stared out the back with her. Neither of us spoke.

When the silence became too much, I said, "What about your client, Mike? Is he okay?"

"I guess so. Said for me not to worry, and to come back later in the day. He's a bit old you know, and some of these older guys, they like to pretend, but not do so much. Good for their, what you call it? Self-esteem, I think."

"Possibly. So, where are you from?"

Her mouth turned up at the corners. "Hong Kong. Don't you remember?"

"Cute, but where before that?"

"Europe—Czech Republic."

"Enjoy the work?"

"Money's good. I can take or leave the rest. Now your turn, where are you from?"

"Sydney—Australia. Been there?"

"No, but people say it's a good place. Maybe one day soon I will go. Do you like this work?"

"Don't know yet. I've hardly started."

"This your first time in security? You a virgin?" She laughed, and threw her head back.

"Very clever—no, only just started on this boat."

"Ha," she said, waving a hand, "fancy you a virgin. That means you not married, right?"

The punch in the gut hit me again. Damn this sensitivity. I didn't like this feeling, but one more thing I now knew—I didn't like questions, even half-joking questions, about my marriage. Too soon.

I sucked up a slow breath. "Was, but not now."

She must have sensed my change of mood, and went quiet for

a minute. I sat, slowly drumming my fingers on the table. Then she said, "I was too, but also not now."

Venus then turned in her chair, placed her hands on mine to stop the drumming, and looked straight at me. Now all serious. "Sorry to make joke. I meant no harm." She kept one hand on top of mine, and with the other slowly stroked the back of her fingers up my arm. "Maybe I could make it up to you. In your cabin, now, if you like. Just for fun. No charge."

For a split-second the temptation hit me. But it… everything…was too soon.

"Great offer—thanks, but ask me later, eh?"

23

The *Golden Empress* slowly made her way toward Macau, passing under the long, gently arcing bridge which connects the mainland to Taipa. At a little after four in the afternoon, we moored a couple of hundred yards short of the outer-harbour marina. I sat on the deck outside the salon, taking in the sweep of casinos dominating the harbour front, as the anchor rumbled down.

Wil Wallis appeared, cigarette in hand. He took a long draw. "You can get the tender out now. Need any instruction?"

"No," I said, "I'm good."

"They need fifteen minutes to get there from the office, so when do I get 'em to leave?"

I did a quick calculation. "I reckon it'll take me ten to get the boat in the water with that crane, and another five to get to the wharf…plus some wriggle room in case of unintended consequences. Say twenty…and so, say they leave in five?"

"I'll let 'em know. Remember…boss' name is Sebastian. Small bloke, sharp dresser. His lady friend is Miss Jay-Dee, I believe. Three guests, all called Mike as you know."

I made my way down to the toy room, pressed a button to raise the starboard door, and hooked the four cables from the crane onto the tender. I pressed a couple more buttons, slowly raised it from the cradle, turned it side on and extended the arms out above the harbour. A gentle pull on a small lever dropped the tender alongside the *Empress*. I unclipped the cables, retracted the crane, jumped in, and kicked the starter over.

As I approached the pier, all was quiet. No sign of anyone. I sat a little way off, idling. A small woman finally appeared.

Her shrill voice bounced across the water. "Yoohoo…are you from the *Empress*?"

"Yep."

"Then we are ready." She turned away and called out, "Sebastian, over here."

I moved the tender alongside the pier, and tied it off. Four men, and the small woman, made their way toward me. Another man pulled a trolley with bags. The dapper man Wallis had described stepped forward and held out his hand. "My name is Sebastian. You are?"

"Todd, Ash Todd. Head of security on the *Empress*."

"Very good, Todd Ash Todd…yes, my father mentioned you."

"Just Ash will be fine."

"Alright, Ash, this is my friend Miss Jay-Dee."

Jay-Dee held out her hand as she stepped aboard. "Helloooo again," she cooed. She looked pretty enough I thought, but that stubble might soon need attention.

I looked at the porter. "Hand those to me." I put the bags together in the middle.

Sebastian then introduced the three Mikes. Two Asian, one European. No surnames, letters only…W, M, and G. Each shook hands and sat at the back of the tender. Sebastian sat with them, and Jay-Dee settled in beside me up front.

I phoned Wallis. "On our way."

A few minutes later I tied the tender up at the boarding platform at the stern. Skip and Wallis stood to attention in their uniforms. The three entertainers, Cherry, Mae, and Belle, stood next to them, beaming. When they turned it on, I thought, they didn't look half bad. Gina took up the rear, holding a tray on which sat a bottle of whisky, and four glasses.

My passengers stepped on to the boarding platform—Jay-Dee first, then the three guests, and lastly Sebastian. Hogan and Wallis greeted each in turn, with Sebastian running the introductions.

Wallis said, "Gentlemen, a drink perhaps?"

Mikes M and W shook their heads.

Mike G looked around, shrugged, and said, "Then I will take." He lifted the bottle and a glass from Gina's tray.

Wallis then introduced each guest to his entertainer—M to Cherry, W to Mae and G to Belle. The guests all nodded approvingly. The entertainers maintained their smiles. Mouth smiles, I noticed. No eyes smiling.

Wallis then said to the group, "Please follow me and I will show you to your cabins."

I said, "I'll have your bags delivered shortly." Wallis handed me a list of cabins and occupants—M in the Heart, W in the Club, and G in the Diamond.

I moved the tender off, stowed it back in the toy room, and

began the bag delivery. Eight bags in total. Three trips up and down required. I began with Sebastian's, to the upper deck. Miss Jay-Dee answered the door.

"Mister Ash— are you new?"

"Yep. Does it show?"

"Here…take this. You might need me some time." She pressed a business card into my hand.

"What about Sebastian? He'll be jealous."

"Oh, he's not permanent."

"Well, thanks, but boys are not really my thing. By the way, is he in?"

"He's with Skip."

I finished off the porterage to the other cabins. I knocked on each door. Not the Spade—I assumed Venus had resumed attending to Mike Z—and at each the entertainer answered and took the luggage.

As I headed back down, the chef and his assistants were hard at work, chopping.

I poked my head in the galley. "What's for dinner? Anything good?"

The chef turned and flashed a sleazy grin. "Nothing for you," he said and he held up his cleaver, still grinning.

I waved him off, and moved into the salon. I felt the vibration as the motors kicked in, and Wallis appeared from the upper deck.

I cast him a glance. "Where to now?"

"Open water," he said. He motioned over his shoulder, "South China Sea. Forty miles or so, then we'll stop for the night."

For a group of heavy-hitters, it seemed a damn strange destination.

24

We travelled for a couple of hours, east for a bit, then south-east. I made my regular trips around the boat, making sure everything was in order. The place was surprisingly quiet. The water was calm, and the motors hardly registered a beat as we cruised. The heavy, pink-grey haze of Hong Kong had been replaced by a lighter-grey version in Macau. Away from the mainland it disappeared altogether, and the later afternoon turned a softer blue.

The humidity remained, but in the air-conditioned luxury of the *Golden Empress*, no-one raised a sweat. Not from the weather, anyway. I stationed myself on the deck off the salon. The guests kept to their cabins and Gina ferried food or booze to them, or up to the bridge, on request. The entertainers occasionally appeared, and when they did, joined me on the deck.

Cherry turned-up carrying a bottle of Coke. She slumped in a chair, pursed her lips, and blew out a long breath. Her shortish blonde hair, which was normally kept perfectly in place, looked ruffled. Like she had blown it around with a hair dryer. Makeup showed no sign of wear. Light-pink lipstick looked like it had been freshly touched-up. Her clothes were intact, but her very short skirt rode up her long, brown legs as she sat. I noticed a couple of things— some scratches on her upper thigh, and no knickers.

I nodded at her. "Hard day?"

She stayed silent for a minute, watching the ocean roll by, then smiled faintly.

"Not really. Just some guys want to do some stupid things." She held up the bottle, placed it down between her legs, gave me a long questioning look and shook her head.

"You okay?"

"Sure. He's deciding what he really wants. But he's not using this," she said, holding up the bottle again, and resumed staring at the sea.

"Let me know if it gets too rough." Cherry just shrugged.

I decided to check in on the bridge and followed Gina up on one of her trips. As we passed the Owners Suite, we could hear voices raised.

"No, don't put it there," one said. The tone was sharp.

"Where then?"

"Put it here," the first voice said.

Gina turned and gave me a quizzical look. I shook my head. The lovers didn't sound happy. We moved on.

Gina knocked on the bridge door, and slipped in with her tray of refreshments. Four bottles of beer. She stepped out with the same tray plus three empty bottles, and headed for the galley. I gave a few quick raps, and stepped in.

Hogan and Wallis sat at their respective stations, both now pulling on a fresh beverage. Hogan didn't move. He checked his screens.

Wallis looked around at me and said, "Ah, security, what can we do for you?"

"Just making sure you don't need anything. And an ETA on when we might pull up, and where."

Wallis said, "We don't need anything. If we do, we'll ask. If we don't ask, assume we don't need it. That right, Skip?"

Skip nodded twice.

Wallis continued, "So you just look after the guests and the girls. Don't worry about us. See you later."

I turned to leave.

Skip half looked up and said, "We'll stop when I say so. But since you asked, in fifteen minutes. And where?" He threw his arms round in big circles. "Out here."

"I'll await further instruction then." I moved to the door and turned back slightly. "By the way, Skip, I think we've met somewhere. Any ideas?"

For a moment, Hogan didn't move. Then in slow-motion he turned his head around, and up to me, his jaw clenched tight. His bottom lip and chin wrinkled from the pressure. He pursed his lips. His eyes narrowed. He shook his head.

"Never seen you before."

Wallis nodded twice. Hogan looked back at his screen.

25

As Skip had promised, the *Empress* slowed to a crawl after about fifteen minutes. She made gentle headway for maybe another five, and then the engines cut out. A calming silence took over.

I sat back on the salon deck, breathed in the humid salty air, and scanned the horizon. Off the port side stern, some distance away, two container ships made steady, slow-motion progress heading south. Another headed north, well off on the starboard. The light was fading and the evening took on a pink-grey hue, as the sun set behind us over Macau. I made a mental note to ask Dick Mayvers to check on the name 'Patrick Hogan'. See if anything came up.

Wallis appeared, took up a position, standing, at the rear of the deck, and lit a smoke.

I said, "Well, what now?"

"We stay here for the night."

"Won't we drift—it's too deep to anchor?"

"We will—but Skip and I take turns on watch, and we correct our position as needed. We'll pretty much be here in the morning."

"And tomorrow?"

Wallis blew out a cloud of smoke. "Who knows? Time will tell. Just concern yourself with tonight. The guests and entertainers will be fed in there, soon." He pointed over my head at the dining area. "And then they'll retire upstairs to the gaming lounge. I want you up there with 'em. They'll be pretty full of booze by then—and we don't want any emotional imbalances. Get my drift?"

"Sure."

Wallis flicked his cigarette butt into the water, and made for the salon. "Any major issues, call me. Otherwise I'll see you tomorrow." He signed off with a two-fingered salute.

*

Ma Junjie rapped sharply on the door of the Diamond cabin, directly opposite his. Silence. He knocked twice again. He heard shuffling. The door opened slowly. Belle stood before him, long auburn-red hair covering her shoulders. Her skin was quite pale, he noticed, and her breasts gently heaved with each breath. They were quite small, but then that fitted nicely with her long, slender body. She was nearly as tall as him, he noticed. Maybe six feet.

He glanced down. Her pubic hair was neatly shaved, into a thin strip. It was a nice auburn-red colour. Her legs were long, he noticed, but in balance with the rest of her. She was a very attractive woman, but then, Cherry, who had been allotted to him, was also a stunner. He was pleased with her. And Grekov, his partner, did have a thing for redheads. He dismissed his thoughts, and stopped noticing.

Belle said, "Oh, it's you."

"Who else were you expecting?"

"No-one."

"Is he in—I need to speak with him?"

"Yes, he's in, but he's asleep."

"Well, wake him."

"He's very tired. He doesn't want to be woken."

Ma tried to peer around her, to see if Grekov was in fact asleep. But she shifted slightly sideways, blocking his view. He glanced at his watch—6:45.

"We have dinner at 7:30. I need to talk to him before. Please make sure you wake him, and I will return at 7:15."

"Okay, Mike, I'll try," she said.

Ma turned and stepped back toward his cabin. Belle blew him a silent kiss, snapping her head up as she did. She held her lips in a pout. There was no smile. A 'piss-off' kiss. Ma had his back to her. He didn't notice.

*

Sebastian Lam pulled the knot on his gold silk tie tight, straightened the collar on his fine, white shirt, and adjusted his deep-red brocade dinner jacket. Red and gold were important colours in Macau—Chinese lucky colours—and he felt it only right they should be worn at such an occasion. The occasion? Dinner he was hosting for his important clients, his lucky clients, aboard his wonderful yacht, *Golden Empress*.

He glanced across to the king-sized bed occupying centre stage in his Owner's Suite. Miss Jay-Dee lay face down and naked amongst the deep-red sheets. He pulled the top sheet off her. Bright-red marks covered the back of her neck—three or four strips each side snaking their way around to her throat. Her buttocks were a similar colour from repeated slapping, and her back was streaked from half-a-dozen fingernail scratches. Her wig had slipped slightly, and now sat at a forty-five-degree angle to her head. A small amount of blood and semen seeped from her backside. She looked a bit of a mess.

Sebastian pulled the sheet over her. “You coming to dinner?”

She stayed still for a moment, silent. Then she said, in a voice muffled by pillows, “How can I, like this? Look at me. After what you’ve done to me, I can’t go out. I’ll eat in here.”

“Suit yourself,” said Sebastian, “but I have a guest calling in shortly. Make yourself scarce, eh?”

Jay-Dee raised her head slightly, and glanced round at Sebastian who was now standing at a cocktail cabinet, carefully pouring two small whiskies. She gingerly hauled herself up from the bed, pulled the sheets back into place, and staggered to the bathroom.

Sebastian lifted the white bedspread off the floor, draped it across the bed and straightened it as best he could. A short knock on the door came moments later.

“Ah, Mr Wang, nice to see you. Come in. A whisky?” Mike Wang stood, unblinking, in his trademark white shirt, black trousers, and black shoes. For dinner, he had added a black coat with three buttons—all fastened. Sebastian handed him one of the just poured drinks.

Wang bowed slightly, said, “Thank you,” and settled into one of the deep-red armchairs.

Sebastian eyed him. “Enjoying the cruise? And Mae is to your liking?”

"Very nice—both—thank you."

"So, you are right to conduct the after-dinner business?"

Wang took a sip of the whisky, swirled it in his mouth and swallowed. "A fine malt," he said.

Sebastian nodded. "Thank you."

"And the business? Yes, that is in hand. What are our guests expecting?"

Sebastian tapped his fingertips together and cocked his head up at the ceiling. "Round figures? Seventy-five million—US. Fifty for the old man, and twenty-five for the odd couple."

"A good number," said Wang. "I will arrange it."

"Less, of course, our small fee." Sebastian looked across at Wang and winked.

Wang looked straight back, unblinking.

Then he smiled.

26

I ate dinner in my cabin. With no entertainment below deck for crew, I slipped on headphones and kicked back to some Elvis Costello and a bracket from Cold Chisel. They finished up with Choir Girl. That got the mind in the right frame for the evening.

At around 8:45 I ventured up to the main deck, dinner plate and fork in hand. The chef and an assistant were busily clearing the dining table. Empty bottles of whisky and red wine lined the sideboard. The white tablecloth was a mess. Looked like dinner was Italian. I added mine to the stack of plates.

I tapped chef on the shoulder. "All finished?" He jumped at the surprise.

"They all go," he said, pointing to the upper deck, "up there."

I made my way up to the gaming lounge. The atmosphere was subdued, courtesy of the wood panelling and dimmed lighting. A few items were backlit...the mountain ceiling motif, the two gaming tables, and the bar. Andy Williams' Moon River spilled from various speakers.

The roulette table sat empty. Mike W occupied the dealing

chair at the blackjack table. Seated opposite were Mike's M and G. W dealt cards out slowly, unblinking. M inspected his hand, rubbed his chin, and placed the cards face down on the table. G hardly moved. I thought he'd fallen asleep.

Fifteen feet away, semi-reclining in a plush, grey armchair, Mike Z sat back with Venus on his lap. She gently stroked his hair and smiled at him, picked up a tumbler of whisky from a side table, and held it for him to sip. He seemed to be in a sort of dream, quietly mouthing the words to the music.

In the middle of the room, directly under the mountain motif, Cherry and Belle took up a couple of chairs. They fiddled with their phones, waiting for instructions from their guests, who were pre-occupied with the card game. I pulled one of the armchairs out from their cluster, moved it to the opposite side of the room near the office, and took up my casual observation position. Out of the way, just as Sebastian had ordered. No-one seemed to notice.

Mr Williams finished his Moon River...and a new one began...Sinatra with My Way. This seemed to be some sort of signal, because Mike Z suddenly sprang to his feet. Venus did well not to dish the whisky over him.

Z searched along a wall in the half-light. "You have a microphone? Karaoke?"

Venus looked about, shook her head, and shrugged. "I don't know."

Mike W looked across from his dealing chair, with a dead-eyed expression. He pointed to a corner of the bar. "Over there," he said. "And not too loud, please."

Z grabbed the mic, flicked it on and blew a couple of times

into it to test the volume. He found a small wall panel behind him, adjusted a knob, and began crooning along with Mr Sinatra.

Mike M looked around, lifted his eyes heavenward, and shook his head. G stirred in his chair, picked up the hand W had dealt him, and said, "I put everything on this." He placed his cards face up on the table.

W stared at the hand, peeled a card off the pack, and placed it in front of him. He dealt two more. He looked up at G and said, "Congratulations, you have won."

"Good," said Mike G, "I'm sick of playing." He turned and looked across at Mike Z. "And his singing, it is shit."

W looked at both men and said, "Mike and Mike, let's settle up." He rose, the other two followed, and the three men made their way across the room, and into the small office beside me. Z finished his sing-along with a powerful finale, and strode back to his armchair.

His singing wasn't that bad, I thought, and the three girls all applauded. Certainly better than the cranky Mike G gave him credit for. He seemed pleased with the attention and gave a theatrical bow as he sat down. Venus settled back on his lap, and he took a long draw on his single malt.

The next number came on. John Rowles. Big voice. Z said, "Please turn this up." Cherry peeled herself away from her phone, and did as requested. Mr Rowles belted out Cheryl Moana Marie. Z sang along, eyes closed, from his chair.

Through the noise I became aware of a different sound. Voices arguing. I couldn't make out the subject, but the three men in the small office next to me were now having a disagreement on something. The one thing I could hear, quite clearly, was Mike

G, who bellowed, "I won't be treated like shit." A few moments later Mike W appeared, straightened his clothes, and strode briskly toward the Owner's Suite. He returned with Sebastian hurrying behind, buttoning-up his shirt.

The four men crammed into the office. It was quiet for a minute, then more argument. This time M exited, followed by G, his belly wobbling from the sudden movement. M stood facing back at the office door with his hands clasped together, as if to pray, his body leaning forward slightly, and his head slowly shaking from side to side. I assumed this meant "no" to whatever had just transpired in the office.

Mike G's face was flushed, and he shook as he thundered, "This is not a fucking deal. This is robbing. Again. I already warned you. Now, you fix it—all of it. And no more of your shit." He snapped his fingers at Belle and Cherry. "We go—you come." G, M and the two entertainers made for the stairs, and their cabins below. Mike W and Sebastian finally appeared, and watched the backs of the entertainers disappear down the stairs.

W didn't blink. Sebastian did, several times. And Z stopped singing.

27

Wil Wallis kicked back in a comfortable chair on the bridge deck, his feet propped on a sun lounge, drawing back on his cigarette. The tip glowed bright-red in the dark as he took each draw. He blew out the smoke and looked up at the night sky. Out here he could see stars, unlike on the mainland which always seemed to be shrouded in some grey haze. He took a swig of his beer.

Off in the distance he made out lights. Ships plying their trade back and forward to China. One of the busiest shipping routes in the world, and the *Empress* was parked in the middle of it. He sucked on his teeth, making a clicking sound as he released the pressure of his tongue, and smiled. He liked being at sea. He liked the smell of salty air—even the heavy, humid, polluted salty air of Asia. He closed his eyes and imagined being retired. Nothing to do but sit back and smoke and drink. On a boat—his boat. What sort of boat would it be, he wondered?

He ran a few options through his mind. One thing was certain—it wouldn't be the *Empress*, or anything like her. Not even close. Way too much money for him. He thought about the yacht club, and wondered about his mates. He hadn't seen most of them for years. Half of them confirmed bachelors, so they said, the other half pretending they were. Or wishing. Drinking, smoking, telling lies and occasionally rooting. Or was it the other way around? Anyway, none of that now.

That was it, decided Wallis, he'd buy another Compass. Maybe he could take her up the coast. The Whitsundays? Blue water, blue sky, clean air, and warm. Why not? He inhaled more smoke and let his mind wander around the Whitsunday coast. He thought about retirement. How could he retire? He needed money to retire. Come to think of it, he needed money to buy the boat. This job paid well, but not that well, and the work was stop-start. Once a month, maybe less. He'd just have to find a way. He resumed visualizing his paradise.

Gradually, though, his peace was being broken. For a few moments, he thought he had been dreaming it…a part of his mind wandering. But the noise grew louder. Slowly he realised Patrick Hogan was yelling. It snapped him back from somewhere off north Queensland, and onto the bridge-deck of the *Empress*. Hogan sat upright in his captain's chair, on the bridge. He was probably fifteen feet from Wallis, but they were separated by the thick windscreen. Only the bridge-deck door was open. Hogan was on his phone.

Hogan said, his voice rising with each point, "I don't give a damn. Why don't you get off your arse and get a job? Why do you have to rely on me? And that useless son—tell him to join the Army. Maybe they'll have somewhere he can go. He could try the Middle East. And stay there."

There was a short period of silence.

Hogan fired up again, "Christine, you can get stuffed. No more money. Got it?" He shut off his phone, stood for a few moments contemplating the call, then moved out on to the bridge-deck.

Wallis looked up. "Lovely evening."

Hogan said nothing, looked out into the darkness, then glanced at Wallis. "That a statement or a question?"

Wallis shrugged. "Depends. Unhappy home?"

"It's not my home. Not now. We've been divorced for years. You know that."

"Sure," said Wallis, "but if she wants money, it's still home, your home, to her."

"Bitch," Hogan spat, "you know what she's done? Called her stinking lawyer, that's what. He's gone to court and said I'm short on alimony payments. Over five years. Reckons the court will be all over me for the cash. The bastard…"

"How much?"

"Fifty grand. Plus costs, and interest. You know the drill. Probably sixty-five, at least."

"Jesus. Is he right—you short-change her that much?"

Another brief silence. Hogan looked at his feet and shuffled. "Possibly."

28

Sebastian Lam and Mike W retreated to the small office in the gaming lounge. W looked straight ahead, emotionless. Sebastian cast me a sideways glance, kind of smiled, and nodded. A nod that said, "Everything's okay, and I'm in control. Business as usual." They quietly closed the door.

But I've seen that expression before, and I knew he was not in control. The smile was forced. Pained. Behind that expression, he was thinking, "Shit, what now?"

Mike Z said, "How about Perry Como. Any of his?" Venus rose from his lap, sauntered over to the CD collection, and began searching.

I looked across at Z, who held his glass close to his lips and sipped at his whisky. I gave him a small smile. "Enjoying your trip Mike, so far?" He looked at me and winked. I took it as a 'yes', and decided to continue the small talk.

"So, what brings you here?"

"None of your business." The voice of Sebastian cut me off, as he and Mike W emerged from the office.

"Care for a small flutter?" W asked Z.

"Why not?" said Z as he rose and made for the blackjack table, whisky in hand. "Hope I get lucky."

Sebastian returned to his suite, Venus put on a Perry Como CD and settled in at the second chair at the dealing table. W began dealing cards. I stayed where I was.

Z and W played numerous hands, interrupted only by a couple of requests for Venus to fetch another whisky for her guest. Every so often W would say, "Oh, you're having a good night," to which Z would simply smile and nod. In order to avoid a slow death from outright boredom, I decided to run a security check on the boat, and made my way down to the main deck. Chef and his assistants, including Gina, were finishing the dinner clean-up.

I strolled along the passage between the suites. I could hear muffled voices from the Heart Suite. Sounded like Mike's M and G. The others were quiet. I reached the end of the hall and knocked on each of the red and black doors. Cherry opened the red, and Mae the black.

I raised an eyebrow at them. "Night off?"

"They not want us," Mae shrugged. She flicked her thumb back over her shoulder at Belle. "We all here, they have meeting," she said, pointing at M's suite. No action here, so I retraced my steps back up to the gaming lounge.

The two card players, W and Z, had now disappeared. Venus had moved back to her lounge chair in the corner, and Mr Como sang quietly.

I headed for my chair. "They've gone?"

"In there," said Venus, pointing at the office. "Sebastian too."

I took up my position outside, and Venus strolled over. She

sat down on my lap, put one arm behind my head, and with the other, lifted my hand and slid it between her slightly open thighs. It was warm, and a little damp. I skipped a couple of breaths.

"We should get together," she whispered.

This was the second move she'd made on me that day, and as beautiful as she was, I knew it was too soon. My thoughts jumped to Sally and Jack constantly, and the 'gut punch' was never far away. My mind said I had to learn to let them go, but the problem was my heart. In there, I didn't want to. I felt I had to hang on, for their sake. I couldn't let them go. Not yet.

I said, "Venus, you're very attractive, but for Christ's sake, not now. If they come out of there, and see us, we're dead meat." Venus sighed, and lifted herself off. She headed to the bar, mixed a drink, and retreated to her chair. She blew me a kiss, and took a long sip.

A shaft of light suddenly appeared across the lounge floor, as the office door was flung open. Mr Como had stopped singing. Venus put down her drink. Quietness enveloped all.

Sebastian Lam came out first, backwards. He was quickly followed by Mike Z, standing tall, who jabbed Sebastian's chest several times with his index finger. The smile, the nod, the wink had gone, now replaced by a scowl.

Z said, "This is ve-ry dis-a-ppoin-ting." Each jab emphasised each sharp syllable.

"But p...please understand, w...we have costs," said Sebastian.

"Then you had better cut them. Either that or I will cut you—out completely. Just fix it. If you don't know how, then ask your father." Z turned, motioned for Venus to follow him, and made for the stairs. A carbon-copy of the M and G exit earlier. W had now joined Sebastian outside the office. He stood expressionless. Sebastian began to wring his hands.

The night was clearly over. They both crumpled a bit, their energy deserting them fast. Whatever deals they were doing in that office, or trying to do, were coming unstuck. No-one was buying.

I looked up at them from my chair. It made me wonder how I would report this to CH...should I report it...because I couldn't be sure it was all Sebastian's fault. But he was clearly the one wearing the blame from the unhappy customers. They both turned and cast me a sullen look...a look of condemned men.

Neither said a word.

29

Sebastian and Wang drew back into the small office adjoining the gaming lounge. Wang sat behind the desk, an ornate timber piece, but small, in keeping with the size of the room. This was his usual position for meetings held here. Sebastian usually sat in a small club chair to one side, midway between Wang and clients, who sat in identical club chairs opposite. Sebastian felt this bridged the gap slightly between the formal side of meetings, which Wang conducted, and the 'I'm on your side really' impression he liked to convey to his clients. This time he sat opposite, in a client chair.

Sebastian said, "Well, what now?"

Wang blinked a couple of times, spread open a thick book lying on the desk, and began to study it. He shook his head slowly, and finally looked up. "I believed you had them organised…that they knew what we wanted, and had agreed. Clearly you have not. You have failed in this regard."

"Mr Wang, I have not failed. These clients were happy when they came on board. I left them in your care. Now they are unhappy. You must have done something to them in the meantime."

"Don't accuse me of anything. I've not made them unhappy—you have—and now you must fix it. I'm retiring for the evening. We must talk in the morning, before we see them at breakfast. We'll meet here at 7:00 a.m. Goodnight." With that, Wang rose, closed his book, shoved it under his arm, removed his coat from the small cloak cupboard, and left.

Sebastian felt defeated. He sat slumped in his chair for five minutes. He ran through the meetings in his mind, but how he could 'fix' things, and save face, was beyond him. He could simply change the deal—that was easy. But it flew in the face of the way his father had taught him. It would show Wang that he had no balls. It would reveal things to his father which, for now, were hidden, and the clients would be in a position of supreme authority. Lam senior would be unimpressed. With everything. Totally.

Sebastian wearily pulled himself up, switched off the light, and headed for his bed. As he crossed the gaming lounge he flicked another set of switches, casting the lounge into darkness. He was about to round the corner into the small hall to his suite, when Patrick Hogan almost flattened him. His heart thumped.

"Damn, sorry, didn't see you coming out of the dark," Hogan rasped. His heavy breath covered Sebastian in a fog of beer. Sebastian winced at the stale smell and let out a small "phhww."

"You okay?" Sebastian squinted at the swaying skipper.

"Yeah, yeah, I'm okay, but I've got a problem and I need to talk to you."

This was the last thing Sebastian needed. Another problem. Someone else's problem. "Can't it wait—maybe in the morning? You might feel better then."

"No, it can't. And I feel just fine now, if it's all the same to you."

Sebastian didn't like Hogan's belligerent tone, but he sure as hell didn't need to aggravate him anymore. "Sit here then." He pointed to the chairs occupied earlier by Zhou and Venus. "What's this problem?"

Hogan sat, and expelled a couple of beer-laden burps. "I've been working for your father for a long time—on and off. We go back a long way, you know."

"I know, yes, I know."

"Well I've run into some trouble with my ex-wife. The one your father met some years ago. You might remember?"

Sebastian did remember. CH had insisted the ex-Mrs Hogan was a dangerous woman. What made her dangerous Sebastian wasn't sure, but he was in no doubt she was not his father's favourite woman on planet Earth.

"Yes, I remember. What sort of trouble."

"It seems, in our divorce, I may have underpaid her slightly. She wants the money—now. To be more accurate, she and her lawyer want the money—now. Given our long-standing relationship, I wondered if you might be able to see your way clear to advance me some? To get rid of her—them—for good."

The thought of handing out cash for someone else's marital problems did not immediately appeal to Sebastian. Given that it would benefit the ex-Mrs Hogan, it would appeal to his father even less. But the real block, was the thought of extending himself at all for Hogan, who treated him with something approaching contempt. Still, he had to keep his skipper appeased to some degree. After all, they had to get home—the crew and the clients.

His mind flashed for a second to the clients. That did not make him feel any better. "How much are we talking about?"

Hogan paused for a moment, as if considering a number. "Two hundred should cover it."

"Two hundred what?"

"Grand."

"Two hundred thousand?"

"Yep—takes care of the lawyer too."

Sebastian paused for a moment, as if giving the request great consideration. Then he shook his head, eyes down. "I'm sorry, Skip," he said, "but we just don't have that kind of money available at the moment. Unfortunately, I won't be able to assist."

"So, that's it?" Hogan exploded. He stood, wobbling, waving his arms around at the gaming lounge, and the boat in general. "Even with all this…this…extravagance. This…floating brothel with fucking ceiling motifs and gold taps. You don't have the money? That's final?"

"I'm afraid so."

"Fuck it…I'll talk to CH about this when we get back. He'll understand."

Sebastian flinched at the thought, but at least that would give him time to get in his father's ear first. Hogan hitched his trousers, belched again, looked down at Sebastian with a withering, drunken stare, and staggered toward the bridge.

Sebastian waited until he had disappeared, then set off again in the direction of his suite.

"No, he won't," he mumbled to himself, "not by the time I've finished."

30

CH Lam stood at the huge picture window of his apartment, overlooking Macau. In front sat the gambling edifices of the MGM and Wynn casinos. One to each side like a pair of guardian Rottweilers. Lights ablaze, they beckoned punters to enter. Between them, he had a gun-barrel view across Nam Van Lake, directly at the building which housed his baby. The Golden Mountain Club.

It was late. Late for CH anyway. He was usually in bed around 10:00, and it was now approaching 11:00. He gazed at the view, seeing little. He saw it every day, and the view was, like all views after a time, just part of the view. The city glittered and twinkled, all of it bouncing in reflection off the water. He looked down to the street. Any moment he would receive a call from the club's driver.

His mind jumped back to the most recent phone call, from Mr Zhou. And the one ten minutes before that, from Mr Ma. He had known them for years, and had never heard them so troubled. Not raging angry exactly, but more than worried. Except for Grekov, of course. He seemed one-hundred-percent angry. Probably half-drunk too.

Personally, Zhou was someone he liked. Educated in England, Zhou was from a powerful family. With strong allegiances to Mao from the 1940s, Zhou's family maintained a connection to the ruling elite which continued to this day. Zhou had style learned from the Europeans, and had seriously big money. The family wealth came from petrochemicals, or more precisely, ethylene. Zhou had one son, Claude, who should now be taking over from his father. The press would call him a *tai zi*—a princeling. Except Claude was dead. A mysterious car crash late at night on a Shanghai motorway. An accident? Maybe. Or maybe other forces were at work. Nobody talked about it, and CH was never going to raise it with Zhou.

Ma was different. More an old-school slogger. His family was important—they had to be. Those who made the big money were all connected politically, but in Ma's case, the connection was local. As mayor in a small city which had now been swallowed by greater Guangzhou, Ma senior had carried plenty of local clout. His brother was the deputy mayor, his cousin the secretary-general. As mayor, he had made both appointments. Ma junior, now fifty-something, had a dream run. As China grew, he grew with it. Connections to banking—another uncle—and city planning—two more distant uncles and a cousin—were all appointed by his father or uncle. CH didn't bother learning the Ma family intricacies, but he knew one thing—Mr Ma had done very well.

Ma had taken on a partner, Grekov. He was from Russia, and had joined forces with Ma about ten years earlier. CH didn't like Grekov much. He drank too much, vodka mostly, and was abusive. To staff, to managers, anyone who happened to be about when Grekov suddenly felt aggravated, which to CH appeared to be often. Grekov apparently had been in construction in Russia, whatever that may have involved. He apparently also had money, but how he came by it was not clear.

Grekov and Ma built things…shopping centres, apartment blocks…whatever needed to be built. CH suspected many were probably not needed at all—just like so much construction in China—but were built anyway to make someone more money. He had read the reports from the west. Reports the great mass of Chinese people never had access to, but his clients—the big punters—did, and which they passed on to him.

Still, how Grekov and Ma made their money was not his business. He used to handle their spare change years ago, when he worked at the big casinos. They were heavy punters and good clients. Now, after years of pitching them, they'd left the big establishments and swapped to him. Now, he just wanted to handle some of it on the way through his little club.

And it was these club transactions that were now apparently causing so much grief. To Ma and to Zhou. And they were so offended, they felt they had to involve CH personally. Whatever the issue, it should not have reached this stage. Damn, Ma and Grekov had only just come on board. So fast? How could they be offside so fast?

Sebastian should have handled it better. That's why he was in charge—to take care of this stuff. But they were on the boat, it was late, and CH felt sure if he called he would get conflicting stories. Thank God, he'd put new security on…someone nobody on that boat would know. Bynow had assured him this man, Todd, was the best. Big, strong, and straight. He needed to get Todd's report…his take on things.

But for now, there was only one course—go to the club, look at the books. He'd rung in. Lily was there, working late, and she would open the computers for him. That way he would know the numbers, the real deal, and then he might get to the issue.

His phone rang. The club driver was approaching. He peered into the street below, as the black Rolls, glinting under the city lights, made a wide, sweeping turn in front of his building. He picked up his coat from the back of a sofa and opened the apartment front door.

"The numbers," CH mumbled to himself, "the numbers never lie."

31

I'd waited, unseen, in the darkness of the gaming lounge, and when there was no further sound of either Sebastian or Hogan, I slipped away to do a quick security check before heading to my bunk. It was nearing 10:30, and no-one, other than our guests and entertainers, had passed through since my arrival, just before 9:00. From the gaming lounge, I scaled the stairs to the sundeck. I was surprised to find Miss Jay-Dee sitting alone in the jacuzzi. All was in darkness other than the dim light offered by the haze-covered moon.

"You alright?"

"Not much." She sobbed a little as she spoke.

"How did you get here? I didn't see you come through below."

"Private stairs—from Sebastian's suite. He didn't want me around, so I came up here."

"Why didn't he want you around?"

"Because of the way I look. You see." She stood up, completely naked. It was a strange sight, this figure with the head and breasts of a woman, but the voice and genitals of a man.

"Surely he knows you look like this?"

"Yes, of course this bit," she said, brushing her hand down her front. "But this…" She turned around, and even in the dark I couldn't escape the welts on her back and buttocks, and around her neck. "He used to be kind, but now he's just cruel. He's gone weird, kinky. I hate it. I think he wants to kill me. I hate *him*."

"Has he threatened you—other than these marks?"

"No, not really. Only this."

"Well, there's nowhere to go here. You'll have to wait until we get back tomorrow—unless the entertainers will take you in. If it gets too rough come and get me—I'll see what I can do. But when I last saw him he wasn't looking too happy. Maybe you'd better go back to him—might cheer him up."

She nodded, but I don't think I'd convinced her. I made my way down to the main deck. The four entertainers, and Gina, drinks in hand, were all sitting on the rear entertainment deck. "Oh, here he comes again," said one of them.

"Got the night off, girls?"

"They don't want us," said Venus. "All three of them in a meeting."

"And my Mike is in a bad mood," said Mae. "He told me to take off."

"Well, have a lovely evening. Shut the lights off when you leave, eh?"

I continued down to my cabin, and organised myself for some sleep. The gentle movement of the boat soon had me out to it.

*

The first sound I heard was a scream. I didn't recognize it as a scream, because it was muffled. I was asleep, in my cabin, when the noise finally woke me. I don't know how long this sound had been going on, but when I opened my cabin door, it pierced the tiny corridor. Came from the galley it seemed. I pulled on some clothes and scaled the chef's ladder fast.

At the top stood Gina, at the corner of the galley. She was sort of bent forward from the hips, and stared around into the recess which housed the dumb-waiter. Her hands clasped each side of her mouth, which was stuck open. The kitchen clock above read 6:33. She screamed again. Beside her stood the chef, meat cleaver in hand, his mouth the same, eyes bulging. Behind him one of his assistants strained to peer over his shoulder, then quickly turned away.

I looked at the group. "Problem?"

Gina's eyes, too, were wide, like saucers. She pointed around the corner and spun on her heels. In two steps, she was over a sink, her pumping stomach dry-retching. I glanced at the chef who appeared stuck in position—mute—like a mime artist.

I poked my head around the corner. The dumb-waiter door was open, and a water jug lay smashed on the floor below it. Gina must have dropped it. The sight would make you drop anything.

Staring straight back at me from the otherwise empty dumb-waiter, was a head. Wild-eyed, clenched-tongue and blood-stained. Hacked-off just below the jaw.

The head of Sebastian Lam.

32

I grabbed a kitchen towel, pinched the handle on the door of the small goods lift, and pulled it down. Didn't need my prints on there. I couldn't leave that head staring out—the sight of it would give the staff nightmares. And me.

I hauled a chair from the dining area, and placed it in front of the lift. I looked around at Gina, the chef, and his assistants. Grey with horror, the lot of them.

"You okay?" They each nodded, slowly, in turn. But Gina shook hers, and leant over the sink again, heaving.

"Chef, if you're up to it, keep making breakfast. Whatever you can do, just continue like normal…if that's possible." Chef nodded. "And nobody goes near the goods lift, okay? Nobody at all. If anyone tries, you let me know." Somehow, the chance of them going near it any time soon seemed remote. None spoke. I don't think they could.

I checked the hall from the galley, which led to the suites. All quiet. I moved along it, and stood outside each door for a moment. The only sounds were snoring from Mike G in the Diamond, and a couple of the entertainers talking in theirs. I ran back through the galley and the casual living room, passed under the giant octopus, and up the stairs to the upper deck. The gaming area remained dark and quiet, just as I had left it last night.

I slowed my pace. What if an intruder had done this? A silent visit from another boat, maybe? I checked outside, scanning port and starboard sides, but knowing it would be futile. Anyone smart enough to pull that off would be long gone.

I poked my head in to the small gaming office. Empty. Then into the adjoining bathroom. Ditto. I moved along to the owner's suite and stood outside—all quiet. I knocked once, pulled out my handkerchief, slowly twisted the door handle, pushed it open, and stepped inside. Empty. The bed was a slept-in mess, and there were clothes thrown criss-cross over a chair. All appeared normal.

I moved carefully around the corner to the dressing area. That was when I noticed the stairway which led to the sundeck—the one Miss Jay-Dee had spoken of. To the left was the bathroom. The carpet leading in had a couple of spots. I knelt down. Looked like blood. I pushed open the bathroom door. That was a sight I was glad not to have every day.

Sebastian Lam's body lay in the bath. Naked. Headless. Blood smeared everywhere—floor, walls, toilet—it looked like an up-market abattoir. I stepped in, making sure I avoided the red trail. The cops would want this intact. I looked down at Sebastian's body. One thing was clear—a solid cutting instrument had been involved. Aside from his head, his gut had been slit and his penis removed. It was now lying adjacent to the plughole. Whoever did this had a score to settle.

I retraced my steps, locking the door behind me. Wil Wallis told me he had a master key for the boat, so that would get us back in. Or I could break it down. I figured the guests may start to appear, and at this stage I didn't want them interfering in the drama. I also needed to make sure they were where they were supposed to be. I let myself into the bridge.

To the right, on the rear bridge wall, sat the phone and intercom system for the boat. I began calling each suite, beginning with Mike M in the Heart. He answered quickly.

"Mike, this is Ash, head of security. We've had an incident on the boat, and I need you to stay in your room."

"What sort of incident?"

"I can't give details, but there's been a death."

"Whose death?"

"Sorry, Mike, but no details. Please stay there until I call again. Breakfast will be delivered to you."

I called each of the suites. The correct person answered each call. The entertainers were alarmed, the guests mostly inquisitive, but that was it. Mike G seemed angry being woken so early. My final call was to the galley, to check on the state of the staff, and organise breakfast to be delivered to the suites. As I hung up from my final call, Wil Wallis appeared.

"Thought Skip told you not to come in here," he said. His voice sounded rough and gurgled...probably from last night's smokes, I guessed.

"Emergency—just getting control of the situation. By the way, where is Skip?"

"Dunno—asleep I guess. What emergency?"

"A death."

"Death? Who's fucking dead?"

"Sebastian—your boss. And it's not good. He's been cut up badly, and I've locked down the boat. Everyone in their quarters. Except kitchen staff—they're cooking, and anyway, they found him."

"What the…what do you mean the kitchen staff found him?"

A sound distracted me. Seemed to come from the hall leading back to the owner's suite. I poked my head out. Miss Jay-Dee, still barefoot but now clad in a pair of shorts and a tee-shirt, twisted the door handle back and forth, trying to get in.

"Sorry, Miss," I said, "you can't go in there."

"I need to see Sebastian."

"Sorry, you can't. Tell me, where have you been?"

Jay-Dee hesitated a moment. "In the bathroom, freshening up."

"Which bathroom?"

She hesitated again. "The one in the gaming lounge."

"Funny, you weren't in there when I checked a few minutes ago."

"No…I just…came down. You know…from the jacuzzi, where you saw me last night. I stayed up there. I was so afraid. You remember?"

I considered this for a moment. Seemed plausible enough. "Well, Jay-Dee, you might want to sit down. Take some time out. Unfortunately, Sebastian's dead, so you can't go in."

"Dead? My Sebastian is dead? It can't be." She began to sob loudly. I held her by the shoulders, steered her back to the gaming lounge, and sat her down to cope with her grief.

Wallis had followed behind. I turned to him.

I said, "Okay now, Skip…he's in charge of this thing, and he needs to start alerting authorities. You'd both better have a look at the body, so you know what you're dealing with."

"Let's go wake him," said Wallis.

We moved back along the hall to the captain's cabin. Wallis banged his door a couple of times, and called out, "Hey, Pat, you up?" No answer. Wallis turned the handle, but the door wouldn't move. "Funny," he said, "never usually locks it." Wallis fished in his pocket, produced a set of keys, and let us in.

Patrick Hogan lay on his bed, arms spread wide, and snoring with a rumble like an approaching storm. He still wore his white captain's shirt, partially unbuttoned and pulled tight over his belly, and shorts. Scattered around him on the bed lay seven or eight empty beer bottles, and a small bottle of rum. Also empty. Given the argument he'd had with Sebastian, I wasn't surprised. I looked at Wallis, shrugged, and moved round to the side of the bed to try to rouse him.

Hogan's right arm lay flopped, off the bed, pointing down at the floor. His hand and lower arm were covered in blood. There were blood smears on the carpet. And resting in the middle of the mess, sat a blood covered knife.

A big hunting knife, about a foot long, with a partially serrated, seven-inch blade.

33

CH Lam was spent. He sat in the back of the black Rolls, as it slid to a halt outside his apartment building. It was nearing 7:30 a.m., the sun was shining hard through a humid haze, and he had hardly any sleep. He was too old for this sort of life now. As he stepped from the limo, the heat nearly knocked him out. He stumbled in to the lobby, and gripped the handrail of the lift as it shot him up to his apartment. Once inside, the air-conditioning cooled him off, and he recovered enough to make some breakfast.

Since a little before midnight, he had sat at Sebastian's desk, studying computer screens. He was computer literate to a point, but would have preferred to pore over hand written accounts. Those no longer existed, relics of a bygone era apparently, so computer it was. Lily had stayed back, long past her usual hours, to help him. He caught a nap at around 3:00 a.m., but was too fidgety to sleep properly. He sent Lily home at 4:00.

He could see from the numbers the club was doing very nicely. Just as Sebastian had said. They had a full house most days—around eight to ten members—and at the minimum two million dollars a day, it had been a good week. Most left their house accounts in limbo, picking up at later visits where they had left off from before. But he could see that Zhou, Ma and Grekov had decided to settle-up theirs.

He had opened each file separately, pored over the transactions, and on the surface at least, could see nothing out of order. The sums were large—Zhou with fifty million dollars invested, and Ma and Grekov with about twenty-five million, but he would have expected this from them. With Zhou, he wouldn't have been surprised to see two or three times that amount. It was harder to tell with Ma and Grekov, being new members and on their maiden visit.

Lily had shown him how to open the members' personal data, the basis of their individual dealings with the club. Zhou Wei Li, his address in Shanghai, his birth date, the date his membership began, bank accounts details for transfers, and his rate. Five percent. He had checked the others—Ma Junjie and Vadim Grekov. Both with Guangzhou addresses. Same rate. This seemed in order. He had scoured some other member files—thirty or more of them. All the same. So why where Zhou and Ma so angry? What had happened on that boat?

He pondered this as he gazed out across Nam Van Lake, absently nibbling at some toast, sipping tea. The answer lay with Sebastian, and he would just have to wait until he returned. And Wang, too. They would both have some explaining. He glanced at the clock—8:12 a.m. He needed to sleep. CH pulled himself up from the table, cleaned away his cup and plate, and headed for bed.

As he reached his bedroom, the phone beside it rang. He sat

on the bed, and picked up the receiver. The club receptionist said, "Mr Lam, I have a call from the *Golden Empress.* They asked to be put through to you. Do you want to take it?"

"Of course, thank you." A short silence, then an unfamiliar voice.

"Mr Lam?"

"Yes, who is this?"

"Mr Lam, we have some very bad news…"

34

I sat at the bridge, in the captain's chair, a few feet from Wallis. "Bloody, Skip," he said, peering at the GPS coordinates, "too pissed to even remember to come on watch." He had just checked our position, and we had drifted quite some way.

"Or too busy killing people," I said.

Wallis moved just outside the door, on the bridge-deck, lit a smoke and puffed hard on it. He finished it quickly, flicked the butt into the water, and lit another. He polished off that one, returned to the doorway, and sucked his tongue against his teeth, making a sharp clicking sound.

We had taken photos on our phones of Skip, passed out and covered in blood, knife at his fingertips. He would wake eventually, and maybe not remember how he got into this state. Whatever he did remember, it was bound to make him mad. If he was responsible for the hacking of Sebastian, he might want to remove all trace. We touched nothing…except the knife. Couldn't take the risk of leaving it, so I found a towel, picked it up by the tip, and placed it on the bridge console.

The photos might be our only evidence, and Wallis and I would have to back-up each other's story. That would make Skip madder—but it *was* what we found. Just depends what he might remember. I went over with Wallis the argument I'd witnessed the night before. That was a motive, though I didn't feel it was strong enough to drive him to murder. And a savage murder at that. Wallis couldn't believe it.

There were others with potential motives too—all the guests had raging disagreements with him, and even Miss Jay-Dee wanted to keep her distance. After we'd locked Skip's cabin door, though he could still open it from inside, I slipped down to the guest suites below. I sat with each of them, Mike W included, one at a time. I asked all the usual questions…whether they had left their cabins during the night…whether they had seen or heard anyone else doing the same…when they last saw Sebastian…and so on. No-one had heard a thing.

They all expressed shock, horror, and disbelief. Sure, they'd had disagreements with him, but that 'meant little' they said. They expected all would be fixed in due course. None could understand why anyone would commit such a brutal attack. Miss Jay-Dee was barely able to speak about it, but she plucked up some courage to voice her own brand of dismay. She really had a 'soft spot' for Sebastian she said, and in fact, often felt maybe she loved him. It was just that at times, he could be 'a little difficult'. That was why she spent the night on the sundeck. Then she burst into tears all over again.

I ran each of the entertainers through the same process. They'd heard nothing. The guests had dismissed them earlier, and after my seeing them on the salon deck, they all made their way to bed.

With two to a room, their stories tallied. Identical.

I covered off what had happened with each of the staff, but like me, they were out to it two decks below Sebastian. The first sign of trouble they had heard was a scream…from Gina as she opened the dumb waiter.

Skip was obviously our main suspect. Whatever had actually happened, whatever Skip would argue when he came to, Wallis and I agreed…he had to be relieved of his captain's position until we reached land. We discussed where to head. We were in international waters, technically. Wallis snickered and said, "The Chinese might have a different view on that." Hong Kong was a little closer, but in the end, we decided to return to Macau. That was where we began, that's where the boat lived, and of course, Sebastian.

Wallis had rung CH. He was distraught. "A shock like this could kill him," Wallis said, stating the bleeding obvious. Wallis looked concerned, and rang back to The Golden Mountain Club, advised the receptionist what had happened, and suggested they send someone over to check on the old man.

For now, we had to return to Macau, and alert the authorities. Wallis slipped down the hall from the bridge, and returned a minute later with a hat. He put it on. It read CAPTAIN. He fired up the engines.

I put a phone call in to the Macau police department. "I want to report a death…a murder." A Chief Feng came on. I gave him details of our victim, what I'd found, the boat and all who sailed on her…or what I knew of them…and an estimated time of arrival.

Feng was terse. "And you are?"

"Name's Todd…Ash Todd…head of security."

"When you anchor, no-one is to leave. Do you understand? No-one. You will advise us when you are on approach. Do you understand? We will come on board. We will take over the boat. Do you understand?"

I assured him I did understand. I couldn't mention that I was also a copper, because right now, I wasn't. But I knew what he wanted to hear. "I give you my guarantee, no-one will leave, we will call you, and you will be in charge." That seemed to calm him.

I settled back in the first-mate's chair, next to Wallis, and began running the scenario for the next few hours through my head. What would we do when Skip woke up? How could I make sure no-one interfered with the crime scenes? There seemed like a lot to cover for one man.

Wallis pointed the big boat west toward Macau, and gunned her. I scanned the horizon, across the vast South China Sea.

It was 8:43 a.m.

It looked to be turning into a beautiful day.

35

We made good time across the ocean. The morning sea was calm. I sat with Wallis, running the scene in Sebastian's suite over and over in my mind.

I looked across at him. "By the way, where were you last night?"

Wallis half-turned to me. "In my room." His eyes narrowed. "Why? You don't think I'd do this?"

"Got to cover all bases. The cops will ask, too."

"Fuck the cops. That's where I was. No proof, but they can please themselves. Anyway, where were you? Bet you can't prove it either, unless you had company down there." He raised an eyebrow. "Eh?"

I shook my head, but he had a point.

Wallis checked a couple of screens, and turned back to me. "Come and sit here, and watch these will you? I need a smoke."

I moved into the captain's chair, and took over scanning the dials. No idea what they meant, so I stared straight at the ocean ahead. Wallis obviously needed some space. He moved on to the bridge deck, and lit up. The wind whipped across him, burning the cigarette twice as fast as he drew on it. His hair flew about, blowing left, then right. His beard flattened onto his face. Finally, he tossed the butt and returned.

"I'm going to do a check on all the others," I said, "you okay here?"

"Sure…no rush."

I took myself along the bridge hall, stopping to listen in at Hogan's door as I passed. No sound. I knocked. No answer. I thought of looking in, but let it slip. I made my way below.

The guests, and Mike W, were seated around in the salon, each in his own chair, reading or staring vacantly out to sea. The entertainers, and Miss Jay-Dee, sat around a table on the adjoining deck, talking, or texting. This seemed like a good opportunity. I motioned to them to come inside.

I moved around to the galley where chef, Gina and the assistants were cleaning breakfast dishes. The goods lift remained closed off, door firmly shut. I lifted the door, making sure again I left no prints. The grotesque head stared back. I shut the door. I tapped chef on the shoulder. Made him jump. "Can you and the staff come out here?"

When all were assembled, I ran through the events of the morning again, so that there was no doubt what we were dealing with. All nodded gravely. Mike Z glanced at Mike W and made some short comment, in Mandarin. W didn't react.

I explained that the police in Macau had been informed, that we would be there in about two hours, and that no-one was to leave the boat. The police would question everyone.

"Hope they won't take long—have to get back to Shanghai," said Z.

"Yes," mumbled G, "this trip is turned to shit."

All nodded in unison. The entertainers said nothing. Miss Jay-Dee began to cry again.

I stood to return to the bridge, and turned to the group. "By the way, we have a suspect."

The room stopped, and looked at me as one. "A suspect?" said W. He blinked a couple of times. "Who?"

"At this point the captain has been relieved of his position. First Mate Wallis has assumed that role, and I am assisting him. The police are aware." The last bit was not entirely true, but I thought it should sound as though we had covered everything by the book.

Everyone looked at the person next to them, eyes wide, shaking heads in disbelief. "Skip," said chef, "incredible," his voice rising to a squeak as he spoke.

"If you need me, call the bridge." I made my way upstairs, and I could feel thirteen pairs of eyes burning a hole in my back as I went. I stopped outside Hogan's room again. No sound. I moved to the bridge door and pushed it open.

Patrick Hogan stood with his back to me, facing Wallis, who was propped against the captain's chair. Hogan turned to face me. As he did, Wallis peered around him, fixed his gaze on mine, and shook his head and mouthed, "No."

Hogan wore a crisp, white shirt, navy shorts, and his brown boat shoes. His head was bare, but his captain's hat sat on the console. He had showered and shaved—clean as a whistle.

"Skip," I said, "how are you feeling?"

"Never better."

"And last night?"

"What about it?"

"How did you spend it?'

"In my room. Had a couple of drinks, watched a show on telly—baseball from the US—and slept like a log. I was a bit pissed Wallis had started the boat without me, but he tells me we have instructions to head home immediately."

"True. And Sebastian? Did you see him last night?"

"No—don't think so—why?"

"He's had some trouble. You absolutely sure you didn't see him?"

"That's what Wallis just asked me. What in the hell is this about? No, I haven't seen Sebastian for…I don't know…since he came on board. Now let me back to my chair."

He pushed Wallis aside and made for his seat as I put my hand on his shoulder. "Sorry, Skip," I said, "no can do."

That's when he threw the first punch.

36

The second wild swing missed too.

As he tottered off-balance for a second, I grabbed his arm and snapped it behind his back, ripped my left arm under his chin, and squeezed tight. Skip grunted at the force of both.

I said, "Time for a reality check, pal. I'll let you go…but no more hero stuff. Got it?"

"Right…okay." I could feel him gasping.

I released him slowly. Skip rubbed his neck and arm, and scowled at me. "Why are you stopping me? And who gave the instructions to head back?"

I looked at Wallis, who had clambered back onto the captain's chair, and thankfully had control of the boat.

I said, "The police in Macau gave the instruction. They'll be waiting for us when we dock."

"Police? Why?"

"Because Sebastian is dead. Murdered."

Skip's face looked vacant. Not comprehending. "Murdered? Sebastian? When? Who?"

"Last night—and at this time, *you* are the number one suspect."

Skip pondered this for a second or two, processing the news. Then he exploded.

"This is bullshit! Why would I kill him? I'm going to see him."

"You can't. It's a crime scene. Door's locked."

Skip glowered at me, then Wallis. "Wallis, give me the keys," he demanded. "The master."

Wallis looked up, contemplated the ocean ahead, and turned to Skip. "Nope. Not this time. Pat, it doesn't look good. This time we've got to do it by the book. The guests can't help you, the girls can't help. All the evidence points to you. You sure you didn't see him last night?"

Skip stood, shaking, quickly turning his head left and right. To me, then Wallis, then back again. "What fucking evidence?" he yelled.

"You with the murder weapon. That one…" I nodded at the towel covering the knife, the tip still just showing. "And you covered in blood, but I see you've cleaned that off. We have the pictures. And last night, I heard you arguing with him."

This appeared news to Skip. He stopped abruptly, still quivering a little, and gave it some more thought. Then the bluster returned. "You two can go to hell." He turned, and made for the door.

"Stay in your room," I said, "it'll be easier for all of us."

Wallis said, "That went well. I need a smoke—look after this will you?" He headed out onto the deck and I sat at the helm, watching him puff away.

I really needed to corral Skip. I just didn't trust him to remain calm, knowing the cops were going to be crawling all over him once we hit Macau. But how and where to hold him was a problem. There was no way to lock him in his cabin, as he could open it from the inside. Same with all the other cabins. There was no obvious cage to house him. Wallis returned from the deck, brushing down his wind-blown hair.

I nodded at the open sea. "How much longer to Macau?"

Wallis studied the GPS and some dials, and said, "Hour and a bit," and then looked up at me from the console. His gaze shifted past me and he said, "Ohhh, shit."

I turned in time to see Skip, moving as fast as his stumpy legs would allow. He reached for the knife on the console at full stretch, and just beat me to it. "This the murder weapon, you bastard? I'll give you a murder weapon…" He lunged at me with the knife. I side-stepped, and smacked him hard behind his ear.

"Arrgh," he grunted, but stayed on his feet long enough to come at me again. This was getting serious. His mind was so distorted I reckoned everyone would become a potential enemy. Guests and entertainers included. I had to put a stop to it.

He made another swipe, but he was too slow. The beer-belly was just too much baggage for him, and he stumbled as he missed. I grabbed the knife-wielding arm, twisted his wrist hard, and snapped it up. He let off a sort of screaming whimper, and the knife hit the floor. I spun him round, ripped him in close to me, and in a single, clean move, rammed my fist straight up under his chin. I eased him to the floor. He didn't make a sound.

"Nice move," Wallis said, "now what?"

"I need to lock him up, for everyone's sake. Somewhere he can't open from inside, once he comes to."

"The toy room," said Wallis, "that has external locks."

"But the tender…or the skis…he could take them."

Wallis looked exasperated. "Well we'll just have to confiscate the keys…won't we? Besides, not even he would be silly enough to jump ship out here."

"Well help lift him onto me, and I'll cart him down."

We hauled Skip to his feet, and Wallis pushed him onto my shoulders for a fireman's carry. The dead weight was heavy, but once I was up he felt pretty stable. Wallis walked ahead, and we made a slow procession down to the lower deck.

As we passed through the salon, the guests and entertainers, who were all still scattered about, sat wide-eyed at the sight. The Mikes looked at each other, and nodded, as they made comment in Mandarin. That annoyed me—the secretive exchanges in a language I didn't understand.

Mike G turned to me. "That the killer?"

"What happened to him?" asked Venus. "Drunk?"

I looked at her, and gave a little, pained smile. "It's been a long night."

37

Chief Feng and three of his officers from the Macau Police Department, the PSP, stood on a small police boat at the wharf of the outer harbour marina. The same spot I'd collected our guests from twenty hours earlier.

I'd rung ahead fifteen minutes out from the harbour. Just as I'd promised. The guests, entertainers and staff were asked to return to their cabins, with the exception of Miss Jay-Dee. She obviously couldn't go back to Sebastian's, so the entertainers took her under their collective wing.

Wallis, captain's hat firmly back on his head, dropped anchor as close as possible…a little over one-hundred yards off…and the police boat slid into action, making a leisurely pace out to meet us. We greeted them on the boarding platform, and all six of us made our way up to the salon. One of the officers began taking notes.

First-up Chief Feng wanted an account of the boat, its history, and the purpose of our trip. Wallis obliged with a detailed summary. How the club was a discreet casino, and its clients were rewarded with lavish trips on the company boat. Feng surveyed the salon again, and said, "Very impressive, indeed."

He asked about the deceased. Wallis explained Sebastian's role, at least what he knew of it, and that he had taken over from his father a short time ago. The chief had heard of CH, but had never met him. He also had heard of The Golden Mountain Club, but had never been inside.

"Probably because it's private," Wallis drawled. He thought for a moment to mention that on a police officer's salary, Feng would probably be slightly short of the financial requirements for admission. He decided to drop it. No point rubbing it in. Chief Feng then asked for details of the guests.

"Surnames Zhou, Ma and Grekov. Oh, and Wang," said Wallis, "though he's more of an associate of Lam's I believe. Travelled with us before."

Well that was interesting…so that was what the initials stood for. Grekov was obvious, but I made a mental note to find someone to line up the other faces and names. I had a feeling I was going to need to know who they really were, if only to make sense of my report to CH. Because now, without doubt, CH would be expecting one.

"Zhou, Ma, Grekov and Wang," said Feng. "Okay, first names?"

"Don't know," Wallis said, "we're told to call all of them, Mike. I think they don't want their identities known."

Feng considered this, and gave three, deliberate nods. "Anyone else?"

"The entertainers," Wallis said, "they came to us through an agency in Hong Kong…Lashings of Love. Names are Cherry, Mae, Belle, and Venus. We also have Gina, but she is more a domestic help—serving food and drinks, that sort of thing."

Feng flicked a sideways grin at one of his colleagues. "No surnames there, I suppose?"

"Of course not," said Wallis. "Then there's the chef, and his assistants. They are employed by the club. We have little to do with them. Oh, I almost forgot. Lam's girlfriend, or boyfriend, or whatever. Miss Jay-Dee—she is also on board."

Feng cast another glance at one of his officers, and turned his attention to me. "Now, again, you are?"

"I'm Todd…head of security for the boat…for this trip."

"Ah, yes," said Feng, "you are the one who rang me. And you found the body?"

"Yes, well mostly. The kitchen staff found part of it first, then I found the rest."

"Mostly? Part? The rest? What *has* happened here?" Feng demanded.

"Decapitation, Chief. The head was found in the small goods lift in the galley, like I said, by the kitchen staff. Gina in fact. When they started the breakfast shift this morning. I responded to their distress call, and then found the rest of the body."

"Which is where?"

"In his cabin—the owner's suite—in the bath."

"Anyone touched it?"

"No, we left it as it was found, and locked the door. The head is still in the goods lift."

"Good. Good…" said Feng, again nodding slowly. "So, who would want to kill Mr Lam? Any obvious motives? And any weapon found?"

I explained what I had seen and heard the previous evening in the gaming room. To my mind, all the guests could have a motive. But such a brutal death seemed over the top for what appeared short-term disagreements.

"But we do have one with more compelling evidence," I said.

"Go on," said Feng.

I looked at Wallis. "Our captain…"

Feng cut in and looked across at Wallis. "I was going to ask…you said you are first-mate?"

"Correct," Wallis said.

"Yes, I wondered about the captain. Where is he?"

I explained what I'd heard between Sebastian and Hogan last night, and how Wallis and I had found him passed out this morning. Covered in blood, and with the hunting knife at his fingertips. I pulled out my phone, and showed him the photos. Wallis did the same.

"Good evidence," said Feng, "and where is the weapon?"

"On the bridge. He cleaned himself up, then attacked us with it when we challenged him," I said.

"Okay, so where is he now?"

"Locked up below—in the garage," said Wallis.

"Excellent work. You two are super-organised. Just like proper policemen." I shrugged the comment off.

"Now," continued Feng, "I wish to see the body first, then where you found the captain. Then I want you to bring me each of the guests, the entertainers, and the staff. One at a time. In here will be fine."

We ushered Chief Feng and his officers to the galley, to Sebastian's suite, and Hogan's cabin…the order in which evidence had been found. They reeled when they saw the head. One of the officers began heaving, and rushed to give the sink another workout, just like Gina.

They reeled again when they saw Sebastian's headless body. When another junior officer spotted the severed penis by the plughole, he began to faint, and had to be helped out by a colleague. Hogan's cabin, by comparison, was a haven from the gore. Some blood remained around where the knife had been, but was otherwise tidy. Cleaned up. Feng ordered an officer to have the blood tested.

We moved the police team into the bridge, showed them the big, serrated hunting knife which still lay on the floor, and demonstrated how I'd been attacked. An officer produced a plastic bag, and slid the knife inside.

We returned to the salon, and Wallis set off to fetch the first of the guests, Mr Ma. He was to be followed by Zhou, then Wang and finally Grekov. The entertainers and Miss Jay-Dee were to be next. I headed to the lower deck to alert the staff.

It took one hour and forty-seven minutes for Chief Feng to finally conclude his interviews, with first Wallis and then me, alternating turns returning and fetching each person. And in doing this, I was able to match up the guests and their names. In between, we sat on the aft deck, outside the salon, doors shut. Sealed off from the conversation. Five times Wallis said, "I could do with a beer." He was right. Instead he smoked about ten cigarettes, casually flicking the butts into the harbour at the end of each.

Chief Feng then said, "In light of the evidence you have presented, and the interviews we have conducted, I am releasing all the guests, entertainers and staff. They are free to go. Now, please take me down to the captain."

We led the chief and his officers to the lower deck, and Wallis fumbled through his pockets for the keys. Both access doors, the internal lower deck, and the rear onto the boarding platform, were secured from the outside with heavy-duty brass padlocks. Wallis found a key and released the first lock.

As he did, Feng called out, "Captain Hogan...Macau police. We're coming in."

Wallis gave the narrow door a gentle push, and stepped inside first, his frame blocking the view. Then he said, "Ohhhh, dear."

"What is it?" said Feng, who followed him in. I was next. Wallis stood frozen, staring. The garage door, the big one on the starboard side through which the toys came and went, was wide open. A warm breeze gushed through, and tiny harbour waves slapped at the hull below us.

Wallis turned to face Feng, moving his head side-to-side like a man who can't believe what he's hearing. Or seeing. Totally bewildered.

"Looks like he's gone, Chief."

38

Feng flew into police overdrive, barking orders at his officers. He fumbled for his phone and frantically dialled a number. Someone answered, and he conducted a rapid-fire conversation with them in an English-Chinese hybrid language. He shut off the phone, and looked at Wallis, then me. "Nobody is to leave until I say so. My officers are now searching the captain's cabin—I need his passport. Unless you two conveniently gave it to him before you locked him away."

Wallis said, "Nobody gave him a thing, except a good smacking from security here." He hoisted a thumb over his shoulder at me. "He was out to it when we left him. I didn't give the big door a thought. Didn't occur to me he might take to the water. Wherever he's headed, he'll have no ID, and no money."

"Yes," said Feng, "the passport?"

"Follow me," said Wallis, "should be in his cabin safe. Your boys will need the lock combo."

We set off up to the upper deck, arriving to find officers peering at the captain's safe, punching in various numbers.

"Let me do it," said Wallis. He put in the code and pulled open the door. "That's interesting."

"What?" snapped Feng and an officer in unison.

Wallis pulled out Hogan's passport and handed it to another policeman. He then drew out some cash and held it up. "This is the money he'll be needing." Wallis slipped it into his pocket.

"That is evidence," said Feng.

Wallis looked at him and shook his head. More a shake of pity. "I really can't see how he killed and beheaded Mr Lam with this bunch of notes, can you?" He pulled out the roll of money and held it up. "How could it be evidence?"

Feng shrugged. "Yes, maybe you are correct."

Wallis pocketed the cash again. "This is what's interesting. You got a cloth?" An officer pulled one from his small kit bag and handed it to Wallis, who reached into the safe with it and drew out a big, partially serrated hunting knife. "This is the knife which belongs to the captain. It was out in the gaming lounge when we came on board yesterday." Wallis looked at me. "You remember?"

I nodded. "Sure was. You were going to get him to move it. Looks like he did, but if that's the case, who owns the other one…the one we found there on the floor under his hand? Unless he has two?"

"No way," said Wallis. He shook his head and closed the safe door.

Chief Feng stood for a few moments, quietly studying the knife. "Bag this," he said to an officer. "We will now fingerprint everyone on the boat. And I want all passports."

We moved back down to the salon, and Wallis set off to fetch the first of the guests. I volunteered my prints. Feng held up his hand to stop me. "Hold on," he said, and pulled me aside as he proceeded to make a phone call. He closed off the call and said, "Why didn't you tell me you were a police officer?"

"Your channels work fast," I said, "but right now, officially I'm not. On leave."

"So why are you doing this? Bit of nooky, nooky, away from the wife, eh?" He grinned, displaying his row of big yellowed teeth, and gave me a knowing wink.

Another clever-dick reference to Sally…and another 'gut punch'…but I managed to push it away. "Just needed a break. Something a bit different…you know…I'd appreciate you not telling anyone here."

"Sure, sure," said Feng, "anyway I don't need your prints. Not for now—they'll be on a file somewhere, eh? Just get the others. And here's my card if you need me."

I helped Wallis bring everyone through, all handing over passports. Except the entertainers, chef and his assistants, and Miss Jay-Dee, who'd travelled with ID cards. Feng's men collected them. Zhou and Grekov protested at the indignity of it. Ma shook his head, but in the end just sighed and accepted his fate. Wang proceeded without a sound, unblinking, as usual.

Wallis was last, and handed his over as requested. He walked over to me and pressed his rough beard against my ear. The voice was quiet, and hoarse. "What about yours?"

"Already done. While you were out," I said. He stepped back and gave me a stare…a look that said, 'yeah…right…I don't think so.' He moved a few paces away, and I could feel the suspicion vibrating from him.

Chief Feng addressed the assembled group. "We are now taking control of this vessel. You have five minutes to gather your personal items. My boats will take you back to Macau, where you will have to remain. We will be checking details, and, all being in order, your passports and ID's will be available at the station from 5:00 p.m. today. You will then be free to leave. The first boat is at the boarding platform. Please move there as quickly as possible."

Everyone headed to their cabins to grab items. "This is disaster," grumbled Grekov. Ma nodded silent agreement.

Wallis pulled me aside, and put his beard to my ear again. "Give me a minute, will you? Make sure they don't come up." He nodded in the direction of the police group.

"Why, what are you up to?"

"Got to get my gear, and Skip's passport."

"I thought you gave it to them."

"I did…his Aussie one."

"He's got another?"

"Of course. He's Irish you know." And he slipped silently up the stairs.

39

The PSP boats dropped us at the wharf where we had collected the guests the day before. The first boat took the three guests and Wang, the next carried chef, his assistants, and Gina. The last ferried the entertainers, Wallis, and me. Miss Jay-Dee, who seemed to have befriended the girls, also came with us.

A PSP officer took us to Customs. I handed over my passport and the officer did likewise with the girls' cards. A sour-looking official took them away.

Wallis slid up close behind me. "Thought you already handed that over...to the chief."

"Yep, and he gave it back," I said. He cast me another flint-eyed look, his beard twitching slightly as he decided whether I could be trusted, or otherwise.

The thing was, Feng, through whatever channels were available to him, had discovered who I really was. Not surprising given the information sharing that took place between police operations across the globe. But I didn't want that known to Wallis, or anyone else on board for that matter. Up here, I wasn't a cop.

The customs officer finally returned with all the documents and a bunch of 'arrival cards'. He gave each a cursory look-over, handed all back, and waved us through.

Miss Jay-Dee pulled off her platform stilettos, air-kissed each entertainer on each cheek, and set off barefoot into the city. The guests each hailed a cab, Ma and Grekov together, and disappeared. Chef gathered his assistants and also set off on foot. Gina joined our group.

Wallis pulled me aside. He said, "I've got some business to attend to. Looks like the cops don't need us…we're free to go…so I'll catch ya later. But I need you to do something for me."

"Depends…what is it?" I was beginning to feel as if Wallis didn't know what to make of me…so any job he might have would not be designed with my comfort in mind. But I needn't have worried.

"These girls have to be paid in, like…folding stuff," he said. "You're still working for CH Lam, so…if you don't mind, can you take 'em to the club, where they'll fix 'em up?"

"Yeah…okay…I guess so. Where is it?" Didn't seem too hard a task, and might give me a look at the operation.

"Got something to write on?"

I pulled out Chief Feng's card and flipped it over. Gina produced a pen from her clutch. Wallis wrote an address and number on the back, and handed it to me. "This is it—The Golden Mountain Club. Ask for Lily…I'll call her and let her know you're coming. You all going?" The entertainers nodded in unison.

Wallis turned and faced the two big casinos off in the distance. He pointed at the towers. "See those two? That's where you're headed. Go straight between them, but round the other side of the lake. That'll put you in the right area."

Wallis looked at the entertainers. "Sorry it's turned out like this. Stick with Ash here...he'll see you get your money." He turned to look at me. "And keep your phone handy. I might need you."

I moved closer to him. "Where are *you* going?" I whispered.

Wallis lit a cigarette, took a long draw, and said, "Got a meeting...with a long-lost friend," and gave me a wink.

Then he stepped back, looked at the group and gave a two-fingered salute, turned on his heel and strode off.

*

Patrick Hogan gave several short, sharp, quiet raps on the old, brown wooden door. He repeated them when there was no answer. Quiet raps, but urgent ones, like someone gently tapping a nail. He did not need to draw attention from neighbouring buildings, and here the buildings stood cheek by jowl. Three or four storeys, hard against one another. It was only a matter of time before a head would appear from a window above, just to see what the fuss was about. He was not trying to cause a fuss.

Hogan was knocked up. He had swum the hundred yards or so from the *Golden Empress* to shore. He had to swim fast, before the cops on board discovered he'd abandoned ship. But not so fast as to thrash the water. So, underwater it had been. Then up for three gasps. And back under. Once...thirty years ago...he was a good swimmer. Competitive, even. But this was the most exercise he'd taken for years, and all in a severely short time frame. By the time he'd hauled himself from the murky harbour, he could barely breathe.

He'd rested on the shore for a few minutes, staring out at his beloved boat. It pained him to leave it, but if those on board reckoned he had killed Sebastian Lam, he could no longer stay. When he had regained some composure, he'd set off, dripping wet and barefoot, through Macau. He'd crossed several busy roads, but as much as possible kept to quieter back streets. His neck and jaw hurt. He was beginning to dislike Todd. Big time. After twenty minutes of darting, he'd arrived at the tiny street, then the building, and toward the far end, the faded brown doorway he was after.

In between knocks he looked quickly both ways along the street. The buildings opposite could not be more than fifteen feet away, and were almost identical to the one he was focussed on. Some with shuttered windows, others with metal barriers, a mixture of doorways, some single, others double. The buildings were painted a variety of colours...green, brown, blue, and yellow mostly. Once they would have been bright and happy looking. Now they were all blistered paint, faded and dull. He rapped again.

The door opened. A small, olive-complexioned woman stared back at him. In her late-seventies she was lined and weathered, her grey hair pulled back taut from her face and tied up behind. She wore a simple, floral cotton dress, and an apron over it. Her hands were covered in flour, which also streaked parts of her face.

She squinted hard. "Captain Hogan, what are you doing here?" She looked Hogan up and down. "What has happened to you? You look miserable. Where are your shoes?"

"Mrs Rodriguez, can I come in please? Do you have a room? I need one...now."

Mrs Rodriguez said nothing for a moment. She chewed at her bottom lip, and her head shook a little. This was taking some contemplation. Hogan resumed his nervous glances at the street. "Very well," she said, and waved him inside.

Hogan jumped through the doorway almost taking her out in the process. He wanted to get off that street. Mrs Rodriguez said, "You can have your usual one upstairs. But do you have money to pay?"

Hogan faltered. "Ah, no…not right now, no. But soon."

"How soon?"

"I don't want anyone to know I'm here. If anyone asks, you haven't seen me, okay?"

"Yes, yes, but when will you have the money?"

"The only person you can let in is an old-looking guy—tall, grey hair and beard. He'll have the money."

"When is he coming?"

"Soon."

"Soon, eh? Well, what's his name?"

"Wallis. Wil Wallis."

Mrs Rodriguez chewed at her lip. Her head shook. She squinted again at Hogan, stepped back, and again looked him over.

"Go on," she said, "but if your Mr Wallis isn't here by dark, you're out."

40

I arrived at the street-front security door of The Golden Mountain Club with my posse of beautiful women. They had tottered and lurched, sometimes one in front and two to each side, but mostly behind, for twenty minutes. Their platform shoes made them jar and jerk as they moved…skimpy skirts riding ever higher with each step. Even in Macau, where the sight of hookers drew little attention, they were a spectacle. And me in the middle, duffel bag slung over my shoulder. Obviously, their pimp.

I pressed the intercom. A woman's voice instructed us to move, as a group, three paces to our left, and face the door. We did as directed. The voice asked, "Is that all of you? Six in total?"

"That's it," I said.

"Please identify yourselves."

I said, "I'm Ash Todd, head of security on your boat, *Golden Empress*, and these women are, from my far left, Mae, Venus…"

"No, I want the girls to tell me."

The women each gave their name. Why I couldn't have just continued made no sense, but I guess it was their club. Their rules.

The voice then said, "Please push the door, and enter. Dong, who is *our* head of security, will escort you from there." The door buzzed, the lock released, and we stepped into the small foyer.

Dong appeared from a side door. Not overly tall, maybe five-eight or nine, and about as wide as he was high. He was dressed in a white shirt, black suit, and a navy tie emblazoned with the Club motif. He bowed slightly and said, "This elevator, thank you. It will take you to reception."

We filed into the lift, and Dong reached in and pressed a button. There were only two buttons I noticed, one with the initial R, and below it, one with G. Moments later we were deposited several floors above, and greeted by a small, pretty, thirty-something woman.

"Welcome," she smiled, "my name is Lily. A very sad time, isn't it?"

We all nodded our agreement.

"Is there anything I can get you? Tea, perhaps?"

I looked at the girls. They all shook their heads. I said, "No, thank you, we've all had a very long day. If you could just settle up the wages, we can move on."

Lily ushered us into an adjoining office, which housed a black round boardroom table and a dozen or so chairs. We all took up positions around it, as Lily disappeared, and then returned with a metal box and a book. She opened the box, and pulled out five envelopes. Each envelope bore the name of each of the women. "Take whichever is yours," she said.

The girls picked out their respective envelopes and without invitation, ripped them open and began counting. Almost in unison they looked up, grinning.

"Now, I need you to sign for the money," said Lily, opening her book, and sliding it to Mae. The women each signed, and Belle, who was last, slid the book back to her.

Lily stood, and said, "I trust this settles everything?" The girls nodded. "Then thank you—I'll show you to the elevator." They followed her out to reception.

I came out last, and quietly pulled Lily aside. "I don't want to appear rude, but I think there's something you've overlooked."

Lily looked up at me with her serene smile. "Ah, you mean yours, Mr Todd?"

"Well, no, not just the money. I expect someone will want my report…"

"Certainly," said Lily, "and a meeting has been requested. As you're already here, now would be a good time. Yes?"

"A meeting? Who's requested it?"

Lily ushered the girls into the lift, smiled and said, "Bye, bye," and sent them down to the security entrance. She turned back to me, the smile gone, her face all business.

"The boss," she said.

"The boss is dead, remember?"

"Yes, yes…but I mean…the real boss."

"CH Lam…he's here? Now?"

"Of course. You don't think Sebastian ran this entirely on his own, do you? Too busy spending money, playthings…you've seen them. Yes, Mr Todd, CH is here…let's not keep him waiting."

41

Lily led me to Mr Lam's office door, knocked twice and showed me inside. I scanned the room, quickly taking in the view, the desk, and the furnishings. Impressive joint.

CH Lam, immaculately dressed in a pin-stripe navy suit, stood at the huge picture window overlooking Macau harbour, his back facing me. Anchored below just off the wharf, sat his boat, the *Golden Empress*. Off-limits now, even to him. He looked to be a carbon copy of Sebastian, only older, with a full head of black hair, greying slightly at the temples. He sighed…the sound of a weary old man…then turned and offered his hand. His grip was surprisingly strong for a man of his age.

"Mr Todd, thank you for staying to meet with me. Please sit." He indicated to a large sofa.

"I'm very sorry for your loss, sir," I said.

CH nodded a 'thank you'. "Tell me, what did you find? What happened to him?"

I hesitated a moment. "I know you wanted a report on Sebastian and his relationships…with the clients…and maybe other staff. But are you sure you want to go into this detail?

Haven't the police told you?"

"The police have told me nothing. They have the boat locked up…that's what I was doing at the window. Staring at my boat. But I can't get to her. They just say they are 'continuing with their investigations'. But you were there…so tell me."

"Not good. I woke this morning to the screams of the kitchen staff. I really don't know how he died…I guess an autopsy will tell…but it was vicious—like a revenge attack." I hesitated again.

CH looked up at me. "And?"

"There's no delicate way to say this, sir. His head was hacked off, and placed in the goods lift. That's what the staff found. I found his body. In the bath, in his suite. And…" Yet again I faltered. Did he need to know about the penis? Would it help?

"Yes?" CH leaned in at me.

"Just a God-awful mess."

CH silently contemplated the floor again. He shook his head, like a man rejecting his tenth whisky for the night. Speaking of which he said, "Do you drink, Mr Todd?"

"Sure, when time allows." It occurred to me, in that moment, I'd had little to drink on the *Empress*. Too much other stuff happening, I guessed. But in a fleeting way, it did feel like a little victory.

"Normally I don't, but right now I'm going to make an exception. What will you have?"

"Bourbon, with ice, thanks."

CH pressed an intercom on a side table, and ordered a bourbon. "And a whisky for me. Double," he said. "Now, Mr Todd, who do you think did it?"

"Well, you know we arrested Skip on the boat?"

"Skip? You mean Hogan? No, I didn't know. Nobody told me that. The first-mate, Wallis, rang me with the news. That's all I heard. Why did you arrest Hogan?"

I explained the various disagreements I'd seen between the guests and Sebastian, Hogan's drunken argument, how we'd found Hogan in his cabin, the hunting knife, and the blood. I showed CH the pictures I'd taken on my phone. I detailed how we'd locked him in the toy room, and once we'd anchored, how he'd escaped through the side door. "The police are looking for him. And we now have a second knife, found in Hogan's room safe. So, I don't know what weapon was used."

CH appeared to take each piece of information without emotion, nodding as he listened. He gave it some quiet thought, and then said, "I can't believe Hogan did this. I've known him, on and off, for a long time. Met his wife once. Terrible woman. He's cranky sometimes, belligerent I think you call it. I think she would make any man cranky. But I don't believe he would kill Sebastian. Someone else on that boat has done this. I think they've set Hogan up."

"Possibly, but who?"

CH stared at me. "Mr Todd, you're the policeman."

I gave him a little smile. "Ah…Bynow's been talking, has he?"

"Before I take people on, I like to know a little about them. Mr Bynow speaks very highly of you, but don't worry, your secret is safe here. Now, he tells me to pay you directly. Ten thousand was the agreed sum, I believe?"

"It is."

"I want to extend our arrangement. I want you to look harder at the people on that boat. The guests in particular. I know them, they're clients here. But I don't count anything out. The police take their passports?"

"All, except the entertainers and locals. And mine," I said.

"How did you manage to keep it?"

"The chief…Feng is his name…found out I'm a cop. He wasn't interested in me after that."

"Good—see that's why we do our homework. Now, you'll need to go to China…that's where they live. I've got all their personal details here and we can arrange a visa for you quickly."

"But they can't travel—not while Feng has their passports."

"Don't worry about them, Mr Todd—they'll find a way." CH gazed off through the picture window, and muttered again to himself, "They'll find a way…"

There was one thought which had been bothering me, and I seized the small break in our conversation to raise it.

"You mentioned you and Hogan have some history," I said. "I wondered about him…and Wallis for that matter. They seem an unlikely pair to be operating the *Empress* for you. From what I saw Hogan didn't think too much of Sebastian, but he sure has respect for you. If the question's not too rude…how did you meet?"

CH gave a little laugh. "No, no…it's not rude. Many years ago…more than ten I would think…when I was still in the employ of one of the big casinos, Hogan appeared. He had money then…plenty it seemed…and was a good client of the business. A decent sized punter. And I looked after his…shall we say…outside activities? As I did for many clients."

"Hmmm…then something's obviously changed."

CH nodded. "He disappeared for quite some time…and then

a couple of years ago he resurfaced…here. He had tracked me down, so to speak. He was looking for work…the money had gone, but I don't know what happened. He didn't say…and I didn't ask. Not my business. Anyway, I'd known from before of his interest…and his skill…with boats. We'd just bought the *Empress*. So, it seemed fate had lined him up for us. I put him on…and Wallis seemed to come as part of the package. I know he can appear a bit rough, but he does a good job for us. So, that is why I want to push this further. So…the job…what do you say?"

"Okay…then how much?"

CH gave me a confused look.

"For the extra work—additional, you know."

"Ahhh…let's say twenty thousand for the extra, and another twenty if you find the real killer? Plus, what we owe you so far."

I thought for a moment. In my very short meeting I'd decided I quite liked CH. He seemed straight enough, and he certainly wasn't entertaining any notion that Hogan was a killer. And if Feng's men found Hogan…which wasn't an 'if', but 'when'…he would be thrown to the mercy of the Macau justice system. Which would mean no mercy. And if he was innocent as CH believed, I couldn't let him go through that. Not on my watch.

"Deal," I said.

CH shook my hand and gave me a card. "My direct number—please don't hand it around. Keep me informed. I'll have Lily get the items together for you in the morning. Oh, and that girlfriend of his. What's her name?"

"Miss Jay-Dee, you mean?"

"Yes, her, maybe have a look at her also."

"Him."

CH stared at me again. "Him?"

"Sorry, thought you'd know. Jay-Dee is a he."

CH looked stunned. "Amazing," he muttered, shaking his head. "Lily will see you out."

I retrieved my bag and let myself into the foyer. Lily greeted me again, and handed me an envelope. "Ten thousand, as agreed. Give me your bank details in the morning, Mr Todd, and I'll transfer the rest. Ten upfront, ten on progress, another twenty on successful completion. Yes?"

"Sure, yes. Thank you." I took the lift to the security entrance, where Dong let me out, bowing very slightly as I departed. I stepped onto the pavement, wondering what my next move would be. I needed somewhere to stay. I pulled out my phone to scan for hotels. There was a sudden tap on my shoulder and I wheeled, ready to smack whoever it was, just in case.

Venus stood there in the early evening glow, the big, flashing lights of the casinos across the water bouncing off her honey-coloured hair. She looked magnificent in the half-light.

I smiled at her. "Thought you'd all gone home."

"Ah, too late for the ferry to Hong Kong." She peered at my phone. "So, Tarzan, where are we staying?"

42

After I left The Golden Mountain Club I called a couple of hotels, both linked to casinos, but the rates were too high. Sure, I was about to make good money from my extended operation…but man, I'm not one of their high-rollers. It was as though the receptionists were looking down on me from their eyries across the lake. '*There he is*,' I could hear them say, '*needs a room fast—for him and his hooker. Let's double the ask.*'

Venus put her hand over mine, and closed off the phone.

"Come on," she said, "we go this way." She grabbed my hand and we walked for ten minutes, maybe fifteen, around the end of another lake, up the hill and into the welcoming arms of the Riviera Hotel. Perhaps a bit past its prime, and with rooms decorated in a dazzling array of bright, confectionary colours. But the rate was right.

Our room was painted jade green, with a chocolate-coloured carpet in some swirling pattern. It looked like the interior designer didn't know what to put with what, so went with everything. But the views were straight from the brochure—over the lake, past the glowing Macau Tower and onto the Taipa

Bridge. Macau and Taipa twinkled in the distance.

We ordered room service. A steak for me, fish for her, a beer for me…first…then a bourbon…gin and tonic for her. A bottle of red to share. I wanted a shower, so did she. She went first, while I gazed at the view. She came out, still a bit damp, wrapped in an oversize towel. I went in and when I came out, oversized towel around my waist, I noticed the food had arrived. I also noticed Venus had moved to the bed.

The doona had been pulled down. Her towel had gone missing. All that was left was a long, tanned slender body. Smooth. Two breasts heaved gently at me. She hardly moved, except for a small kinking upward of her right knee. Her legs slightly parted. She crooked her left index finger, and mouthed, 'come here.' I moved to the edge of the bed, as she gently took my towel in her hand, and slowly unwound it.

"What do you want to eat first," she asked in her quiet accent, "the meat or the sweet?" Her hand moved lower to my groin.

"Well, as we seem to have started this course…"

Venus pushed herself up from the bed, pulled herself tight into me, turned me round and gently pushed me down, backwards onto it. She then sat astride me and ever so slowly began to move her hips back and forth, back and forth.

"Good choice," she purred, "but we mustn't take too long or your meat will go cold."

At that moment, a surging wave of guilt hit me. My mind fled from the hotel, and flashed to the car. And then to Sally. She could see me, I was sure. I heard the sound of scrunching metal. I saw the hospital. And the teddy bear. Look what I'd *done*. I gasped, sat up and without any force pushed her off me.

"I…I'm sorry," I said, "but I can't do this. Not yet, not now."

"Why, what is wrong? You don't like the look of me?"

"No, no. You look wonderful. It's…just…me. I'm sorry…"

Venus seemed genuinely hurt. She picked up her towel, and her clothes, and retreated to the bathroom. I dressed, and took a couple of solid gulps of my beer. When she emerged, we ate in silence. We drank the bottle of red. Not a word spoken. And then she said, "You want to talk about it?"

"No…not yet."

Venus shrugged. We went to sleep—separate beds. In the morning, she was up at six, showered again, dressed, and by 6:45, on her way. As she left, she handed me her card.

"Look after yourself. If you get better and are in Hong Kong, look me up. Okay?"

A weak smile escaped me. "I will. Sorry…"

She put her finger to her lips. "Shhh…bye, bye." And she was gone.

43

Patrick Hogan sat at the small metal window, gazing out at nothing. Darkness was consuming all outside. Dim lights came on in the apartments opposite, and a couple of equally dim lamps lit the tiny street. A short, two-minute shower had wet the street paving, so that it glistened a little. Hogan stared straight through it all.

He replayed the events of the evening before, over and over, in his head. He could remember not much. That was the trouble with booze. It made you forget. That was good sometimes…like when he could forget Christine. Now, he remembered, he'd spoken to her earlier in the night. She wanted money. "Fuck, Christine," he thought.

He concentrated hard, trying to recall more. He could remember shutting the boat down for the night, and retiring to his cabin for a couple of drinks. Well, it only seemed like a couple. Maybe it was more. Then what? Ah, yes, that was right. He tracked down Sebastian and asked him for a loan. Two-hundred grand. That was a bit cheeky. He only needed sixty or so to get rid of Christine, but she would keep coming back for more. He wanted to be rid of her, and her leeching lawyer.

But Sebastian said no. What a turd. If anyone could afford to lend him money it was Sebastian and The Golden Mountain Club. Shit, they'd keep that much in the petty-cash tin. That made him mad, and he remembered storming back to his cabin for another couple of nerve-settlers to think what to do. Then he'd woken. It was morning, he was still dressed, and his arm and hand were covered in blood.

He could remember nothing of what had happened in between. The night was a blank, so he'd cleaned up the mess on the floor. How that blood got there was a mystery. And where was it from?

Then Wallis, and that big bastard Todd, had arrested him. Arrested *him*. For what? Murder? "Bullshit!" he muttered, trying not to make any noise which might remind Mrs Rodriguez he was still in her house. No, if he was going to kill anyone it would be that damn Christine, or her lawyer, or his useless son. Not the bloke who paid him…even if it was really his father who paid…and even if he wouldn't lend him money. Don't bite the hand that feeds you—that was the motto. His best mate, Wallis, had done this to him. And Wallis and Todd had it wrong. He felt betrayed.

He moved slightly in his chair. The sharp pain in his neck and jaw made him wince. Then he remembered something more. That's right…he'd threatened them with the knife. The knife on the bridge they said was a murder weapon. But that wasn't his knife. Couldn't be. He'd stashed his in the cabin safe.

But he couldn't remember anything after threatening them. He could only guess that it was them who locked him up. Maybe it wasn't them. But someone did. Probably for his safety. And theirs. As ship's captain that's what he would do if he were threatened that way. They were just doing their job. Now he began to feel guilty about feeling betrayed.

Still, they'd made one mistake—they didn't lock the outside garage door on the boat. He had to get away from there, to save himself. But maybe it wasn't a mistake. Maybe Wallis and Todd made sure he could escape. No…not Todd…but Wallis might. Who knew? And the big questions remained…what had happened to him during the night…had he really killed Sebastian in a fit…where did he get the knife which wasn't his…and who owned the knife?

So, holed up in old Macau in this little old upstairs room, in a little old apartment building, in a little old street, owned by a little old woman who would soon enough throw him out, with nought but the shirt and shorts he was wearing…and no money, no passport, no shoes…a bigger question loomed large. How was he going to get out of *this* shit?

He heard a small noise outside, underneath. It was too dark to make out the source, but it sounded like knocks on the front door. He heard Mrs Rodriguez shuffle toward it. The door creaked a bit as it opened.

"Yes?" said Mrs Rodriguez.

"Do you have a Captain Hogan here?" a voice said. Sounded like Wallis.

"Who are you?"

"I'll take that as a 'yes'. Name's Wallis…First Mate Wil Wallis."

"Do you have money?"

"How much?"

Mrs Rodriguez hesitated a moment. "Five hundred—US."

Wallis said, "Don't know that he's worth that much. Nope…" He turned to leave.

Upstairs, Hogan's heart skipped a beat. No, two. He was about to tear down the stairs and rip Wallis apart, when Mrs Rodriguez said, "Alright, four will be good."

Wallis fished in his pocket, and held up some notes. "Three is all I've got—for both of us. Tonight only. Deal?"

There was a long silence as Mrs Rodriguez considered the offer. Hogan sat mummified in his chair. Why was Wallis playing this game…with *his* life? He had to have way more than three-hundred on him.

Finally, Mrs Rodriguez said, "Okay, a deal. But I want you out by ten tomorrow. Unless, by chance, you find more money."

Upstairs, in the quiet darkness, Patrick Hogan allowed himself a little fist-pump and a small, triumphant, "Yes!"

For the first time, that day, he felt human.

44

Chief Feng sat back heavily into his cheap, black, leatherette, PSP issue chair. His office at the rear of the second floor of the PSP headquarters at Praceta de Um de Outubro overlooked nothing in particular. Just apartments, all similar. Twenty storeys, faded white, enclosed balconies, air conditioners. It was nearing 9:00 p.m. and he was dog-tired. He fixed his sights on a balcony, and then on an adjacent air conditioner, glowing under the apartment light. Thirty-feet away, fifty maybe. He tried to concentrate on his newest case, but nothing would come.

Two-and-a-half hours earlier he had received the four clients from the *Golden Empress*—Zhou, Ma, Grekov, and Wang. All demanded return of passports as promised. Their stories matched, at least to the extent of what they were doing, or knew. Or said they knew. Whether they were colluding was hard to say. Their background checks were clean. So clean, in fact, that Feng had nothing on them at all. He had never seen background reports with so little information.

Most people had something on record. Education, minor

infringements like traffic, or bigger things like, say, political involvement. In China, definitely political involvement. But the reports said simply: *Zhou Wei Li—Petrochemical Industry, Shanghai; Ma Junjie—Property, Guangzhou; Vadim Grekov—Property, Guangzhou; Wang Bo Hui—Finance, Beijing. End of Report.* And Grekov was Russian. Not even one line of additional information on him. But Feng's thirty-years and two-month police career had taught him one thing—if the Chinese authorities were prepared to supply so little information, there was nothing to be gained by pressing harder. Probably just the opposite—there could be much to lose. He handed over the passports.

That left him with just two—the main suspect, Patrick John Hogan, the captain of *Golden Empress*, and the first-mate, Wilson Donald Wallis. Feng had no idea why Hogan might want to hack his boss to death, but the evidence Wallis and Todd had presented was compelling. Hogan was missing, and Wallis was, well, out there somewhere. He had to find Hogan, and in Feng's mind, the easiest way to do that was to set the dogs free.

In this case, the dog was Wallis. He seemed to know a lot about Hogan, how to get into his safe, what was in the safe, and so on. Chief Feng's great hope was that Wallis might know more than he let on, and would lead them to Hogan. From the moment the PSP boat had deposited Wallis on the shore, he was tailed. All Feng could do was wait. He looked away from the window and back to his notes.

His desk phone rang. Feng lifted the receiver.

"Boss, we've got them," said Sub-Chief Lau.

"Both?"

"Yes, sir."

"Where?"

"An apartment in the Travessa de Sancho Panca."

"You think they're still there—no rear escape?"

"We think so—just more buildings the same on the back. Unless they've punched a hole through. We've been watching the area for half-an-hour."

Feng allowed himself a glimmer of a smile. "Good…bring them in."

45

It was just after 9:30 a.m.

Lily, personal assistant to Sebastian Lam, deceased, and now to his father, CH Lam, greeted me at The Golden Mountain Club reception. I had been escorted to the floor by Dong, the ever unsmiling head of security. He bowed in his customary manner as I departed the lift.

"Mr Todd, good morning," Lily smiled, "enjoy your evening?"

"Very much," I lied.

"Good, then CH is ready to see you now. Come on through."

I followed Lily into the vast office. CH rose from an armchair, hand outstretched.

"Morning, Mr Todd. Got your bank details?"

I pulled a small notebook from my top pocket and held it up.

"Fine…then let's plan this attack, shall we?"

CH motioned for me to sit at his desk, opposite him. Three computer monitors sat on it, and behind a whole wall was occupied with screens. Most were off, but a couple flickered away, showing muted images of clients in gaming rooms. I wondered what all this was about. CH noticed me staring at them.

"Early starters," he said. "Some of them will play all night, or all day." He glanced at his watch. "Almost ten o'clock. Not so early then." He waved his arms at the screens. "But this is Sebastian's doing. He loved control. Now Mr Todd, look at these please."

CH spread three sheets of paper on the desk. I read them carefully. Each sheet related to a client on the *Empress*. Name, address—home and business—phone numbers, occupation, and a summary of their membership at The Golden Mountain Club. Written in both English and Mandarin. Below each summary was a neatly drawn map. Street names and numbers, again in English and Mandarin. At particular points CH had marked a small asterisk.

"Now turn them over please," said CH.

On the reverse side were bigger maps, again hand drawn, showing where each of the smaller maps fitted into each city. One of Shanghai, one of Guangzhou.

"Only one in Guangzhou?" I asked.

"Ma and Grekov work together—same office. Ma lives above—fifty floors up. Penthouse. So, only one asterisk. Grekov moves about—sometimes China, sometimes Russia. Hard to track him. Stays in hotels."

"There's one missing. Wang—you've given me nothing on him."

CH stood from his desk and moved over to the big window overlooking the harbour. "Did you enjoy our boat, Mr Todd? Beautiful, isn't she? Look at her down there—and I can't get to her. It is very distressing."

"She's certainly beautiful, CH, but what about Wang?"

"Leave him Mr Todd. Wang is different to the others—more like a friend of the business, you know? He wouldn't have done this to Sebastian."

"How can you be so sure?"

CH turned to me and stared—the same unblinking stare I'd observed in Wang on the boat. "Because I know him, Mr Todd. So, we'll leave him. Understood?"

I nodded. "As you wish. Now where am I headed first?"

"I've booked you on a flight to Shanghai—at two o'clock." CH pointed to a package on a nearby coffee table. "Those are your documents. Return tickets from Macau, plus one from Shanghai to Guangzhou, return, and one more from Shanghai to Hong Kong. Oh, and your tourist visa."

CH scribbled a note on a sheet of paper, folded it and handed it to me. "When you get to Shanghai, call this number. Name is Ho. He will be your guide. Should you need to go to Guangzhou, Ho will give you a contact there."

I took the note from CH, picked up the packet from the coffee table, and tapped it against my hand. This lack of interest in Wang might be a cause for concern, but I figured I had three others to begin my chase with, and I had to start somewhere. And Hogan may come to depend on it…wherever he was.

I picked up my bag, slung it over my shoulder, and turned to CH as I opened the door. "By the way, CH, these clients—did they win or lose here?"

CH was silent for a moment. Thinking. "I believe they won, Mr Todd. Yes, I would say they won."

"So, they must have been very pleased with the club, and

Sebastian. Tell me, did he have any enemies?"

"No, Mr Todd." CH slowly shook his head. "I can't think of a single one."

46

The walls of cell twelve in the basement of the PSP headquarters, were coloured cream. A filthy, dirty cream. Cracked, dark-green linoleum covered the cement floor. A solitary light, dim with no shade, hung about one foot below the middle of the ceiling. A few feet further away a dusty, round air-conditioning duct hummed. Every so often it clanked. A toilet, with no seat, stood in a corner, not far from the bed. A metal hand-basin hung at the midpoint of the wall opposite. The door was a metal grate. Black, heavy, big lock.

Wil Wallis reclined on a bed in a corner of the small, stark room. Alone. Now and then a police guard would cruise past, in slow-motion, and cast him a cursory glance. Otherwise the room was empty…and so nothing else to see. But the guard looked in, anyway.

Wallis had little idea how long he'd been here, because the light had been left on. Without interruption. With next-to-no sleep, he'd lost any sense of time. But he knew it was around 10:00 p.m. in the evening when he'd arrived. He knew that, because the last time he'd looked at his watch, it was 9:12 p.m.

and Patrick Hogan had said, "I'm stuffed. Let's get some shut-eye and we'll sort this crap out in the morning."

So, Wallis had done as requested, and shut off the light in the small bedroom he and Hogan were sharing in Mrs Rodriguez' apartment. He'd barely got to sleep, perhaps ten minutes later, when there was a loud thumping from below. Voices yelled, "Police—open *now*."

The commotion startled Wallis, and Hogan even more, because he was already asleep. Hogan sat bolt upright and yelled, "Who's that?"

Wallis whispered, "For Christ's sake, shut-up." They heard the front door open. Seconds later the bedroom filled with light again. Half-a-dozen uniformed police officers stormed in. One said, "Captain Hogan, First Mate Wallis, you are under arrest. Stand up."

They struggled to their feet and an officer grabbed each of them, spun them around and slapped the cuffs on. In that sharp procedure, Wallis felt his watch-strap snap, and the timepiece slip off. Another fifteen minutes passed, and they were driven through an automatic door in the rear of a building, in the middle of the city, and separated. The building, and its location, were a mystery to Wallis. This small room, where he had since been confined, was not.

He knew a police cell when he saw one, and this was one. He did not like police cells. He felt a wave of claustrophobia overtake him, and a gnawing need for a cigarette. He heard a guard approach, raised himself from the bed and called out, "Hey, Officer, you wouldn't have a smoke, would you? I'd kill for one right now."

The guard appeared from the side and stood in front of the metal grate door. He looked at Wallis for a few seconds, stepped back and shook his head. A fast shake. "No smoking in the building," he snapped. "But now I know why you killed Mr Lam. For cigarettes."

The guard marched off. Wallis slumped back on the bed, stunned. They had to be kidding...killing for cigarettes? No...this must be a dream. No...not a dream...a nightmare. Trouble was...it was just beginning.

*

Chief Feng sat at a small metal table in a windowless PSP room. Dark brown walls and minimum light. There was no noise. Soundproofing made sure of that. In one corner, a hulking giant reclined in an armchair. He wore plain clothes, and sat expressionless. Only occasionally did he crunch his knuckles. His favourite power-move.

Opposite Feng, barefoot and dressed only in a shirt and shorts, sat Patrick Hogan. After a day and a half in these same clothes, and on the run, Hogan was beginning to smell a bit.

The smell did not make Feng any happier. What he wanted was a quick confession, so he could get out of there, and let somebody else take charge of the stinking prisoner. He had more pressing matters to attend to, in particular the annual PSP awards that night. Chief Feng was to receive the Excellent Service Medal, in recognition of his thirty years in the force. He had been questioning Hogan for nearly an hour, and getting nowhere.

The evidence was clear to Feng. Sebastian Lam had been stabbed a number of times, his throat slit, his torso gutted, like a fish, from navel to chest. And his dick had been severed. That one threw Feng. Why would someone cut that off? A frenzied attack. Feng had never seen such violence. The murder weapon had been found in Hogan's company…indeed he had even threatened his own colleagues on the boat with it. And those same colleagues had photographs of Hogan, sprawled on the bed, and covered in blood, knife at his fingertips. *Damn this prisoner,* thought Feng, *why doesn't he just own up?*

Feng rose from his chair, and stared down at Hogan. "One final time, Mr Hogan. You cannot deny the evidence. We showed you the pictures, and the knife. Just make it easy for yourself."

Hogan stared straight ahead. He was tired, but he was not giving in. "I've told you, the knife was not mine. I remember nothing. How can I admit to something I don't remember? Tell me that. And one more thing—something you haven't come up with—where's the motive? What reason did I have to kill Sebastian? Tell me that too."

Feng said nothing, and looked away at the man in the corner.

Hogan smirked. "That's right…you can't tell me because you don't know. There is no motive. Ha…see…a bullshit case."

Chief Feng had had enough. He nodded to the man in the corner, and moved to the door. "Your choice, Mr Hogan." He opened the door, stepped out, and pulled it closed with a gentle click.

The next sound Patrick Hogan heard was a grunt. His own grunt, as something hit him hard on the neck. After that he heard little. He felt some things though…the floor as his head smacked into it, a racking pain across his back as something crashed into his kidneys, and a blurred feeling of leather and laces, all at once, taking out the side of his face. He felt blood well up in his mouth and nose, another jolt across his back, and all the breath leave his lungs.

His mind flipped for an instant to the bridge of the *Golden Empress*, and Wallis lighting a smoke. Hogan didn't smoke. Hated the smell. But for a split-second now he could smell it. And for that split-second, he liked it.

At that point, in the inside world of Patrick Hogan, the lights went out.

47

I sat in the lobby of the Holiday Inn Hotel, sipping at a coffee, my mind wandering back-and-forth between thoughts. Things about this case were worrying me. Things like the possibility of two murder weapons. Which was the real one? Things like the strange collection of clients on the *Empress*, and CH's determination for me to pursue them. But not Wang. Things like the police interrogation of those same clients. Was there any?

Things like Sebastian's apparent lack of enemies. That is, according to his father. In his business? With his lifestyle? All that cash, fancy suits, fast cars, and still he beats up the tranny he's shagging. Yeah, right. The old man must be delusional. And things like our 'arrest' of Hogan, and his escape. Did Wallis plan that?

I had a few hours to kill before my flight to Shanghai. I'd made my way from my meeting with CH, around the lake, across the city, and now sat in the hotel coffee shop gazing across the street at the arse-end of the ugly, yellow building which housed the Macau police.

I sent a text to Bynow…best to keep him in the loop I figured. It read, *Big drama on the boat…CH's son dead…on my way to Shanghai. Be in touch.* Bynow responded in kind with, *Be careful…call me if in trouble. No hero stuff, eh?*

I finished my coffee, grabbed my duffel, strode down the street and rounded into the Praceta de Outubro. I bounded up the steps, and into police reception.

"Chief Feng, is he available please? He gave me his card," I said, flipping both his and mine onto the counter.

The receptionist glanced at each, and picked up her phone. She spoke fast in Chinese, then pointed across to two lifts and said, "Second floor. Chief Feng will meet you."

Feng was waiting as I stepped out, smiling as he ushered me in to a side office. Those glistening yellow teeth again.

"So, Mr Todd, what brings you to our fine establishment?"

I told him of my concerns, and that I'd been hired to follow up for the Lam family. In a private capacity. Not that they didn't trust the police. Oh no, not at all. They just wanted to make sure there were no other issues between them and their clients. And being the thorough investigator I was, just as Chief Feng was, I should check everything. Feng nodded, without a word, through my explanation. Whether he believed it was not clear.

"I don't want to get in your way, or interrupt your work, Chief, but I would like to see the murder weapon. Both…if possible."

Feng picked up the room phone and made a call.

"You can see them, Mr Todd, but I doubt they will do you any good." A young policeman appeared at the door with a box. Feng flicked a finger in its direction. "Help yourself."

I opened the box, and slowly slid the two hunting knives on to the table. They were remarkably similar—except the handles. I studied them up-close—one brown and dimpled, and the other black with a small worn motif of some type. I couldn't make it out, but Feng had no issue with my photographing them. I thanked him, and the young policeman took the knives away.

"So," I asked, "any other developments in the case from your end? And what did you mean that the knives wouldn't do me any good?"

"Because there are no prints on the black one. Maybe you cleaned it—with your towel?"

"No way, Chief, no time. And as a cop, I wouldn't do that...would I?"

Feng gave a small smirk. "The brown one is covered in Hogan's prints. And as you also know Hogan escaped, which to me indicates guilt. And I had Wallis followed once he reached land. So, Mr Todd, yes there are developments. We now have both Hogan and Wallis in custody."

My thoughts flipped to when I had discovered Hogan's knife...the brown one...when doing the rounds with Wallis. And how I'd placed my handkerchief over it as I picked it up, so as not to leave prints. And Wallis had made some crack about me being on the run. Well, it didn't look so silly now, did it? If I hadn't done that, I might now be joining them. Feng had worked fast...but my 'inner copper' kicked in. I had a job to do—to find a killer.

"Have they confessed?"

"Not yet, but we are still working on them." Feng winked. Twice. Smiled. His yellow teeth glistened.

"Not physically, I trust?"

Feng looked away. "No…no, not physically Mr Todd."

I didn't like the sound of that. "So, have you charged either of them?"

"Not yet. But shouldn't be long."

I thought hard for a second, stared at my feet. Now I figured I had another job—to get Hogan and Wallis out of that slammer, whether I found the real killer, or not. It seemed to me Feng had decided they were the ones who would pay. He needed a result, and they were convenient. And it was now apparent I needed to get on with it.

I looked up at Feng. "One favour, Chief…hold off charging them until I get back to you. Can you do that?"

"And where are you going?"

I faltered before answering. Too many people knowing my moves couldn't be helpful, but I needed his co-operation. "Shanghai."

He nodded. "Big city, Mr Todd…big, difficult city."

"That's why I need your help. Just…a bit."

Feng copied my earlier move and stared down at his feet. There was an extended silence. Finally, he said, "Only because I know you are a policeman, Mr Todd. So, you have forty-eight hours. Forty-eight hours only."

48

The Broadway Mansions Hotel stood brooding in the Shanghai dark. Twenty floors of art-deco, dark-brown brick. Like something from a 1930s New York movie set. It overlooked the small Wusong River, towered above the old Waibaidu Bridge, and stared almost straight along The Bund. Close by on the left, the Huangpu River, the lifeblood of Shanghai for centuries, snaked its way north. Now, at night, it was quieter, but boats and barges still pushed their way up and down without a sound.

On the opposite shore lay Pudong. The future of Shanghai. No…'lay' was not accurate—it stood up and screamed. A million buildings a million storeys tall, it seemed. Each new one more futuristic than the last. All lit. A neon overload. A never-ending battle for supremacy in the architectural world of China.

I sat alone in my room at the Mansions. Bottle of bourbon, one glass, ice. Level ten, north-east corner. Nice room. Big view of all the above. I'd flown in a couple of hours earlier. Checked in, and taken an early evening stroll along The Bund. People everywhere. Refused the offer of shoes and watches from a dozen or more pushers. Back to the hotel.

I'd made two phone calls. The first to Mr Zhou. He was pleasantly surprised to hear from me. Of course he would be happy to meet with me.

But he was also curious.

"What is this about, Mr Todd?"

"I'll cover that at our meeting, but it's a follow-up on Sebastian's death."

"Whatever I can do," he said, "come over at nine o'clock," and gave me the address. Of course, I already had that…from CH. I resisted the urge to gloat.

The second was to CH's man here. Ho. A gruff but cultured English voice had answered. I introduced myself, and asked if he could pick me up from the hotel.

"I've been expecting you, Mr Todd. May I ask where we are going?"

"An address in Huqui Road."

"And we are meeting?"

"A Mr Zhou—a long-term client of CH's. You know him?"

There was a brief silence. "As he is a client of the company, obviously I know who he is. I may have met him once. I'll be at your room at 8:30."

I'd spent the next hour running a script through my head. Likely questions from Zhou. Why was I here? Who sent me? Why did I think Zhou could help? Did I really think Zhou had done this? You do know my standing with the Club?

And my questions. You and Sebastian argued. What about? Did he owe you money? Did you owe him money? You left the meeting at 10:00 p.m. Did you return to the gaming lounge? You threatened to cut Sebastian out. Did you mean that literally? Tell me again—what did you argue about? I ran and re-ran the script. Still seemed a pretty weak probe from my side.

There was a knock on my hotel door. I peered through the security viewer, and opened it to a stocky, muscular Chinese man. Mid-thirties, jet-black wavy hair. Dressed in a close-fitting black suit, white shirt, black tie, driving gloves.

He peeled off a glove, bowed…just the slightest dip…and offered his hand. "Ho, Mr Todd."

"Call me Ash."

"Thank you, Mr Todd, nice to meet you. Follow me—the car is waiting."

I followed Ho down and out through the lobby. He made a quick call on his phone, and as we hit the street, a black Mercedes pulled up in front. Big—S Class. Ho opened a back door for me as the driver exited, leaving the door open for Ho to take over. I gave him the address.

Ho swung out of the hotel, took the first left, left again, along a couple of blocks, and left again. We crossed the Wusong River, travelled one block, and Ho pulled into the entry of a mid-level apartment block. Down across the river I could clearly see my hotel—an eerie, dark sight silhouetted against the dazzle of Pudong.

"That was fast—could've walked it," I said.

"I don't think so, Mr Todd. Much safer with me. Do you want me at the meeting?"

"Thanks, but no need—shouldn't take too long. Can you wait?"

"I'll be right here."

I found the number of Zhou's apartment and pressed the intercom. I smiled at the security camera as he answered and clicked to let me in. Should look a bit friendly, I thought. The lift took me to the top floor, and I buzzed again at his door.

Zhou, dressed in an open-neck blue shirt and grey trousers, offered his hand. Behind him lay a vast expanse of blue-carpeted living area. Beyond that, floor-to-ceiling glass framed Pudong across the Huangpu, like a giant painting. The view that is offered to the world.

I stood a moment, mesmerised at the sight, but recovered my senses as I realised Zhou was staring at me. "Beautiful view, Mr Zhou."

"Thank you, come in. Now I believe you have met."

A figure rose from a chair, his back to me, turned and stood expressionless. He made no move to greet me. Just stood blinking, and nodded. The Pudong view may have stunned me a touch, but this one stunned a little more.

"Hello, Mr Wang," I said.

49

The meeting with Zhou and Wang didn't take long. Possibly fifteen minutes. I declined the offer of a drink, and we settled around a long, marble-topped desk in one corner of Zhou's living room. On it sat a book. Wang's book…the one I'd noticed on the *Empress* near permanently clasped under his arm. I wondered what was in that book.

Zhou asked a number of questions—most followed the scenario I'd run over and over in my head at the hotel. I explained that both Hogan and Wallis were in custody. They seemed pleased to hear that. I also explained that CH didn't believe our two suspects had killed Sebastian. That didn't go over so well. Wang just blinked. And further, I was now officially on the case, to try to find the truth, and with the blessing of Macau Police. That may have been a stretch, but it got them looking at each other. A sharp, nervous glance from both.

I decided to try a different tack.

"Mr Zhou, what do you do? Other than gambling."

"What do you mean?"

"Business—what line are you in?"

Zhou turned in his chair and looked out at Pudong. When he turned back, his demeanour had changed. The ever-smiling, suave, good-timer had been replaced with a serious old man. The creases around his mouth deepened from the pressure of clenched teeth. He stabbed his index finger a couple of times on the desk. I noticed he wore a ring. A ring with a black motif, which I thought I recognised. But his hand moved too fast. Too fast to see clearly.

"Mr Todd, you are entering dangerous territory. What is your issue here?"

"I just want the truth—for CH and Sebastian. You appear to be a man of considerable wealth. In this country, I guess that also means power. You and Sebastian argued. You said you'd cut him out. I'd like to know what it was over. And you, Mr Wang…" I glanced at him. Wang showed no emotion. "You argued too—both accused each other, but I'm not sure of what. Stuffing up? And what do you really do? Care to explain?"

Wang shifted in his chair. The first sign of any discomfort I'd seen in him. Maybe I was hitting near a nerve. They both fell silent.

In a swift move, Zhou stood and barked at me, "Wait here. Wang, you and I will talk." He motioned for Wang to follow, and they made for an adjoining room.

The door clicked shut. Wang's book remained on the desk. Alone. I moved to it quickly, and leafed through pages. Numbers, numbers. I flicked to the back, the newest entries I hoped. Chinese text. Impossible for me. Then some in English. Names, names of people, names of what? Companies? I recognised Zhou's name.

Two pages back was Grekov. Another page. A heading—Zhang Yu. Further back—more numbers, more Chinese characters. Numbers in millions? Hard to say. No commas, no zeros. I flicked pages faster—they might be back any moment. Another list of names. Possibly seven or eight. This time all were listed—Ma, Grekov, Zhou. At the foot of the page, in smaller writing was Wang. Then a number—fifteen—followed by…? Couldn't make it out.

One page further back, a heading. Jinshan. I heard a click, and snapped around toward the door. The handle moved. I closed the book, shoved it in front of Wang's chair, and slipped back into mine. I could feel my heart racing as he entered. No, I could hear it. Thud, thud, thud. Had he spotted me? Thud, thud, thud. I gulped a breath. Zhou followed behind.

Wang stood at his chair, and stared down at the book. Silence. His gaze shifted to me, eyes narrowing. He blinked, and stared back at his book. My heart thumped again. And again. I was sure Wang could hear it, too. Like being whacked in the chest by a hammer. Zhou finally spoke.

"We have decided, Mr Todd. We will need a meeting with all parties. Ma and Grekov will be there. You can represent CH Lam. Hong Kong, tomorrow evening. I will send you details in the morning. Maybe then you can find your truth."

I considered this for a moment. A trap? Possibly, but what else did I have? If these people killed Sebastian, they weren't going to admit it. The meeting would allow me to push a bit harder. Might find a crack. That is, *if* they turned up.

I stood. "As you wish…I'll let myself out." I made for the door and turned back. "I'll expect your call by midday."

I found Ho, still parked at the port-cochere in front of the apartment block. I slipped into the back seat, shut the door, and let out a long breath.

"Hotel, Mr Todd?"

"Thanks, Ho."

We travelled in silence for a few blocks, away from Zhou's apartment and away from my hotel. Turned right, a few more blocks, then right again. Back toward our destination. Streets alternating between old Shanghai, and new. Some dark, others bright, some with buildings low-rise, others full of towers. I began to think of Wang's book.

Ho stood hard on the brakes and yelled, "Hang on."

He ripped the wheel of the Mercedes. The car spun through 180 and he planted the pedal. We took off, the force shunting me back in the seat and snapping my head onto the headrest. We screamed for two blocks. Then he slammed the brakes hard again. A car crossed in front of us. Missed by inches.

Ho planted his foot again, and the big car shot across the intersection. One block later he shut off the lights, and turned into a narrow alley. A car sped past the end of the alley, not more than fifty yards in front of us.

"What now, Ho?"

"We wait."

Another car crossed in the opposite direction. Same car? I couldn't tell. But Ho looked worried. He eased the big Mercedes forward, right up to the intersection. That was when two cars appeared. One up front, and one right behind.

We were going nowhere.

50

Ho sat, eyes straight ahead, both gloved hands gripping the wheel, frozen. The car in front had stopped side-on to us, the one behind nose-in to our tail, headlights blazing.

A figure appeared at Ho's window. A second appeared next to mine. Ho slid down his window. Someone dressed in camouflage uniform stood close, and in the black of night I could just make out gloved hands moving. He asked Ho a question. Ho answered. Another question. Another answer. In Mandarin, as usual. I understood only one word. Todd.

The camouflaged figure pointed at me, and banged on the roof. Ho glanced in the rear-view mirror and said, "They want your window down. I'll do it." As he lowered it, the second figure, also in camouflage, ripped a pistol from a holster and shoved the barrel at my forehead. He barked an instruction.

Ho said, "Don't move."

"Got it."

Another instruction.

"They want your passport."

"Back at the hotel."

Ho passed the information on. Camouflage 1 moved away, and the pistol bearer shoved the barrel an inch or two closer to my head, to reinforce the 'don't move' instruction.

Camouflage 1 reappeared at Ho's window, and flicked his glove. Ho hit the central locking switch, and the passenger side rear door opened.

A third man, early fifties I guessed, slid in. He was dressed in a green uniform, with heavy epaulets on each shoulder, and five rows of medals across his chest. In his left hand, he held a green cap trimmed with gold, and big, red star on the front. He looked like a General.

"Mr Todd, is it? What is your purpose here?" Polished English. His tone was sharp. Businesslike.

"I'm chasing a murderer."

"A murderer? Where was this murder?"

"South China Sea."

"That's a long way off. What makes you think anyone here would be involved?"

"People here were at the scene. I'm following up—assisting Macau Police."

"When are you leaving?"

"Not sure yet."

He nodded at the pistol waver. The weapon smacked into my cheekbone. I put my hand to my face and felt a small spot of blood ooze.

The corner of his mouth twitched a fraction. "Wrong answer. Ever been inside a Chinese prison?"

"Not had the pleasure."

"Very cold, Mr Todd. Cement floors, cement walls, no light. Bunk beds, and ten men, or more, to a cell. One hundred to a toilet. Limited food—saves cleaning up around the toilets, you see. If you don't eat, you don't shit. Excellent re-education programs featuring electric batons, and a blasting bowel cleanse. Of course, if you are selected, they are compulsory. You interested?"

"Depends on the rate."

The mouth twitched again. "Ah, quite cheap. As little as asking the wrong question can get you a twelve-month stay. Similar to providing the wrong answer." He nodded again at the man with the pistol. The hammer clicked. "So, what do you say?"

I thought for a moment. "Not really my kind of deal."

"Then go home, Mr Todd. While you can."

The General slipped from the car, and the two camouflaged accomplices withdrew. In a moment, both vehicles disappeared as quickly as they had arrived.

"Who were they, Ho?"

Ho shrugged, shook his head, and said, "Where to?"

I wasn't sure if Ho was now part of the solution to this, or the problem. Maybe he knew more than he was letting on. A lot more. But then, possibly, he was just CH's man here, and was now caught up in my little mess. I played it safe.

"Hotel to collect my gear, then the airport." Leaving seemed to be a good option.

Ho pulled out onto a main road and sped back toward my hotel. As he pulled up he said, "Be careful when you open your door. Make sure you don't have unwanted guests. I'll wait."

I unlocked my hotel-room door, gave it a shove and stepped back. Just in case. On Ho's advice. No sound. I stepped in.

"Damn, damn, damn it," I muttered. The contents of my duffel were scattered to the four corners.

The unwanted guests had already been.

51

In a suite on the eighteenth floor of the Zhujiang Hotel in Guangzhou, Ma Junjie sat at a long, rectangular glass-topped table. His eyes were not more than a few inches above, as he studied an unrolled sheet of paper which covered most of the glass, turning it one way, then the other.

Fifteen feet away, Vadim Grekov occupied a cream armchair. His belly and backside were too large for the chair, or maybe the chair was too small for him. Either way, he was wedged into it. A cut-crystal glass and a bottle of vodka sat within easy reach on a small, wooden coffee table. He clicked at a gold cigarette lighter, and in a deliberate move brought the flame up to a cigar clenched between his teeth. He blew a small stream of blue smoke up at the ceiling. Ma caught the smell and looked over at him.

"You shouldn't be smoking in here," Ma scolded.

"I don't give a shit. They have no rooms on the smoking floor and I am a regular customer, so this is the price they pay." He took a slug of vodka. "What do you think of the plans?"

Ma studied the paper further, saying nothing. He rose, took himself to the window and looked out over the Zhujiang River which split the city. He saw nothing but his own reflection in the glass. Night had fallen and he hadn't noticed. He turned his attention back to Grekov.

"The plans look okay, but do we really need another twenty-five levels of apartments above five of commercial? We already have two towers empty, and my cousin tells me there are another ten proposed for our section. No-one can sell."

"Don't you worry—the government will have to loosen credit soon. They've had the banks shut for eighteen months—no housing lending. Can't last forever, and when they let it go—*whoosh.*" Grekov's short, fat arms flew in a big circle above his head making his point, sending a fine spray of cigar ash across the carpet. "All your stupid countrymen will dive in again. Can't help themselves. Like—what do they call them? Yes, lemmings over a cliff." Grekov allowed himself a chuckle at the thought.

"But there's five years supply just sitting out there now, and you want to build more? Madness. And the money—where will we get that?"

"Don't you worry—I always get the money, don't I? That's what my friends in the Party are for. You forget, my father helped these people start in the 1940s. Travelled from Russia to advise them, through all that shit weather—snow and mud and sludge. My family association goes all the way back to then. They haven't forgotten." Grekov looked sullen at that thought, and took another hit of vodka.

"Yes, and you forget that my family is vital for us to get these deals. Without my uncles and cousins, we have no business."

"Your family? *Ha,*" said Grekov. "Peasants. Just farm workers."

Ma stiffened at the insult. True, his family had been 'just farm workers', but through smart political manoeuvres locally, they had made good. He didn't like anyone smearing his family reputation, least of all a fat, old, half-drunk Russian.

"Who are you to insult my family like that?" Ma exploded. "They may have been poor, but not now. They helped you get rich. And they have morals, not like you. They don't sit around smoking and swearing and drinking to excess and…and… wetting themselves."

"What the…?"

"I've seen you." Ma spat out the words. "Can't control your bladder when you drink. You got a problem down there? I think you must have. That is why you can't screw the ladies on the boat. That's what they say."

Grekov sat slightly stunned. "Listen, you skinny shit, don't talk to me like that. Besides, you like to use other devices. Coke bottles, eh? I heard them—the girls. They talk about things, too. So, what's wrong with yours? Or are you a faggot?"

Ma began to shake. "I should give you a good belting…"

Grekov bashed the arm of his chair. "Just try—remember I can have you taken out anytime. *Anytime…*"

"Do that…and you'll never leave the country."

Silence fell across the room. Grekov gulped another vodka. Ma stared at the dark window, at his own reflection.

Ma broke the standoff. "So, what about our other money? On the boat."

"Wang should have fixed it," Grekov said, "Wang and Sebastian."

"Yes, but someone fixed Sebastian first. Now what?" He looked over at Grekov.

Grekov took another vodka slug, and shrugged.

52

Zhou Wei Li farewelled Wang, who set off to book flights, poured a whisky and sat erect in an ornate, high-backed chair. Carved gold frame, red velvet upholstery, heavily padded. A striking contrast with the vivid-blue carpet in his living room. It looked important, regal even. His kind of chair.

He stared across at Pudong. He often marvelled at the energy being consumed keeping Pudong's lights ablaze. Couldn't even begin to imagine how much was required. The numbers were beyond comprehension. Not that it mattered much. Pudong was just one small piece of China. It was important, sure, a national showpiece, but there were thousands of Pudongs across the country, each competing like hell in the electricity burning stakes.

No, what pleased Zhou was that the country had lost none of its insatiable desire to consume energy of all kinds. The type didn't matter to him. So long as the political leaders were intent on becoming the biggest economy in the world, energy was needed. Every year the numbers exploded.

Zhou let his eye wander off to the left, further north. Toward Baoshan, away off in the dark, where the Huangpu empties into the East China Sea. The industrial heart of Shanghai. And home to his beloved petrochemical baby, Zhangchem. Ethanol…that was his corner of the energy market. Keep consuming, baby. He grinned at the thought, and sipped the whisky.

His mind wandered back, closer to home, to when he was a small boy. Off to his right, several blocks away, to the old French Quarter. Xintiandi, to be precise. To the old shikumen house he had grown up in, back in the 1940s and '50s. All knocked down now. 'Renovated' the government called it. Some renovation, he thought. Obliterated, more likely. But it was still the nicest part of town. Some of the older houses remained. Quieter, more refined, his kind of neighbourhood. Elegant. That was it, elegant.

Long ago his father was a successful man, an importer. Nuts, figs, dates, all sorts of things, mostly from the Middle East. Not wealthy, but successful enough. He took a keen interest in politics. Zhou was too young to understand, but his father was often missing in the evening. "At a Party meeting," his mother would say. To little Zhou, that made no sense. The two words, party and meeting, just didn't fit together.

One day his father came home and declared, "It won't be long, we'll soon have a new government. A new Party. A new way of life."

His mother looked worried, shook her head, and said to her husband, "I hope you know what you're doing."

His father held his finger to his lips. "Shhh, it will be fine."

And, for the most part, it was fine. From that day for months on end, his father was absent. Zhou and his mother lived well enough—lack of money didn't seem to be an issue. Father was just gone. To Beijing, a lot, it seemed. Young Zhou had no idea what or where Beijing was, but it took away his father.

One evening, when Zhou senior was home, he brought an important guest to dinner. A Mr Mao. Some other men also came, but they didn't seem so important. When Mao spoke, everyone listened. They all laughed in unison at some of the things he said. At one point Mao said, "Mrs Zhou, your husband is a good man, very smart. He has placed your family business with our Party so it can be used for the benefit of all Chinese. He has renounced capitalism, and will now work with our Party for the advancement of China."

Mrs Zhou looked across at her husband. She showed no outward emotion, but he knew the look barely disguised her horror. Mr Zhou smiled politely at Mao, and the others. But he did not look at his wife. From that day on, Zhou senior became a very busy man. For the Communist Party. The family continued to live in their old shikumen house, and for young Zhou Wei Li life went on as normal.

At some point, on an otherwise nondescript school day, Zhou became aware of a problem on the street. He was still only five, and could not understand the commotion, but some people seemed to be marching, and others were shouting. His mother fetched him from school and bustled him home, saying nothing.

He sensed some danger. "Where's Father?" Father could fix danger.

"Away, for some time," his mother said. She looked worried.

"Is he coming back?"

His mother frowned and said, "I hope so." His father did return, some weeks later. He was very tired, and slept a lot.

Zhou went to junior school, and then senior school. His father made him learn English at home. At school, he learnt that capitalism was bad. His father stopped travelling so much, and went to work in an office a few blocks away from the Zhou home. Not far, in fact, from the luxury apartment Zhou now owned.

Zhou went to university, and studied economics. He learnt about production targets, and how to plan for them. He learnt about cash flow forecasts, and how to get them right. He learnt that even when they were wrong, they could be made right. He also studied politics. Everyone did. He learnt that their leader was a great man, and that the Party was right in just about everything.

When he was nearly twenty, his father came home one evening, pulled Zhou aside and said, "Sit down. We must have a talk." For the next two or three hours, his father began to carefully unravel the beliefs Zhou had ingrained in him for the past fifteen years. The ones that had changed so abruptly on that day in 1949.

He discovered many things that evening, the most important being that his father decided to join the Party and give up his business because he believed that was the best way for the family to prosper, long term. Otherwise they would have to have fled the country, to Hong Kong or Taiwan, like nearly all other business people. Either that or stay and fight, only to be jailed, or killed. That sent a shockwave through young Zhou.

"Would they really do that, Father?"

"They did do just that...but forget you heard it from me."

His father went on to explain that for his loyalty and excellent work for the Party, he was to be appointed the head of a company which would import oil. His new office would be at Baoshan, where a refinery was being built. Further, he had arranged a job at the oil business for his son, once his studies were finished.

"Will you come with me?" asked Zhou senior.

"I suppose so."

"Good…and so to complete your studies, you need to go overseas. To England. I have it arranged from now. You can leave in two weeks. There you can try to learn the English way. And when you come back, I will show you how the system really works."

"How it really works?"

"Yes," said Zhou senior. "If you want to not just survive, but prosper also, you have to pretend that what you have learnt up to now is written in stone."

"To pretend? And then?"

"Then you do the opposite."

53

Zhou finished his economics degree in London, and returned to Shanghai to work with his father. They were given shares in the oil company, which performed well despite the vast wage bill. As China grew, so did their operation. As their operation grew, so did the Zhou family wealth. The wealth that was for the benefit of all Chinese.

Zhou had learnt an appreciation of fine living when away at university—Savile Row tailoring, top-end restaurants, Rolls Royce cars, and whisky. These seemed to be standard fare for the families of many of his student friends. He decided that, when the time arose, some of these would be good to incorporate into his life back in China. Patience would be required.

Zhou travelled—on business of course. Much of it to Hong Kong, where his tailor was located. He also established a couple of bank accounts there. The Party would never condone this, and to be found out could mean jail time, or worse. So Zhou kept a low profile. He travelled alone…without fuss…and at home dressed like everyone else.

At a later point, two Party officials from Treasury came to the office and demanded to inspect the accounts. They seemed pleased with what they saw. They asked Zhou why he travelled, so often, to Hong Kong.

"To keep up to date with latest accounting methods," he said. "I must continually improve my knowledge for the good of China."

The officials were very impressed with this news. They asked if it was possible to open a bank account in Hong Kong—a separate one under another company name. That company would be owned by Zhou and the two officials. "To help pay for your continuing education expenses," they explained.

"I suppose so," said Zhou, "I've never looked into it. I could make a visit there and report back."

The officials agreed this was a splendid idea, and if possible, Zhou should open just such an account. He made the trip and opened the account. Without delay the officials transferred a bonus, for their joint excellent work, which they would equally share. Zhou was smart enough to leave his share where it was, though, in the company account. To move it to his own bank might be just the trigger they were after.

In time, Zhou senior became ill, and stepped back from day-to-day work at the refinery. Zhou took over the role, as Head of Operations. The boss. The bonuses grew, and the refinery acquired a new partner. The People's Liberation Army. The PLA was appointed by decree from Treasury. The two officials remained as part of the team.

Zhou was pleased—sort of. The PLA could have you removed for any reason. Terminated. Your footprint on planet Earth gone. No history. Or they could be your friend. With them by your side, there was no competition. You owned the playing field. And outside trouble never came your way.

The business continued to expand. Zhou married, and had a son. Claude. The Treasury officials came to visit with another business proposal. A nightclub. These were part of the capitalist system which had been dismantled and banned by the Party following 1949. But, the officials explained, the human spirit must prevail. Men needed an outlet, to prevent trouble from developing. Zhou agreed it was important to prevent trouble.

The nightclub, just off Fuzhou Road, was a great success. Other clubs opened, all underground. A sort of secret society, where only Party members, who knew the password, were granted access. Zhou decided that the Party knew nearly too much about him. Protection could be required at any time, and other groups were busy ensuring their own interests were protected. Zhou didn't waste time.

He recruited eight men—three from his refinery whom he knew could defend anything, and five more from their network. Ruthless, hard-arsed bastards. Some had been jailed, the rest probably should have. But he made them tidy themselves up, and present a clean image. He made sure by day they all had work at the refinery, and by night they guarded the club. And his home. He named the group Zhangyu.

Zhou expanded the business into petrochemicals. Ethanol. Money flowed in. The PLA was pleased. The Treasury officials were pleased. Claude completed schooling, and like his father, went off to London to university. To learn to run an ethanol plant, Zhou hoped. The nightclub prospered. More money flowed in. The PLA and Treasury officials were more pleased.

In time, a couple of competing nightclubs opened nearby. The money flow slowed. Zhou sent a couple of his men from Zhangyu to check out the new clubs. Try to figure out the ownership. Test the strength. Zhou's wife had been to Hong Kong to visit family. Claude was home from university, and took Zhou's new Mercedes to the airport to collect his mother from her flight. Neither made it home. Two cars hit them…one from the side, the other from the rear. The Mercedes flipped, skidded wheels-up down the freeway, mounted a concrete retaining wall, and smashed onto another road forty-feet below. Then two months later, Zhou's father died.

Zhou threw himself into his work, to get past his grief. The two competing nightclubs closed. The PLA fixed it. He met a man at his club one evening. He had become a regular visitor, and asked to be entertained by the same young lady each time. He was called CD.

Zhou was intrigued. "No other name, CD?"

"That's all you need to know."

Zhou learnt that CD lived in Hong Kong most of the time, but travelled often. To many different countries. He operated in money markets, was not married, and spent a lot of time in Macau. Gambling was a major source of entertainment for him. Over a dozen or more visits, CD and Zhou got on like family. Then CD came up with a business proposition.

He wanted to establish a small private casino. In Macau. He had the man to run it. He had the connections in Macau to get a licence. He had the cash to start it, but wanted a background partner to help fund it. Would Zhou be interested?

To Zhou this was manna from heaven. Not that he believed

in heaven, so it was manna from wherever it came from. Zhou could move a little further away from the state—the all-seeing and knowing grasp of the PLA, and the Party. A little insurance. He was in. A silent partner in The Golden Mountain Club.

But now he returned his attention to current matters. Pudong came back into focus. Tomorrow he had a meeting to attend. This Ash Todd was getting too close. Better to nip it in the bud now, before it all got messy. He picked up the phone, and dialled.

"Zhou," a gravel-voice on the other end said, "a problem?"

"Some potential I think. Tomorrow night, I want you in HK."

54

"Well, you taking the man's advice?" Ho pulled the big Mercedes into a tight, airport parking space. "Going back to Australia?"

"Not yet. More work to do, but when it's over...sure. Straight home."

"I think you should go now."

"Thanks—I'll keep it in mind."

Ho's insistence was a bit worrying. Maybe he did know more than he was letting on. But I still had CH's work to do...his maybe-innocent captain and first-mate, stuck somewhere under the Macau police headquarters. And, of course, there were forty thousand other reasons to keep going. Each with a dollar sign in front. But it was the recurring image of Hogan and Wallis copping a beating... something Feng refused to deny...that weighed on me. This meeting with Zhou carried some risk...that was obvious...but abandoning CH's men was not on. I'd caught a few hours fitful sleep in the departure lounge, and grabbed an early morning flight.

And now at 9:30, I was sitting in a suite on a high floor in the Wynn Macau Hotel. Funny thing, but the view from this room took in two things—to my right across the lake, The Golden Mountain Club, and around to my left, still moored, the *Golden Empress*. Coincidence? Probably.

The suite was occupied by Bruce Bynow. With the turn of events in Shanghai, and mindful of my upcoming session with Zhou and friends, I'd thought it only right to keep him in the loop. After all, he *was* the Asian crime expert, and it was *his* job that had now catapulted me into this situation. And the night before I joined the *Empress*, as he left my hotel, the last thing Bynow said to me was, "Toddy, if you're in trouble…call me." I wasn't yet in trouble, and I don't much like being called Toddy, but I put those aside, and made the call. Insurance.

As it turned out he was headed to another job in Macau, and was staying at the Wynn. So here I was, sitting across a table from him, while he devoured a plate of eggs and toast, and I threw back a coffee.

"Tell me again what happened," Bynow said.

I gave him another rundown, this time with a bit more detail on Sebastian's death…some specifics on the dismembering… CH's desire for me to chase-up the clients…and the follow up from Zhou's meeting with the General in Ho's car.

Bynow picked at his teeth and paced up and down, then grabbed his phone and dialled. "Johnny, can you come up here? I need your advice." He shut his phone, looked at me and said, "You need to meet this guy…only be a minute."

After three minutes, a knock at the door. Bruce opened it to a small, older Asian man. Grey hair brushed back, little goatee beard. Tailored cream suit, white shirt, floral silk tie, matching pocket square. A couple of big, gold rings. Gold Rolex. Natty. He introduced us.

"Ash this is Johnny Cho. Johnny, meet Ash." Johnny shook my hand and bowed a little. Bruce continued, "Johnny is my eyes and ears in gaming here. Knows everybody in the casino world. Been around it for twenty years or more. Right, Johnny?"

Johnny nodded and said to Bynow, "We got a problem?"

"Ash has been helping with a client of mine...you know him...CH Lam...runs the casino..." Bynow said.

"Owns the casino, I think," I said.

Johnny scanned both of us, twice, and said, "Sure, I know who he is. You got a problem with him?"

"His son's been murdered, and he's put me on the case," I said.

Johnny stroked his goatee. "Anyone else involved?"

"Some of his clients, maybe."

"They have names?"

I looked at Bynow. "It's okay," he said.

"Zhou, Ma, Grekov, Wang."

Johnny again nodded quietly, and stroked his goatee some more. "You work in exalted company, Ash. I hope Mr Lam is paying you well for this. What is your next move?"

"I have a meeting tonight with Zhou, and maybe the others. In Hong Kong. I somehow think they're involved in the killing, but I can't put a connection together yet. Wang keeps a diary of some sort—I got a quick look at it but so much in Chinese and I can't make it out. Very hard to separate him from it."

"What is this meeting for...tonight?" Johnny asked.

"They say they want to give me information—so I can get to the truth of the matter. They're going to call with an address. But I don't trust them totally."

Johnny considered this again and said, "I will tell you some things which might help. First, they are very powerful men. You are right to be concerned. Second, Chinese is a complicated language, and all is not as it may seem. So, when they say they want you to get to the truth, more likely they don't want you anywhere near it. Third, Wang is not a client. He is a part of CH Lam's team."

Point one was pretty obvious. Point two I kind of had figured. The news on Wang was from left field though. But it did help explain the strange way he dealt with everyone, and maybe his argument with Sebastian. It also explained why CH had told me he was more like a friend, and to leave him out of the hunt.

Johnny looked at Bynow. "You going back today, Bruce?"

"Yep…later."

"Then I think we'd better help. You okay with that?"

"Yeah, sure, as long as you don't keep me out all night."

Johnny looked at me. "When you get that address, let Bruce know. We will be outside at the meeting time, in Bruce's car. You can't miss it—a BMW. Red."

I moved toward the door. "Thanks, boys—I'll call you later."

"Ash," said Johnny, "if you want to solve this, you have two tasks at that meeting."

"Yeah? Only two?"

"First, you must get that book of Wang's. If he's there. You get that book and I can probably help sort it out, but that book will be vital."

"Okay, and second?"

"You must get out of there alive."

55

I left the meeting with Bruce Bynow and Johnny Cho, with Johnny's words clanging around in my head.

"Get that book, and get out of there alive."

It sounded so simple, but I knew it wouldn't be. Couldn't be. Not with Wang's grim determination to keep hold of the book. And my life? Well that would depend who else was at the meeting.

In the meantime, I wanted to follow up with Miss Jay-Dee. Something told me Chief Feng and his men had barely spoken to her, yet she seemed to have as much motive as anyone to want Sebastian removed. And CH had suspicions about her. I found the business card she'd given me on the boat, and dialled the number.

Her husky voice soon answered. "Ash Todd here, Jay-Dee. I need to have a word about Sebastian. Can we meet now?"

"Okay, you come to my place." She gave me an address.

I grabbed a passing cab, repeated the address to the driver as best I could, and ten minutes later found myself inside an old apartment block. I knocked on the unit number, and Miss Jay-Dee, unmissable in a canary-yellow pantsuit, her standard bright-red lipstick, and barefoot, ushered me in.

She looked me up and down. "What you want to know, darling?"

"I want you to tell me again why you were up in the jacuzzi the night Sebastian was killed. What happened to you?"

"Like I already told you, he was sometimes rough, and I wanted to get away."

"So, what happened? Run me through it…give me some of the finer points."

Jay-Dee smiled a little smile. "You want to try it? Just for fun, we can do it same way."

"No," I snapped, "I don't want to screw you. Just show me."

Jay-Dee's smile vanished. "Okay, then it is like this. Sebastian lie on his back, his legs in the air." She slipped on to the floor and adopted the position. "This is how gay do it, you know? One of the way. You see the picture?"

"I get what you mean. What next?"

"I have this piece of rubber, my hands are not so strong you see, so I have this tube which I tie round his neck, and I wind it and wind it tighter. He can hardly breathe, but he loves being screwed while I do this."

"You mean like some sort of erotic choking?"

"*Yes*, darling," Jay-Dee shrieked, "he's a *gasper*."

"Hmmm, did it go too far that night—you forget to let go of the noose?"

"No, no. When I have finished he then gets me to lie like this," she said, rolling over on to her stomach, and lifting her buttocks slightly off the floor. "Then he does same to me, but he uses his hands around my neck. Often, he scratch me—you saw my back—and slap hard. It hurt. He squeeze so hard, I think I am going to die. That is what he did to me. That is why I go away to the jacuzzi."

"Do you really like doing this stuff?"

Jay-Dee sat up on the floor, looked across at me and then dropped her eyes. Sad eyes. She said quietly, "Not this rough stuff. I'm gentle, you know, I not like it much at all. That is why I prefer men who are kinder, you know, like the others on the boat."

That sat me up. "What 'others on the boat'?"

Jay-Dee's eyes widened as she realised what she'd said, and tried a quick cover. "Well, like you. I'm sure you not rough like that."

"Jay-Dee, you know I'm not into boys. And you wouldn't know whether I'm rough or not. There's a murder at stake here, and you're in it up to your neck. Literally. You must have had someone in mind, so smarten up—what 'others' did you mean?"

Jay-Dee was quiet again, slowly shaking her head.

"Jay-Dee, if you want to get out of this I need help. Names?"

"You must promise not to tell that I told you?"

"Okay, if that's possible."

"Mr Grekov."

"No kidding? Grekov is a client of yours?"

Jay-Dee smiled at the thought. "Yes, a nice gentle client."

"Did Sebastian know?"

Another quiet pause. "No, I don't think so."

56

With my duffel over my shoulder, and armed with a newfound understanding of the sexual preferences of my late employer Sebastian Lam, and his client Grekov, I beat a hasty retreat from Miss Jay-Dee. I grabbed another cab, and made for Macau police headquarters. I particularly wanted to assure Chief Feng I was on the case, and make sure he hadn't changed his mind to act against Hogan and Wallis. And I wanted to eyeball them as well.

Feng agreed to see me, but his face was not that of a happy man. He was sharp, dour.

"Your investigation, Mr Todd, any breakthrough?"

"Maybe, Chief, maybe…but it's still early. Got a meeting tonight—might produce something. But a favour—can you keep holding-off on the two inmates?"

"Forty-eight hours I said, Mr Todd. That leaves you twenty-four."

"Then can I see them now?"

Feng considered this for a moment. "Why do you want to see them?"

"Just to let them know I'm still on it."

"I can do that for you—let them know."

I stood and scanned Feng's wall. Three framed certificates lined-up, one above the other, and a couple of fading photos sat to one side. Police squads…all in full uniform…and each member appearing as unhappy as Feng now did. My mind drifted back to my early days in the Feds, and the words of one of our FO's. '*The Asians, Todd, love pomp and ceremony. Their uniforms mean a lot…and they love awards. I mean…they fuckin' love 'em.*' I returned to the certificates.

"You've done well, Chief," I said. "These are no doubt important, and I can't read them, but am I correct in assuming the top one is a great honour?"

Feng smiled and nodded. "Supreme Courage Award, Mr Todd. Some years ago now…but a young couple drove off the street and into the harbour…avoiding something…and I happened to be on patrol nearby. Their vehicle was sinking, and I jumped in and managed to rip open a door and break a window, just in time to get them out."

"Congratulations…you must be very proud. I'm envious."

"You don't have any awards?"

"A couple…but nothing as impressive as this." I cast the certificate another admiring glance. "Oh…and Hogan and Wallis…just a few minutes with each?"

Feng let out a tiny laugh, and slowly shook his head.

"Very well, Mr Todd…five minutes only. And twenty-four hours. After that I charge them. Murder, for both. And once I enter the charge in our system, it gets very hard for them. So, don't take too long to get back. Yes?"

"Yes, yes…twenty-four hours."

Feng picked up a phone and barked at a junior on the other end. "Take Mr Todd down to the prisoners."

The young cop appeared and I followed him down to the basement. He ushered me into a dimly lit room with a couple of chairs at a desk, and another off in a corner. "Wait here please," he said. I sat at the desk.

A minute or so later Wil Wallis was led in by the young copper. Wallis' eyes narrowed, and darted, then blinked…like a man with some condition…as he saw me. A smacking sound came from his lips, as his tongue sucked hard against his teeth.

"Jesus, where have you been? Get me outta here, can you? Can you get me a smoke? I gotta have a fuckin' smoke, *now*." Rapid-fire conversation, all one-way. His arms circled his back, like he was giving himself a bear hug. He slapped himself a few times and jumped up and down on the spot. His nerves were right on the edge. Desperate for a nicotine hit.

I looked at the cop. "Can you get the man a cigarette? Look at him—this is torture."

"Sorry, no smoking. Orders."

I stood up, pulled myself to full height, and moved in tight next to the young policeman. About an extra three-quarters of a foot and one-hundred and fifty pounds over him. I spelt it out, "The man needs a smoke. Right. Now." The policeman glanced up at me, head shaking, and bolted out the door.

I looked at Wallis. "I've only got a minute. Try to keep calm—don't give them any other reason to keep you here. I'll be back tomorrow, no matter what."

The young cop reappeared with a cigarette and lighter in

hand. Wallis nearly fainted when he saw it. His hands trembled and he couldn't flick the lighter. The cop lit it for him. He dragged the smoke in hard, and started to settle.

"Did you hear what I said?"

Wallis nodded, and shook, and puffed on the smoke.

"I'm going to see Hogan now—have you seen him?" Wallis shook his head. The cop moved in to lead him back to the cell.

"Officer—give him half-a-dozen more smokes, will you?"

The cop gave me back a blank stare. "Six," I said, "six more cigarettes for the prisoner. Please. Now."

The cop said, "Okay, okay," fished in his pocket and produced a fistful of smokes.

"Thank you," I said. I looked at Wallis. "And don't smoke them all at once. Pace yourself."

Wallis kept his head down. Puff, puff. The cop clicked his fingers and said, "This way." Wallis followed like an obedient dog. His mind was clearly elsewhere, but where was not so apparent.

Soon the young cop returned. "Follow me," he said. We moved down a corridor, turned a couple of corners, and stopped outside a cell. He opened the door, and let me in. Patrick Hogan lay on a single bed, his back facing me. I gave him a small shake. He whimpered, pulled his pillow over his head, and shifted further away, closer to the wall.

His rancid body odour nearly felled me. I gave him another poke. "Skip, it's me. Ash."

With some effort he turned over. The left side of his face was swollen and blue. His left eye was nearly closed, and he had cuts around his lips. I helped him sit up on the bed. The young cop watched in silence.

"Who did this to you?"

Hogan held the side of his stomach, wincing as he took each breath. "Some big bastard."

"Feng?"

Hogan shook his head. "No—another bloke."

"What have you told them?"

"Nothing—except they can't prove anything and they can go to hell."

"Great approach, that. No wonder you've got injuries. Listen, if anyone comes for you, tell them I'm coming back tomorrow. Tell them to wait. Now we'll get you cleaned up."

I pulled out my wallet and slipped the young cop some notes. "Make sure he has a shower, some clean clothes, and get someone to look at his face, will you?"

The cop just shrugged.

"You make sure it happens, because I'm coming back. Any crap, and I'll personally see to it you end up looking like *him*. Now I'm going back to see your boss. I'll let myself out." I poked him in the chest. "Do you understand what I'm saying?"

"Yes…sir…I'll fix it."

"You do that."

I took myself to the stairs and up to Chief Feng's floor. He was sitting at his desk, still looking sullen.

"What's your problem, Chief? You don't look happy today."

"Pressure. Comes with the territory. You see your friends?"

"Yep, and they're not too good. They may be a bit difficult, but no more rough stuff…okay? So, this pressure, who's applying it?"

"None of your business."

“Good—then it’s nothing to do with me?”

Feng looked out his window. Silent.

“Right…I’m out of here, but I’ll be back…tomorrow…you said another twenty-four hours, yeah?”

Feng nodded.

“Well, please look after them…by the book, eh?”

I picked up my duffel from Feng’s floor, and made for the door.

“You know the People’s Liberation Army?” Feng blurted. “You know their power? What they do?”

My mind flipped to the General in Ho’s car, and my hand made an automatic move to my cheek where the pistol had smacked me.

“A little…why?”

“That’s where the pressure is from…that, and the deceased’s father.”

“CH Lam?”

“He carries some clout, you know? Wants me to give you ‘every co-operation’. So…another twenty-four hours, Mr Todd.”

“Very kind, Chief…but the PLA?”

Feng gave me a sour look, his mouth turning down at the corners. “I don’t know what you did in Shanghai, but they aren’t very keen for me to help you. Believe me, Mr Todd, I have no interest in annoying them. I just want a peaceful retirement in a few years.”

“The PLA, eh?” I mumbled. “What have they got to do with this?” But now, the General in Ho’s car, if that’s what he was, started to make sense.

My phone buzzed with an incoming text. I glanced at the

screen. It read: *Meeting tonight, 10A On Lok Lane, Wan Chai. 7.30 sharp. Zhou.* I took in a deep breath, pursed my lips, and let it go.

Feng looked at me. "Problem?"

I shook my head.

"No…no problem—just a little pressure."

57

I caught a ferry to Hong Kong, and arrived at the terminal a little after 4:00. Sent a text to Dick Mayvers—*Mate, what a blast this is, up here. Hey, can you check any info on a Patrick Hogan for me? Cheers.* Now I had time…time to kill…but something else occurred to me on the crossing. Venus had spent time with Zhou. She was assigned to him on the *Empress* and she might have picked up something. I needed all the background on him I could get. She'd given me her card. I made the call.

"Ah, Tarzan." Venus' warm Euro accent rippled right through me. "You feeling better?"

My mind fell back to our night at the Riviera. Back to my embarrassment at not being able to perform. But Sally and Jack were the reason, and I had to find a way past it. To ditch the guilt. I was determined.

"Yeah, much better. Look, I need to go over some things—for Sebastian's murder, you know—can I meet you somewhere?"

"This a professional engagement, or otherwise?"

I hesitated a moment. "Otherwise. Just a chat."

"I'm at home now—you can come here if you like." She gave me an address.

"See you about five."

The cab dropped me on a corner outside a 7-Eleven in Wood Road, Wan Chai. The air was heavy, humid. Overcast sky. The street smelt of cooking—ducks from the shop four doors away, I reckoned. Traffic honked at the end of the street. Above, hundreds of air conditioners rattled and clanked. I walked along the street, one way then the other. "7B," she had said.

I found a restaurant at number 5, and another shop with a name in Chinese only at 9. Both had metal-shutter doors firmly closed. Between them sat a single door, half wood, and half glass. I peered above it. An old metal 7 was attached to the door frame. I looked harder. In faded ink, it read A + B. I guessed this must be it, and pushed the security button.

The intercom crackled, someone spoke but I couldn't make it out, and the door released with a "bzzzchwd" sound. Inside, a dimly-lit tiled hall led to an old elevator, which had stopped a couple of inches below floor level. I pressed button number two, and we lurched upward.

The elevator stopped with a shudder, a couple of inches above the floor level. The door clunked open, and Venus stood, smiling. This hallway smelt of more cooking. More ducks…as though the street smell had wafted its way up through gaps in the building. She gave me a kiss on the cheek. "Come in, Tarzan," she said.

Her apartment was small but tidy. Newish furniture—two yellow sofas, a dining table, three chairs, pictures of people. A man, maybe thirty, an older couple around sixty. A boyfriend? Perhaps. Family I guessed.

She moved to the kitchen. "You want some tea? Black, white? Sugar?"

"Thanks—white, strong, no sugar."

She laughed. "Just like you."

"Very funny."

She clicked on the kettle, and began to rattle cups. "So, what do you want from me? If it's only information, then I don't know how I can help. I'm not much good in that area."

I stashed my duffel into a corner and settled onto a sofa. "You were with Zhou on the boat. You spent time in his room. I'm not interested in what he did, but what he was like. He always seemed so happy. Smiling. But was he always like that? Anything strange about him you noticed?"

"Hmmm," she said, pouring water into the cups, "I don't know. He seemed okay. Very particular, I would say. Dresses well, very neat."

"Sure, and likes whisky, and singing. Anything else?"

Venus thought for a moment. "He is circumcised, you know?"

"No, I didn't, but is *that* important? What I mean is...does he act strangely at all? You know, like different to how you'd expect him to?"

Venus placed my tea on a small table next to the sofa, and looked up at me. "Are you circumcised, Mr Ash?"

"Does it matter? Anyway, you've seen me at the Riviera—or weren't you watching?"

She turned away, bouncing a bit in her stride, to fetch her own cup. "I don't think it matters. But he's Chinese, and I notice nearly no Chinese are circumcised. Like the men in my country. Maybe that is strange."

"Maybe, but I don't think that will help much with my enquiry. Anything else you can think of?"

She handed me my tea. "No, no I can't. Now, what are you doing tonight?"

"Got a meeting. With Zhou—7:30."

"Where?"

"On Lok Lane—here in Wan Chai somewhere."

"We can Google that to find it—so many little streets around here. How about something to eat first. Build you up for your meeting? The restaurant next door will be opening now."

I hadn't thought of eating at this hour of the day, but then realised I hadn't eaten anything much since breakfast on my flight from Shanghai that morning. Only a couple of coffees, hours ago. "Sounds good," I said, throwing the last of my tea down.

Venus grabbed her bag and phone, and we made our way down in the lurching elevator, taking care to step up at ground level. The restaurant owner was raising his shutter as we approached, and inside a couple of staff were busy in the open kitchen, mixing and chopping.

The owner squinted up at me, his eyes narrowing to the point they disappeared completely. He looked at Venus, smiled and said, "Good evening, Miss Venus. For two?"

"Thank you, Chong," she said as we passed by the cooks. She peered over the counter at them. "What are you chopping? Ah, duck I see."

The cook nodded and smiled at her, saying nothing. "Look," she said to no-one in particular, peering again at the dissected fowl on the bench, "that knife is just like the one in Zhou's cabin."

"What did you say? What knife?"

"That knife of the cook's…it's like the one I saw in Zhou's cabin on the *Empress*."

I looked over at the knife. I pulled Venus over into a better light, opened my phone, and brought up the pictures of the two knives I'd taken at Chief Feng's station. One brown, one black with blurry motif. "These?"

She pointed to the black one. "That one—I'm sure."

We asked the cook to borrow his knife, and Venus held it up next to my phone. I said, "You're positive he had one like this? In his cabin?"

She nodded. "Yes—I'm sure. Why, is it important?"

"Just a bit."

I checked again. No motif on the cook's, but there was no doubt.

Identical knives.

58

I sent a text to Bruce Bynow's phone—*Meeting 7:30, 10A On Lok Lane. Red BMW, right?* And another to a mobile number on CH Lam's card—*CH—progressing okay—will update you tomorrow. Rgds, Todd.*

Venus ordered the food. We ate slowly. Course after course, all small. Green tea. Soup, vegetable. Duck, vegetable. Chicken, vegetable. Things which were wrapped up—pork rolls maybe. More vegetable. Green tea. Sweet things—no idea what they were. More green tea.

A text came in from Bynow—*Right, red. Be careful. And Johnny says, "bīng bù yàn zhà."* Bing bu yan zha? What could that mean?

I pondered the knife issue as we ate. Why would Zhou want a knife like that? He was wealthy. Refined. Had an almost English air about him. He didn't seem the hunting kind, nor the killing kind. If he wanted someone topped, he'd employ a pro. Or get a minion to do it.

I guessed he had minions—I still didn't understand his business. He refused to discuss it. And that's partly what this meeting was about—if he could be believed. So, if the knife wasn't Zhou's, whose was it? And why was it in his cabin?

I poked at the food, picked up a dumpling, and ate a small piece. "Come on, Ash," said Venus, pushing a plate at me, "you have to eat more. Get your strength up for tonight." I took some more dumpling.

In my mind, I retraced some of the events of that night on the *Empress*. Maybe there was some logical progression. There must be—things can't always be random. I said to Venus, "Think hard…when did you notice the knife in Zhou's cabin?"

She was quiet for a minute or so. "It was there during the afternoon. You know, on the trip over from Hong Kong."

"And later?"

"I can't remember—don't recall seeing it again."

"Okay, so did anyone else come to his cabin?"

She shook her head. "Not while I was there."

"Yes, but you weren't always there were you? Remember, I saw all you girls on the salon deck at one point. You said the men didn't want you. They were in a meeting."

Venus nodded.

"Do you know who was at that meeting?"

"All of them, but Grekov and Zhou went first. And Wang I think."

"Then, any one of them could have moved the knife."

"I guess so," she said. That gave me something to think on.

The restaurant clock said 7:07. I opened up Google on my phone and typed in On Lok Lane. I showed Venus the map. "Ah, not too far. A five-minute walk—that way," she said, pointing to her right.

"I have to go—it's time. I'll get this." I motioned to Chong for the bill.

Venus put her hand on mine. "Ash, if you get stuck, you know, if you need somewhere, just call me."

"But you'll be out somewhere—working."

She shook her head. "Not tonight…and not any more. I have no need, and I'm sick of it. I'll be around."

I paid Chong, who took the money without a word.

I said, "My gear is still at your place. I'll have to drop by to collect it—maybe first thing tomorrow."

"I'll be there."

As I stood she gave me a small kiss on the cheek. "Take care, Tarzan."

"I'll see you tomorrow." I had a quick thought, and opened the messages on my phone.

"Chong," I said, "can you tell me what this means?" I showed him Bynow's text—*bīng bù yàn zhà.*

His eyes narrowed, and disappeared again, and his face wrinkled from his mouth to his forehead. Then he tilted his head up at me, eyes still closed. But he did smile.

"You must have an interesting time ahead. It's an old Chinese saying. *Nothing is too deceitful in war*."

59

My walk took me out onto the busy Wan Chai Road, along a few blocks, until I stumbled onto On Lok Lane on my left. A tiny split thoroughfare leading, between skyscrapers, to even busier Hennessy Road. The air was heavy, and people yelled, buses honked and cars tooted around me. Night was closing in.

I checked out the area. Wan Chai Road seemed to be mostly old-style shops—jewellers, shoes, food, medicines, a parking station. Apartments further down. And above. More air conditioners. Opposite, a hotel—The Charterhouse.

I turned into the lane and walked through to Hennessy Road. Plenty of people, similar shops, more apartments, more traffic. The warm air smelt of food, and fuel. I hadn't spotted 10A, so retraced my steps. Checked the time—7:27.

The door to 10A lay between two blank walls, recessed slightly into a building. Plain door—could have been anything. Fire escape exit maybe. There was no sign, only a small metal number screwed to the wall. The obligatory security intercom sat above the number plate.

I pressed the button. There was no voice, no welcome—just the sound of the door releasing. I stepped inside onto a small landing, about ten feet square. All bare concrete—just like a fire escape, only the stairs led down. I took them, one deliberate step at a time, listening for any sound. Nothing.

One floor below, another landing, same size as above. No more stairs. Dead end. Only a door, and a dull light above. No intercom this time, and no handle on the door. I looked up—security camera overhead. I waited, held my breath. No sound. Then a click. The door moved a touch. I stepped back.

The door opened further—a very thick door. That explained the silence—everything soundproofed. A thought occurred to me that you could die down here, and no-one would find you. No-one would hear. No way in, and no way out. Until whoever killed you, took you out.

The door opened right up. Someone stood there, holding it, camouflaged in near darkness. "Greetings, Mr Todd. Please come in," said the gravel voice. He stepped into the light and pointed for me to enter the hall. I caught my breath, but gave him nothing. No emotion.

I said, "Ahh, nice to see you again Ho."

60

The dark corridor would have been impossible to navigate, but for a tiny glow…from one mellow footlight. Ho followed. I counted my steps—at eleven the corridor turned hard right, and after three more I entered a small room. All concrete, no windows, lit by a dull pinkish light from a single bulb overhead. Another door, on the opposite side to where I entered, was shut. Two air-conditioning ducts hummed above it.

A blue, armless office chair sat in a corner to my right, a grey metal cabinet about three feet square alongside. A rectangular wooden table sat in the middle of the room. One small wooden chair at the table closest to me and four bigger, padded chairs opposite. They were occupied by Zhou, Ma, Grekov and Wang. Just as Zhou had promised. Zhou nodded. Nobody else moved. On the table, in front of Wang, lay a book.

"Please sit, Mr Todd," said Zhou. "You know everyone here, I believe?"

I looked at each in turn, then around at Ho, who had taken up a position behind me on the corner chair. "I do."

I turned my attention back to my hosts opposite, and sat on

the small wooden chair. Hard, but not sturdy. Loose joints. Uncomfortable. A rope appeared from nowhere and dropped over my shoulders. In that quick movement, Ho had me lashed to the chair.

"For your protection, and ours, Mr Todd, until we establish your motives," said Zhou. For my protection? Yeah, right. This was unexpected problem number one, and we hadn't yet started.

"As I told you yesterday, I have only one motive and that is to find the truth. For the Lam family." I looked around at Ho, who had returned to his corner. "The family I thought you worked for, Ho."

He stared straight back at me. "As you were told yesterday, you should go home."

"Well I didn't, and I'm here now."

"Let's cut to it," said Zhou, "you believe the captain didn't kill Sebastian? And you think someone here did? Is that it?"

"Pretty much."

"And your proof? Motives?"

"Proof? Don't have that yet. Just a matter of time. Motives? Let me see? Try this—you all argued with Sebastian that night. Right down to you, Wang. Ma and Grekov—you accused him of robbing you. Zhou, you said you would cut him—maybe out completely. Or maybe *you* gutted him like a fish. And finally, Wang, you accused him of causing all these disagreements. My first guess is this had to do with your money. You've all got shitloads—the numbers are huge. Maybe Sebastian wanted some, and you didn't want to give. How am I doing for a motive? Shall we call it greed?"

The next thing I felt was a hard thump to the side of my head, then a stinging sensation. My arms were pinned, so I shook my head to try to clear the pain. I looked around in time to catch a second swipe from Ho, who was wearing a heavy leather glove. It took my right eye and forehead. My head slumped forward while I tried to re-focus.

Zhou dipped his head down at a slight angle, at the table. "I think you are on the wrong track, Mr Todd. Any more theories?" His voice was calm. Measured. With a thumping head-pain, and an eye fast closing, I had to think of something…something that wouldn't get me killed. Zhou had the power…over me and the others. They said nothing. Just watched. He was in total control.

"Sure do. There were two knives, nearly identical. One belonged to Hogan, but it was in his safe. Whoever did the killing planted the murder weapon on Skip. He was too drunk to do this—passed out. Perfect for a stitch-up."

Something crashed into my right shin. A fireball of pain shot down to my foot. I swung my head again, and through the blurry eye caught sight of Ho holding an iron bar. I wondered what else was in that cupboard. I was powerless to move. Maybe Zhou was right…and I was on the wrong track. Another swipe took my left leg. Unexpected problem two had arrived. "Hrrrrgh," I bellowed.

Zhou looked up from the table. "Australia now looking like a better option, Mr Todd?"

I shook my head. "Haven't finished."

"I don't know if you are brave or stupid," said Zhou, "go on."

"Jealousy. Jealousy and sex. Tell them, Grekov, tell them how you're fucking Jay-Dee, Sebastian's boyfriend. Or don't you want anyone to know?" I glanced at Grekov through my one good eye. He didn't look happy.

"You, you, you...piece of..." he said.

"I know, I know, I'm a piece of shit. Just like everyone else, right?"

Zhou nodded. Ho produced a knife in front of my face. About a foot long, and with a partially serrated blade. Seemed familiar. Unexpected problem three.

Zhou smiled—just. "We have an old saying, Mr Todd, 'death by a thousand cuts'. Ready to experience the first?"

"I've seen your work already," I said.

Zhou nodded again. Ho grabbed my hair and reefed my head back and to the side.

I pulled my head away as Ho raised the weapon, and yelled, "*No*, you bastards." The knife came down slowly. I could go nowhere. I felt its shiny tip, smooth just above the serrations, move down the left side of my face, about the length of my ear. It didn't hurt so much, but then I felt the warm trickle of blood down my neck. And then came the sting.

That was enough. Time to tackle the unexpected problems. I stood as best I could, and caught another iron-bar blow across my back. I grunted with the pain, but smashed my full weight down on the flimsy chair. It gave, but didn't crack. Ho moved to grab the knife. I smashed down on the chair again. The four men began to move. The chair disintegrated. The rope hit the floor.

Zhou thumped the table. "Stop him."

"Yes, stop him," Grekov said, his voice rising and cracking with the effort.

I turned as Ho moved in with the knife. The blade caught my chest, a small slit of blood appearing through my shirt. I didn't feel a thing. Speed was what I needed to stop this.

I gave Ho two hits. The first, a single-knuckle smack under his jawbone. He screamed through clenched teeth. Dislocated. At least. A quick one-two count in my head and I delivered him the second, another single-knuckle punch to his sternum. It cracked like a snapping branch, his eyes bulged, air flew from him, and he hit the cement floor. Hard.

I grabbed Ho's knife, turned to the ashen-faced group, and took a step toward them. They all backed off, except Wang. He moved to snatch-up his book.

I raised the knife and gave it a small 'swish' under his nose. "Leave it."

Wang backed off…hands up. I picked up the book. "Gotta go…no need to see me out. In fact, don't even bother. Look at Ho. It's just not worth it." None of the men moved.

I limped backwards to the door…watching them…and opened it. No sound. I stepped into the hall, and pulled it shut. Turned in the darkness. The one mellow glow gave me just enough light for my one working eye. Fourteen paces—three plus eleven. I moved fast. My legs were killing. Got to the soundproofed door and pushed it open. Nearly missed the first step. Ribs hurt. Up the stairs. At the top, I stopped. Listened. Voices coming behind. Ten feet to freedom.

I pushed open the street door. Water everywhere, people everywhere. Dark, and raining hard. Neon lights bouncing off the rain, the pavement, and puddles. With only one eye, it was like stepping into a house of mirrors. Still, I had Johnny Cho's two tasks accomplished—I had the book, and I was out alive. Just.

And now, in this night-time kaleidoscope, I had to find Bynow's red BMW.

61

I hobbled and jumped on hurting legs, book in one hand, knife in the other, down On Lok Lane toward Wan Chai Road. Hennessy Road was too busy I figured, so Bynow couldn't wait there. Besides, I could call him, but I needed to get away from 10A as fast as I could. If there was one thing I was sure of…Zhou wouldn't take this lying down. There would be henchmen on my tail.

People stared at me—this cut and bashed giant hopping at them. When they saw the knife, they ran. On the positive side, it was so wet there wasn't the usual crush about. And most people were intent on getting through the storm, so many didn't notice. Still, some screamed. I wished they wouldn't do that. I didn't need the attention.

I made it along Wan Chai Road to the parking station I'd passed earlier, and slipped inside to a corner near the front. Heart thumping, drenched. I grabbed my phone and held it up to my good eye. The screen was wet. I brushed it on my shirt to clear it. Now it was smeared red with blood. "Damn, damn…" I said, rubbing it hard on my jeans. Somehow, I could just make out Bynow's text. I pressed call.

I listened, breathing hard. Four rings. "C'mon, c'mon," I growled.

Bynow answered. "Where are you?"

"Parking station, Wan Chai Road. I don't know—along from The Charterhouse Hotel, toward Central."

I heard Johnny Cho say in the background, "I know it—give us two minutes."

Then I heard someone else say, "That's him, the big one over there."

I looked up to see two Asian men coming at me. They had iron bars. Unexpected problem four. "One would be better," I yelled into the phone. "Gotta go."

I pocketed the phone just as the two attackers arrived. The first I greeted with a kick which caught him in the chest. He flew backwards, tripping off-balance into a car which had turned into the station. He and his bar hit the cement floor, the car sped on, and the book and knife slipped from my hand.

The second hit me with his bar—across my back again. Ohhh, man it hurt. Tears welled up. Blinded. Didn't matter for my right eye, but I needed one working. I blinked fast. He moved to grab the book, or the knife. I grabbed him instead. I gave him a hard, sharp smack to the back of his head with the heel of my hand. He stopped moving for just a moment. That was all I needed and I picked him up by his shirt and belt. "Wrong move, pal," I said. I face-planted him into the cement-block wall. Twice. He stopped moving…for good.

More voices appeared, coming from the other direction deep in the parking station. Echoing. "Here, here, here," they screamed. They were running, and pointing, at me. More iron bars. Did Zhou have an army out there somewhere I wondered? And where in the hell was Bynow? I snatched up the book and the knife, and made for the station entrance. The gang was maybe twenty yards away. Five paces for me to the front. Three if I hurried.

I reached it, belting rain making it near impossible to recognise any type of car. Gang ten yards away. I had to make a decision. A car skidded to a stop in front of me. The back door flew open.

"Get in, Toddy," a voice commanded. It had to be Bynow. I couldn't see, but nobody else called me 'Toddy'.

I dived headlong into the back seat. Bynow floored it, door still open. "Legs, legs…in," he snapped. I pulled my legs in tight. The door smashed into something on the street, and slammed shut.

Johnny Cho turned from the passenger seat, peered down, and shone a small torch over me. "A successful meeting, I hope?"

"So far. At least your two tasks are done," I said. I held one hand up. "I've got the book, and I'm alive."

Johnny looked me over again.

"A matter of opinion, I would say. Where to now?"

62

I asked Bynow and Johnny to drop me at the intersection of Wan Chai and Wood Road. I didn't know where else to go. Venus had said, "If you need somewhere, just call." My gear was stashed behind her sofa…and I was in need of a clean-up, and probably a good patch-up too. It was a lot sooner than 'tomorrow morning', which I'd told her, but I couldn't wait until then. Bynow had taken off so fast from the parking station, he was long past Wood Road when I told him the destination. He swung round a couple of blocks, and headed back the way we'd come.

Johnny Cho said, "Ash, can I take the book? I'll look at it tonight and I promise you'll have it back in the morning. See if we can work out where all this has come from."

I didn't really feel like letting it go, but I figured I had to. I'd worked hard for it, and the pain of that work was now beginning to bite. Everything hurt. Still, there was no way I could understand the thing. I needed Johnny's help.

"Sure, Johnny, and we'll meet first thing tomorrow, eh? I've got to be back in Macau by midday, or two probably innocent mugs are going to be slugged by the Macau justice system." I handed over Wang's constant companion.

Johnny and Bruce agreed to call me first thing. But Bynow refused to leave me at the corner. "Ash…mate…I've got you into this…sort of. But I'm not leaving you here…not with those thugs out there. We've just passed a few more…not that you'd be able to see them. Not with that eye. They're still hunting you."

"I reckon I could handle them," I said.

Bynow glanced at me in the rear-view mirror. "Toddy, you're becoming delusional. You haven't seen yourself."

He dropped me outside 7A. I stood for a minute in the warm rain, knife in hand, to collect my thoughts.

I buzzed Venus' intercom. She said she'd be in. She was. What she saw on the screen apparently didn't please her. "Oh my God, what has happened to you, Ash? Come up." I mustn't have looked too good, because for once she didn't call me Tarzan.

Bynow and Johnny waited in the idling, red BMW. Once I was inside, I turned to wave them off.

But they'd gone.

63

I tripped as I stepped in to her dodgy lift, and she was waiting for me when I tripped as I stepped out. I muttered a couple of oaths with each misstep.

"Oh, my goodness," she said, "your face, what a mess. Come and I'll try to fix it."

"My face? You should see my back. And my legs. It feels like they're at war with the rest of me. I need a shower."

I finally got a look at myself in the bathroom mirror. Bynow, Johnny and Venus were probably right. My right eye was a purplish-blue, and almost closed. I had a two-inch, red-clotted scar down near my left ear, a blue, swollen bottom lip and another slit about an inch long on my left chest. Blood covered nearly all my right cheek, and rivers of the stuff had streaked from the two cuts and soaked my shirt. Each leg had a long, blue bruise running on an angle across. They burned when I pressed them. And then there was my back…

I showered and wrapped a towel around me. Then I lay face down on the bed. Just as Venus instructed. She had some cream which she said was for bruises. She rubbed it gently where the two iron bars had hit me. On a couple of spots, I yelped. Just a bit.

"Maybe you've broken some ribs," she said.

"They'll have to wait. More work to do."

"What is it with you, why do you have to be so tough on yourself?"

My mind flashed to Sally and little Jack. I pushed the thought away. "Probably some form of punishment I guess."

"Turn over," she instructed, "so I can fix your face."

Venus carefully smoothed something over my right eye. I reckoned I could see a little through it. I could make out a light near the bed, and part of her face. It was a thing of beauty, even if a bit blurred. A little makeup, dark-pink lipstick, manicured eyebrows. Small, straight nose.

"That cut," she said, "I think it needs stitches."

"Not going to hospital."

"I know—honey," she said.

"Thank you, darling." I grinned at her. It took her a moment to get the joke.

She smiled back. "Stop that, you're a sick man. I'm going to put honey on your cuts, so they won't scar so badly."

She found the honey, sat beside me on the bed, and leant over to get a good look at the wounds. I could feel her weight pushing onto my stomach. I could feel her boobs yield to the push—flattening against me.

I could feel her finger touch my cheek. It made me gasp. "Turn your head this way," she said. Through my good eye I could see she had perfect fingernails. I wondered if they were real. She was wearing a pinkish polish, and a couple were a little chipped.

Maybe she hadn't painted them today. She had a ring on the middle finger of her right hand, and two more on her left.

She ran a thin strip of honey down the cut on my face, then licked her index finger and smoothed the strip. I could feel the damp of her wet finger as it hit the skin around the cut, but her touch was light. She was concentrating hard on the procedure, and her warm breath tickled the hair on my chest as she worked.

I looked at her eyes. Green. Not so round, maybe slanted a little. "Are you part-Asian?"

She looked up at me. "That's a funny thing to ask now. No, why?"

"No real reason—just wondered."

She moved on to the chest wound, and repeated the treatment. As she moved down, her weight shifted, resting on my groin. Her breasts pressed further down my stomach. I noticed her hair. Brownish-blonde, about shoulder length. Slightly wavy, and shiny. I thought I could smell shampoo. I felt the wet tip of her finger again.

"Now…your legs." She leant across me to retrieve the tube of bruise cream she'd casually tossed on the bed. Her skin was slightly tanned and smooth. It brought back the memory of it in the Riviera Hotel. I wondered if it was her natural colour, or whether she used one of those tanning salons. I picked up a little waft of her perfume.

"You smell good—what are you wearing?"

"You're so full of questions. It's Jo Malone, but that probably doesn't mean much to you."

I lifted my head closer to her neck, and breathed in. "Smells like fruit."

"Lime."

I breathed in again. "I like limes. I like to suck on them—if they're sweet of course. Nobody wants a sour lime."

"Of course."

Venus turned, moved down the bed, and carefully smoothed more cream onto the big welts across my shins. With each stroke, my hand pushed against her back as a sort of defence reaction, and I gasped a little as the pain burned.

"Sorry to hurt you," she said.

"No, no." I sucked in air. "It's good pain. I think."

"That's it then, all done for now." She sat by my legs, and looked me up and down. I lay there for a moment, eyes closed, trying to will the pain away.

Then I felt her place her hand on my chest. She drew a couple of circles around it with a fingernail, and lightly dragged her finger down my stomach. Two inches below my navel she stopped. She drew two smaller circles there.

I opened my eyes. She smiled. I put my hand up and stroked that beautiful face, then copied what she had done to me. As I moved my finger down her stomach, she arched herself back over me, so I could easily reach her navel.

I stopped two inches below it, and made two small circles. Then I moved my hand down another two inches.

She made a little breath. "Ahh."

"Some bonus circles," I said. "Want more?"

She said nothing, propped up on an elbow and placed her hand at the bottom of my towel. She inched her finger up my inner leg…stopped at a spot…and drew a small circle.

I said, "Ahh."

"First, your bonus," she whispered. She lifted my towel, drew another circle on the opposite leg, bent over and kissed me several times where she'd made the circles. Her lips were like velvet. Damp velvet. "Okay, your turn," she said.

I slipped my finger further down, and she dropped closer in to me. I felt the towel slide away. My mind was a blank. My body numb. Nothing hurt anymore. No thoughts, of anyone or anything.

She smiled at me again. "You think your Macau illness has gone?"

"I think so." My voice croaked, as a warm wave of something swept through me.

"Then we'll make sure of it with some proven Hong Kong medicine." Her hand moved up a little more, and the sensation sent a shudder right through me. A gentle, pleasing shudder. I felt her leg cross over mine, and she slid on top. Nearly weightless. She pushed down hard against me. I pushed back. A little faster, a little harder.

Outside it was raining again. Wet. Inside was now the same.

The air conditioner rattled.

I could smell her Jo Malone.

And through my swollen, blurred right eye, I could just see her switch off the light.

64

It was 7:45 a.m. when my phone buzzed with a text. Bruce Bynow's number. The message simply said, *Interesting stuff you need to see. Get here ASAP.* At the end was an address in the Mid-Levels.

I looked down at Venus, who seemed asleep still. She was lying on her stomach, hair flopped over her face. The only hint she was alive was the gentle rise and fall of her back as she breathed. The room was warm—air conditioner clunking away, struggling with the dripping atmosphere.

I stroked the small of her back. It was damp with a light sweat. I bent over and kissed it. She moved a little. I licked the sweat. She rolled on her side, and gave me a half-asleep smile. "You want breakfast in bed?"

"Sounds like an offer I shouldn't refuse, but I've gotta go." I looked at the bedside clock again. "Only got a few hours before everyone's favourite ship's captain, and his mate, are in the shit. And right now, that's priority one. Whatever it takes, I've got to get them out of there. Even if the truth takes a small hammering."

Venus said nothing, and rolled back on her stomach. I

showered and dressed, made myself some toast and coffee, and packed my duffel. She appeared in a white cotton robe.

"Let me look at your wounds," she said. She peered at my busted eye—it was sore to touch, but I had some blurred sight from it. "That cut, you'll have a big scar I think. Needed stitches."

"No time…too late. I'll keep it as a memory of you."

"When you finish this job, where will you go?"

"Back home I guess. Sydney."

"Not here?"

I pondered the question a moment. She was certainly a beautiful companion, and smart. But her occupation—she said it was over, but I wasn't so sure. No way that I wanted to be sharing her with the world.

"I'll think about it—maybe you could come down there?"

She gave a little half-smile. "Maybe I could."

I bent and kissed her cheek, and she wrapped her arms around me. "Take care, Tarzan," she whispered. Then she kissed me hard.

"I will, and hey, thanks. For everything."

I left Venus standing in the doorway of her flat, slung the duffel over my shoulder, negotiated the stuttering lift to the street, and found a cab. I gave the driver Bynow's address, and settled back. My phone buzzed with an incoming text. From Dick Mayvers. It read, *Mate…how are u going? Bynow looking after u properly? I knew the break would do u good. Nil current notes on a Patrick Hogan. Last one 5 years ago. Presumed dead. Take care and call me if u need anything. Fothers sends love. Cheers.*

I ran a check over my body. Head hurt, vision out of whack. Cut on chest seemed okay, ribs hurt, especially on the left side when I breathed in. Then again on the right side when I breathed out. Legs ached. I shut my eyes and took a deep breath. So, this was Mayvers' idea of a break doing me good?

'Look on the bright side, Todd,' I thought to myself, 'you can see, you can walk, and you can breathe. You *are* alive.' And that made me suddenly think of Sally, and little Jack. They *weren't*.

Funny though, that was the first thought I'd had of them all night.

65

Bruce Bynow lived on the tenth floor of an apartment block in MacDonnell Road, in the Mid-Levels on Hong Kong Island. The block was unremarkable—it looked like any other of the thousands of apartment blocks squeezed into the city. Bynow's apartment was modern, with tiled floors, a couple of bedrooms and bathrooms, and a long balcony. His furniture...brown hard-looking sofas and a couple of similar armchairs...looked like replicas of something from the 1960s. The best thing about this home was the view. Straight down into the towers of the city, with the Bank of China building and its zigzag window patterns holding centre stage.

"Nice outlook, Bruce," I said.

"Sure, Toddy, but you get used to it. Now Johnny, tell Ash what you found."

We sat at a small, round timber table. Johnny opened Wang's book. He had tagged pages through it.

Johnny propped an elbow on the table, and rested his chin on his hand. "It's no wonder they wanted to frighten you off. My guess is that if you hadn't got yourself out of there, we'd be reading about you in the press. Past tense though. Once someone found you, that is. And that could take a very long time. These people don't take prisoners, and they don't like to leave traces."

"So, they're not who they seem to be?"

"Oh yes, they are who they seem to be. And a few more things as well."

"Can you give me a summary? Time is short today…"

Johnny fixed me with a stare. "Right, I think it goes like this…and this is a combination of what I can work out from the book, and what I hear around the traps. Okay?"

I nodded.

"There's a company called Zhang Yu. But it's more than just a company. There's a club in Shanghai also called ZhangYu. And there's a group called Zhangyu. Different spelling combinations, but the same thing. Operations are based in Shanghai and here."

"What do they do?"

"Like most things, it's all about money. And control. They have nightclubs in Shanghai, and the spin-offs which go with it—hookers, gambling—you know?"

"Drugs?"

"Possibly. Control comes from small groups of men in both cities."

"You're talking triads?"

Johnny shrugged. "Sure, triads. The story goes it started with a group of eight thugs in Shanghai, and expanded from there."

"So, who controls it—this Zhang Yu?"

"Why your Mr Zhou, for starters. He is Numero Uno—upfront. But his major partner in the whole thing is the PLA."

"People's Liberation Army?"

"One and the same. They controlled much of the so-called 'private' business in China. Without them, it would have been nearly impossible to do much thirty, forty years ago. You needed their protection—they could make things happen—but of course there are all sorts of other power bases within that one, big power base. So, who ultimately controls anything is nearly impossible to work out from here."

I gave this some quiet thought. The PLA is a partner with Zhou. And the PLA is now pressuring Chief Feng. And warning me off. And now it made sense.

"Go on," I said.

Johnny opened the book at a marked page.

"See here," he said, pointing at some Chinese characters, "this says Zhang Yu BVI as a heading. This I would take to be the controlling company. There are eight names. Some of them could be anybody, but some you will find interesting—Zhou, Ma, Grekov, Wang." Johnny gave me a quizzical look. "Interesting, yes?"

"Very. BVI eh? Registered in the British Virgin Islands."

"Probably an older company," said Johnny, "many were registered there years ago for privacy. To hide things. Harder to do that there now though."

"It's all bullshit." Bynow's sudden burst made us both flinch. "It might be a bit harder now, and governments think they can stop this stuff—but the sheer bloody weight of money worldwide opens up new havens. They crack down on one—and the pressure builds and builds. Another one quietly pops up. Like a band-aid on an ulcer, it doesn't fix the issue. Just moves it. Called the law of unintended consequences. And governments are fucking masters at it."

I turned to Bynow. "The politicians have to *appear* to be doing something. You know that. They're always 'cracking down'. But they're hooked on revenue—they can never get enough—and those who are bankrolling them don't want the issue 'fixed'. They all need somewhere to hide. That's why they use only band-aids. What else have you found, Johnny?"

"Here, another heading—Jinshan. Below that, a list of companies. A couple here in Hong Kong, and half-a-dozen more elsewhere. Possibly Europe. Then at the bottom of the page, more names—the usual four, plus one more—and numbers, some crossed out."

"The new name?"

"Lam."

"Interesting."

"And the numbers look like shareholdings—percentages. It looks like Zhou, Ma and Grekov had thirty percent each, and Wang and Lam five. Those numbers had a line through them, and another set showed Lam and Wang with twenty-five together, and the other three with twenty-five each. They have also been crossed out, and each of the three is back to thirty, with Wang now on ten, and Lam zero."

"Sounds like someone's wish list," said Bynow, "or an ongoing negotiation."

"Hard to negotiate when you're dead," I said.

"Let me do some quick research on these companies—give me ten minutes," said Johnny.

Bynow said, "I'll make the coffee."

"Think I need it," I said.

66

Chief Feng was becoming more agitated. It was mid-morning, and he'd just taken his fourth call that day regarding his two suspects from the *Golden Empress*.

First there was a call from Mr Zhou, who seemed to now be *the* spokesman for the guests on the boat that fateful evening. He had called once before, and was not happy that the two hadn't been charged immediately. "But it's obvious they did it," he had demanded, "or at least that captain did. They found him with the weapon. And his offsider tried to cover it up. Why don't you get it over with?"

This morning Zhou seemed more insistent. When he was told that a process was being followed, and he would have to wait, his next two words were, "Look, Feng…" and then hung up.

The second call was from another of the guests, Mr Ma. He seemed much more reasonable, and had explained that Zhou was really just very concerned for his reputation. He assured Feng that they all wanted to see justice administered properly. He went to some length explaining that Zhou's reputation was indeed something worth protecting. When it became apparent Feng was not going to move faster, Ma began explaining how at times, Zhou could become quite fierce.

The third call was from someone called Wu. He had called once before, and claimed to be an officer with the PLA. Feng could never confirm his story. He'd rung the local branch of the PLA, but nobody could, or would, admit to Wu's position. But Wu appeared to know all the details of the case. He vouched for the character of the guests, and said this could be supported by anyone senior in the ranks of his organisation. He pressed Feng to proceed to a charge, and for the second time suggested any delay could be a detrimental career move.

The fourth call was the most worrying for Feng. It was from a superior in his own organisation. Not his immediate boss—they got on well—but someone further up. A Commissioner Qin. Commissioner Qin was not someone Feng knew, but after this call he was left in no doubt. The PLA was closing in. They had transferred their push to a senior PSP officer, and now it was a matter of time. If Feng didn't play his hand right, his career and thirty years of pension, might vanish.

Qin wanted action. Feng asked for more time. He bluffed. He explained there may be a new development in the case.

Qin sounded agitated. "What new development?"

"Better not to confuse the case right now," Feng said, "it may not lead anywhere. It might only involve other innocent parties, and we don't want that do we, Commissioner?"

"When are you going to charge them?" Qin demanded again.

Feng looked at his watch. 9:52a.m. He'd given CH Lam an undertaking—a loose one—that he'd give some help to Todd. And he'd agreed to allow Todd another twenty-four hours. That would end at midday. It was cutting it close…for everybody. "Give me two hours, Commissioner," he said.

There was a brief silence. "Fine," said Qin, "but if there is nothing from you then, and you keep stalling, it could be fatal. Don't test me."

Feng put down the receiver with purpose. To make sure Qin was gone. He looked out from his office at the nearby building, pulled a few quick breaths like he was hyperventilating, let them go, and leant back in his chair.

"Jesus, Todd," he muttered, "you better have something good. Hogan's life is not worth this."

67

Johnny Cho closed off his laptop, took a sip of coffee and directed his gaze out over the towers of Central.

"Investment companies—scattered all over the place," he said, "one of my contacts, lives in Monaco, knows of a couple of them. Says they own property in France."

"Tell me, Johnny," I said, "do you know what any of our four do? I mean their legitimate businesses."

"That's pretty easy—Zhou produces ethanol, Ma and Grekov are in property—shopping centres and so on. Ma's family are all local Party officials—that's how they get their deals done. In the gambling world that's how they are known. But Wang—no, I don't know what he does. All I know is he is close to your man." Johnny cast a sideways glance at Bynow. "Or Bruce's man…CH Lam."

"So, other than Wang…they are all long-term gamblers?"

"Pretty much. Triad groups used to bring them down to Macau—you know, organise the gambling trips, and these few have been at it a while. Except Zhou broke off from the big casinos when Lam set his up. The other two have only recently moved across."

"There has to be more to it," I said. "Something's missing. Some connection. But what?"

"Hard to pin them," Johnny said. "They're all from different backgrounds. And no-one really knows what's behind Grekov either. But they've all done damn well out of communism. Makes a mockery of it all, doesn't it? All men are equal. *Ha*...this lot make capitalism look bad."

"Yep—*Animal Farm*."

Johnny looked at me. "What animals?"

"It's a book—ohhh, never mind. Tell you later. What's this missing connection?" I wondered out loud.

"Written by George Orwell," chimed in Bynow, "you should read it, Johnny."

"So, in short," I said, "we have Zhou who's a loaded industrialist from Shanghai. He's in bed with the People's Liberation Army, and they own nightclubs and only God and the Devil know what else. We have Ma, whose family is in local government in Guangzhou, and we have Grekov, who comes from Russia and nobody knows his money source. But together they get all sorts of major property deals done. And of course Wang, who seems to have no history of anything."

"That's about it."

"They all make a truckload of hooch from business in China, and they gamble it away in Macau. They should have nothing left. Yet they share in companies around the globe, which they appear to control. Doesn't add up. Johnny—those two companies Jinshan and, and..."

"Zhang Yu?"

"Yes, Zhang Yu. What do those names mean? Anything?"

"Jinshan means a golden hill. Zhang Yu is an octopus."

"Golden hill, eh? Maybe a mountain?"

"I guess so," said Johnny.

"Well that's a start. Lam's club is The Golden Mountain. And the Jinshan, or golden mountain group, is owned by the gamblers. And Lam and Wang with smaller shareholdings."

"If the book is on the money, yes."

"There's still something not right. How does Zhou get hooked up so close to a casino in Macau? How does he make that jump? I wonder whose casino it really is?"

"Let me make a call," said Johnny. He dialled a number and retreated to another room for the conversation.

Bynow raised an eyebrow at me. "What are you thinking?"

"Just a hunch."

Johnny returned. "CH Lam used to work in the big casinos. Good reputation. Then a heavy-hitter with money took him and set up this private casino. A man known only as CD."

"You heard of him before?"

"Nope," Johnny said, "and my contact didn't know him either."

I thought a moment. "An octopus, you say?"

Johnny nodded.

I slapped hard on the little table. "That's *it.*" Bynow and Johnny jumped.

"Go easy, Toddy," said Bynow. "What's *it*?"

"I think I can put this together." I looked at my watch. "Holy shit. It's nearly 11:00 and I've got to be there by 12:00. I'll never make it. Feng's going to charge Hogan and Wallis unless I get there with a solution."

"What about the chopper?" said Bynow. "It's close—I'll have you on the helipad in fifteen, twenty minutes. Trip over only takes about the same."

"Then why don't you both come. My shout—and if I'm right, there's twenty grand in this we can share. Besides, I may need an interpreter."

Bruce and Johnny looked at each other and shrugged. "Why not?" said Johnny.

Bynow called up the helicopter company, booked tickets, and hollered into the phone, "And we'll be there in fifteen…make sure she's powered-up and ready to fly."

I scooped up Wang's book, slung the duffel over my shoulder, and dialled Chief Feng. He was on the phone. I left a message with the receptionist, "I'll there by twelve—have Chief Feng meet us at The Golden Mountain Club. Oh, and in the meantime, ask him to call me will you, with the autopsy result?"

I called the Club. Lily put me through to CH. "I think I've got it," I said.

CH sounded surprised. "You do? So fast?"

"Only a few loose ends—we'll be there by midday. I have two assistants coming along, and Chief Feng will be there also."

Johnny joined us, pulling on his suit coat, as Bynow shut his phone and said, "Three tickets booked, 11:30 take-off."

I slapped them both on the back. "Let's go."

Bynow flinched. "Steady…not so hard." We stepped into the lift.

"And, Johnny," I said, "there's one more call I want you to make. Or maybe two. I'll tell you in the car."

68

Take-off from the Shun Tak helipad was clocked at one minute after 11:30. Customs proved a challenge. They were about to confiscate the hunting knife with seven-inch partially serrated blade, which they discovered in my bag. Apparently, they felt it could be 'used as a deadly weapon'. The Customs officer said he might have to call the cops. I produced my Australian Federal Police ID. At that point, I was grateful my resignation had been rejected, and I still had my card.

"The knife—it's already been used, last night," I said. "Look." I pointed to the scar down my left cheek. "I'm investigating a murder and this is evidence. And…Macau PSP is waiting for me to deliver it."

Customs screwed-up his face at me "Your visa says you are a tourist. You're not working here. I *am* calling the police."

"No time," I snapped. I grabbed the knife from the floppy hold Customs had on it, and pointed the tip to his throat. His eyes widened. "Sorry, pal, gotta go." I looked at Bruce and Johnny. "Come on, let's move."

I sprinted to the chopper, Bynow and Johnny hot on my heels.

The pilot was waiting—engine whirring, blades turning. He checked dials and glanced about the helipad surrounds. I jumped in next to him, threw my duffel to Bynow in the back, slipped the knife up to his face and said, "Macau, buddy. And make it fast, eh?"

I glanced behind. Two Customs officers, and a cop, shooter drawn, sprinted toward us. Johnny tapped the pilot on the shoulder, prised his headset loose, and yelled something in Chinese. He jabbed his index finger up. We made lift-off as the cop unleashed a couple of rounds. They missed.

We landed at the Macau Ferry helipad at 11:47. I scanned the area as we touched-down. On the street, half-a-dozen cabs were waiting for fares, their drivers seemingly dozing-off in the midday heat. No way out except through the Customs office. We sprinted to it, Bynow lugging my duffel. I was still flashing the knife.

The Customs officer was the same one who had seen me through with the PSP cops from the boat. His eyes widened and head shook at the sight of my injuries.

"You have had a rough time, sir?"

"Bet your arse I have, and I don't need any more." I waved my arrival card at him. "We right to go?"

"Sorry," he said, "no can do." He flicked his fingers, and three PSP officers rounded a corner off to our right, guns drawn.

I glanced at Bynow. "Taxi time," I bellowed, and sprinted for the door.

Bynow yelled back, "They're not going to like this."

"Stop! Police!" commanded one of the cops. I heard a couple of pops. A slug took out a window to my left. Johnny passed me.

He was fast. Or shit-scared. We hit the street. More bullets shattered glass behind us. We dived in the front cab, and I smacked the driver across the head to wake him from his slumber.

"Move it," I yelled. He turned the ignition. The motor wound slowly. I shoved the knife in his face. "Get us the fuck out of here." Another missile smashed the rear window of the cab. He looked terrified. The motor fired. He planted his foot.

With a tyre screech that would do a Hollywood movie proud, we finally cleared Customs.

69

At 11:58 we slammed to a smoking halt outside The Golden Mountain Club. I'd rung ahead and said to the receptionist, "We're on our way—cops in pursuit. We'll need a fast transfer." In the middle of our chopper-ride and cab-sprint, Feng's assistant had called with the autopsy result, and Johnny had made the extra call I needed.

We jumped from the taxi, and I could feel the heat from the brakes. The air smelt of burning rubber. I slipped the driver a few hundred extra for the window. No time to count it. Sirens rounded the corner a block away. Dong appeared, said nothing, and bowed slightly, and quickly ushered us to the lift. The door clicked shut behind.

I looked at Bynow and Johnny. Sweat streaked our faces, our shirts. Bynow handed me my duffel, and I replaced the knife. I felt inside for the book. All in place.

On the second floor Lily said, "Nice to see you again, Mr Todd." My face made her double-take. She pursed her lips, her tiny mouth forming an 'ohh'. "Mr Lam is expecting you."

We followed Lily to the office door, behind which lay the

stunning view, Sebastian's lavish furnishings, his deep-red sofas, his bank of computers, his huge desk and his amazing Purpleheart parquetry floor. And his father, CH Lam.

I ushered Bruce Bynow and Johnny Cho in first, and I followed.

All those things were indeed in place. And a few unexpected ones in the form of Zhou, Ma, Grekov and Wang. And Chief Feng. And one other man I'd never seen.

"Welcome back, Mr Todd," said CH, barely disguising his horror when he saw me, "with some news, you say? But your face…who did this?"

I stared down the gang of four. "I'll fill you in later."

"Fine—and you know everyone I believe? They have come to offer their condolences."

I nodded. "Very thoughtful of them, CH. Now, these are my associates—Bruce Bynow you know, of course, and Johnny Cho."

Bynow and Johnny shook hands with everyone in turn. "Nice to see you again, CH, but I wish under different circumstances," said Bynow.

"Thank you," said CH, indicating for us to sit.

I looked at Feng, and then at the unknown person beside him.

Feng caught my gaze.

"Allow me, Mr Todd—meet Commissioner Qin."

70

CH had everyone sit around the big, black boardroom table, with its view out to the Bank of China building. He sat at the head, the group of four from the boat down one side, backs to the view, and opposite sat Bruce Bynow, Johnny Cho, Chief Feng, and Commissioner Qin. With twenty-two chairs available, I had plenty to pick from. I stayed on my feet.

"Well, Mr Todd," said CH, "you say you have something. Please proceed."

I stood at the far end of the table, opposite Zhou, and friends, so I could watch their reaction. The smallest movement could be helpful. And it made me wonder what pressure they'd put on CH to be invited to this meeting.

"It had me baffled, CH—the way Sebastian died," I said, "the vicious nature of it, and the motive someone would have for such an attack. But my inquiries have uncovered not one, but a number of motives. These, I believe, give the clue to what really happened."

Zhou shifted a little, Ma the same, Grekov's head appeared to drop, and Wang sat unblinking. Just as I'd come to expect.

Chief Feng sat upright in his chair, his interest sparked. He turned side on to watch me continue.

"Some of this is old ground, but I'll go over it again, to make sure we are all on the same page. Okay?"

"Yes, yes, go on," said CH.

"Well first let's look at our victim. Sorry, at Sebastian. We know he had expensive tastes. He loved making money, and spending it. He believed he was doing a wonderful job at the Club, making it super successful."

CH gave a little "ha."

"Hmmph," snorted Zhou, "with no help."

"And we know he had unusual, shall we say, romantic leanings." I glanced at the group. "Miss Jay-Dee, of course, being the object of his attention."

Now Grekov reacted. "Haaahh—the little shit."

I ignored all the comments—but it was good for Feng to hear it. Might help the cause over at headquarters…strengthen the case for Hogan and Wallis.

"However, Sebastian wasn't content—not with his lifestyle financially, or sexually. He wanted more—more money and more and unusual sex. He started making demands, first on the Club, and then on its partners."

"But," cut in Chief Feng, "why wouldn't he just ask his father? He owns the Club, and Sebastian had twenty-four-hour access."

"Because all is not as it seems, Chief. CH is not *the* owner of the Club—he is an owner, but he had, and still has, partners."

"And who would they be?" asked Feng.

"They're sitting opposite."

Chief Feng and Commissioner Qin scanned the four faces across the table. They all held their ground—no reaction from any. Only CH gave it away a bit—with a little nod. I picked it up—nobody else noticed.

Feng looked back at me. "You have proof of this?"

"As much as I think we'll ever get, Chief. I have a book—a book which is usually in the very firm keeping of Mr Wang. However, I was fortunate to have it fall into my possession recently. I've had its contents analysed. Each of these men is named in it, as is the name Lam. It doesn't specify which Lam, so I've assumed it is the family. CH and Sebastian."

I pulled the book from my bag, and placed it on the table. Wang stared at it.

"You don't read Chinese," said Zhou. "How could you analyse it?"

"No, but my associate Mr Cho, here, does. He can confirm what I'm saying."

"Yes...correct," said Johnny.

"And now we know, that you know something about it, Mr Zhou," I said. "Thank you for that."

Zhou's head gave a small shudder.

"There are companies," I continued, "two main ones we know of, maybe more. One is called Zhang Yu, which means octopus. Registered in the British Virgin Islands. These men all have shares in it, and there are four other shareholders, names we don't know. Eight in total. The one feature of that is that there is no Lam shareholding at all."

Johnny Cho and Bruce Bynow nodded confirmation. Chief Feng kept staring at the group opposite. I couldn't make out

Commissioner Qin's reaction.

Grekov stirred. "Robbing little shit," he grumbled.

I glanced at CH. He was staring down Zhou, and then Wang. First a questioning look, and then his face turned to thunder.

I continued. "The other company is called Jinshan. It means golden hill. I take that to be code for The Golden Mountain Club. This is registered in Hong Kong, and it controls other companies around the world. Property companies and the like. Its main feature, as far as we're concerned, is that the Lam shareholdings increased over time. Until now. Now Sebastian is dead, there are no Lam shares at all. These four men have the lot."

Feng pointed across the table. "And you believe these men over here, have all conspired to steal the Lam family shares in these companies?"

"Not quite. We don't know who owns the ultimate holding in Zhang Yu. But I'd wager CH still controls a big share. Say around half? CH—maybe you'd confirm that?"

CH said nothing. He continued his focus on the four opposite. He wasn't happy.

"I think the argument came from Sebastian—he wanted a bigger cut. He figured he was doing all the big money tricks for these others, so he started demanding from them."

Feng cocked an eyebrow. "What money tricks?"

"Chief, go with me here. Opposite are four men—each very powerful in China. They all have long-term connections to the ruling Party. Stretches back to 1949, and the communist takeover. They have all made a fortune under that same communism. But—and this is where it got me—they come down here and blow the lot through your casinos."

"Sure, but there's a long line of mainlanders doing that," said Feng.

"But not at this level. This lot lose millions, no…tens of millions…they should have nothing left. Yet they still control so much wealth offshore? Chief—it doesn't wash." I waved my arms in a big circle, to take in the whole room. "This enterprise is not about gambling. This is a very convenient, shall we say, 'private funds transfer operation'? They don't want their money hanging about in China—political risk is too high. What if an 'unfriendly' gets to the top—changes the rules? What if the economy tanks? Or the government fiddles with the currency? They have to get it out. And they can't get it out fast enough through legitimate channels, or through the big casinos. No control there."

CH and Zhou stiffened in their chairs, and sat up. Ma did the same. Grekov napped, and Wang sat, unblinking, staring at his book.

Commissioner Qin turned to me and said, "So what you're saying, Mr Todd, is that this is major laundering—these men are defrauding the Chinese Government?"

"Laundering? Definitely. They don't lose it. They appear to lose it—the casino…this casino…takes the money, less a fee. But then it re-invests it overseas. Into property and businesses which these same men just happen to control. Defrauding? Depends on your point of view I guess. But that would be a long, hard case for you to take on, Commissioner. I'm more interested in a motive for killing Sebastian. And with Sebastian attempting to blackmail them into more shares…a bigger cut…I think we have *the* motive for them to get rid of him."

"And what led you to believe there is a connection between

them and this casino?" asked Qin. "You say there are companies, and shareholders, but none mention this club by name."

"That had me stumped, I admit. But I figured there had to be a connection. Johnny made some enquiries. Tell them what you found, Johnny."

"Two connections," said Johnny, "which ties it together. Number one, CH had a partner who set up this casino—a big player in Macau gambling. A man with no apparent history. Hard to trace. Number two, Mr Zhou has been in partnership for a long time with the PLA. They have given him clout, and protection—in return for a major share. The Zhang Yu company…the octopus…was set up a long time ago in the BVI. Eight tentacles on an octopus, eight partners. A lucky number. But, and this took some digging, only two founding partners—Mr Zhou, and the elusive whale who started this casino. A common partner in each business."

Chief Feng drew in a long breath. "Let me get this straight. This person…this…whale…financed Mr Zhou's business, and also this casino with CH? How would he finance Zhou's business—forty or fifty years ago? Under communism?"

"Well there's one more thing," I said.

Qin looked flustered. "What now?"

"I've established, or should I say, my associate Mr Cho has," I said, turning to Johnny for some added effect, "that the whale was a heavy hitter in the PLA. Maybe the heaviest hitter. An original in the regime, and he was able to move about the world, unchallenged. That's how he got control—of businesses, and money. And he could be virtually anonymous. He made the rules."

"Phew," said Feng.

"And you say," said Qin, "they all conspired to kill Sebastian, because he wanted more, and threatened to expose them if they didn't pay?"

"Yes—with another, quite unrelated motive."

Seven sets of eyes now turned to me.

"Fascinating—go on," said Feng.

"As I said earlier, Sebastian had an unusual sexual preference. He was into men—or to be more specific, young men. But he wanted, or needed, to appear interested in women. So, he engaged the services of lady-boys. One in particular, a Miss Jay-Dee, became his regular lover. She accompanied him on this trip."

"Heaps of men do the same here, Mr Todd," said Feng, "you'd be surprised how many. It's a big industry."

"True, Chief, and one of those men sits opposite you—Mr Grekov."

All eyes now swivelled to the Russian. He snorted, "Hmmpfffh."

"The night Sebastian was murdered, I found Miss Jay-Dee late in the evening, alone and upset in the jacuzzi. Sebastian had been arguing in meetings with our four guests here—and all had left in some sort of rage. Grekov included. I asked Jay-Dee what was wrong—and she showed me the wounds Sebastian had inflicted on her."

"He was belting her?" asked Qin.

"That and a bit more. She'd about had enough. Anyway, my subsequent enquiries uncovered one more thing."

"Yes?" Feng and Qin said in unison.

"Miss Jay-Dee was also in a relationship with Grekov. Sebastian knew nothing of it—it was their little secret. And I believe Grekov, in a rage after his meeting, found an additional motive to get at Sebastian. Revenge on behalf of his lover. You would have found *his* handiwork in the plughole."

"Ahhh," said Feng, "you mean the severed dick?"

I nodded.

CH flashed a startled look at me, and then at Grekov.

"Hmmpffhh," grunted Grekov again, "you're fucking mad. Guessing. You can't prove a thing."

"Well, what about your man, Mr Todd...the skipper?" asked Feng. "He was found with a knife, and covered in blood."

"True, but he was framed. He was too drunk to do this. Sure, he had a rage against Sebastian too, but he could hardly stand. No Chief, this murder needed strong, steady hands—or a number of them. And they're sitting opposite."

"Absolute garbage," spat Zhou. "Pure fantasy. I'm not staying for any more of this." He started to rise.

"Stay put, Mr Zhou," demanded Qin. Zhou glared at him, and at me, and sat down.

"But the murder weapon—we have two knives," said Feng.

"Yes, you do," I said, "and remember how Wallis found one in the captain's safe. That was his knife. It is different to the murder weapon—it has a brown, dimpled handle—and it was kept there for security. Along with his gun. But the actual murder weapon is the other knife—the black-handled one. It has a distinctive pattern and motif—hard to see from wear over the years, and it took me a long time to realise what it was. But this morning I got it."

Qin let out a long, loud breath. "Got what?"

"The motif." I moved over to my duffel which I'd replaced in the corner, and pulled out the hunting knife. "This will be an exact match for the murder weapon, Chief."

Feng looked hard at it. "Where did you get this?"

I pointed at the four men opposite. "From them…last night. This knife did this." I pointed to the scar on my face. "And another here." I pointed to my chest. "Courtesy of one of their thugs—one who you sent to look after me in Shanghai, CH."

CH thought a moment. He looked startled again. "You mean Ho?"

I nodded. "He's working with Mr Zhou here." I looked at Zhou. "And *that's* not fantasy, is it, Zhou? By the way, how is Ho? Recovering?"

Zhou said nothing, and turned away to the big windows.

I went on, "So if you look closely, Chief, you'll see the small motif, here." I pointed at it. "Same as on the murder weapon in your office."

"What is it?" asked Qin.

"Same as on the ring on Zhou's left hand. I think if you attended certain nightclubs in Shanghai controlled by Zhou you'd find it on the door…and it can't be coincidence…it's the same as on the ceiling in the salon on the *Empress*. It's this little group's symbol, and it's on everything they own."

"Come on, Todd," demanded Qin.

"It's an octopus—a Zhang Yu."

Nobody spoke. The four looked straight ahead. Qin and Feng gave each other a quick glance, and turned to me. But they didn't notice CH. His left hand made the slightest move, pressing something under the board table. Behind him, off to my left, the office door flung open. Two people jumped through it.

Dong and Lily. Dong was packing weaponry. Looked to be an FNP 45. Seemed to be a favourite of this crowd.

The polite club smiles were gone. They moved with stealth, eyes fixed on the four, gun trained on them. They'd practised this. They stood one at each end of the board table, Lily next to CH, and Dong between Qin and me.

Grekov snapped from his slumber and yelled, "That Sebastian is a fucking thief. A money-hungry low-life. We want an explanation about our money, and we get this. Threats. I'm leaving." He made a move to stand. CH nodded. Dong fired. He didn't miss. Grekov's chest exploded, sending a spray of blood across the huge windows. The force knocked him backwards, crashing behind Ma's chair.

Grekov was on the money with one thing. He *was* leaving.

Permanently.

71

The shock of the shot caused the remaining three to put their hands up—like in an old western.

CH glared at them, eyes narrowed. "Anyone else wish to complain?" Nobody spoke.

Qin and Feng gave quick, nervous glances, trying to decide their next move. Upsetting a trigger-happy Dong seemed risky.

An impulse suddenly hit me. Dong's explosive arrival flashing his shooter about— with CH's blessing? And Grekov's near-final utterance, "…an explanation about our money." What else was going on here?

I said to Lily, "Can you open the club computer? Sebastian's personal files? I want to check something."

CH nodded at her. "Open it," he said.

Lily moved to Sebastian's desk and fired up the computer. Dong kept his pistol trained on the three.

I opened and closed file after file. Fifty or more, each with a horde of sub-folders. A maze. Then I found one headed AMUSEMENT. Looked promising. Inside sat a folder titled KHABAROVSK. I Googled the name. Russian city on the

Chinese border. Back to the folder. Inside that were links. I clicked on some.

Pictures opened. Some women. Ages, names, where they lived. All Russian. Some men—same deal. Hundreds of photos. Each with a note underneath—Hong Kong, Philippines, Macau, Vietnam. But most just said 'Waiting'.

I closed the folder, and found another, titled WORKING. I opened it. More links. Escort services. And brothels. Mostly women. A couple for men. More for lady-boys. An even spread across the same places as the photos.

In each file, at the very end of the links sat a document, one titled DOLG, and the other ZHAIWU. I opened them. Inside DOLG was a number—5,000,000. Nothing more. And inside ZHAIWU—7,338,000. I called out to the group around the table, "Anyone know what Dolg means?"

Silence.

I spelt it out, "D-O-L-G. Anyone?"

Dong took two quick steps backwards, spun around and trained his pistol on me. "Why do you want to know?"

"Easy, Dong, easy," I said, lifting my hands from the keyboard, "it's just the name of a folder in here."

Dong cast a quick, nervous glance back at CH. The pistol flicked about as he moved. Each person flinched as it passed. CH nodded at him and said, "It's okay."

"It means debt," Dong said. "Russian for debt." His accent had changed. A small shift. Less Chinese.

I nodded. "Thanks." Dong turned back to guarding the three. That gave me a clue. I clicked back into the Khabarovsk folder, and opened more pictures. And there, I found what I was looking for.

I looked across to Zhou and asked, "What did Grekov mean 'Sebastian's a thief'?"

Zhou eyed Dong nervously. "He's right," Zhou said, "owes us millions. And never pays."

"So, can I assume Zhaiwu means the same as Dolg? Chinese, perhaps, for debt?" I said. Zhou nodded.

I opened the WORKING file again, and clicked the links. Then I found one which registered. Lashings of Love. That one I knew. Home of the entertainers.

Finally, Commissioner Qin said, "Mr Todd, would you care to tell us what you've uncovered, if anything?" His tone was urgent. Dong's pistol in his face may have been the cause.

"My take on it," I said, "Sebastian's sideline businesses. Hookers—all genders—and brothels, across Asia. And people trafficking. Russians—all piled up around Khabarovsk, just near the Chinese border. A feeder line for his sex trade. All waiting for Sebastian to find them a gig in his network. I'd say he was siphoning proceeds from here, and channelling it to his own empire. Money that was supposed to be invested somewhere else. Zhou's share he'd used—the Zhaiwu—over seven million. And Grekov—the Dolg—another five mill."

CH shook his head. "This just cannot be," he said under his breath.

Zhou nodded three or four times. "Very clever work, Mr Todd."

Feng let out a long whistle. "Jesus," he said, "what a game. All those illegals." He shook his head at the thought, then looked up at Dong. "By the way, how did you know what the Russian word meant?"

Dong ignored him.

Qin joined the hunt. "You," he snapped at Dong, "how did you know? Answer me!"

"Because he's one of them," I said, "Dong is Russian, with a new name, new identity."

"And how do you know that?" asked Qin.

I turned the computer screen around to face the room. "Because he's right here, with his history underneath."

The whole table turned to see a sullen-faced picture of Dong staring back at them.

In that moment Dong abandoned his interest in the three, and turned sharply to Commissioner Qin, who was sitting close by on his left. His pistol jammed hard against Qin's temple and he shouted, "I'm not going back."

Qin stood. Dong's gun followed him up. Qin pointed his finger at Dong, stabbed him in the chest and said, "You'll go back if I say..." That was as far as he got. The shot took out the far side of his head. Blood, bone, and brains splattered along the boardroom table.

Everyone got a taste.

72

Dong moved fast. Across the office, gun pointed at me. "No moving," he yelled. I stayed put. He jammed the pistol against my temple. I wondered what Bynow and Johnny made of this shit-fight I'd led them into. But I figured to some degree this was Bynow's shit-fight, and he'd led me into it. I was supposed to be here getting over the death of my family…not facing my own.

"Careful, Dong," said CH. But he was having none of it. He jabbed the gun at me again.

"You will not send me back. I want to stay here—free. You will agree to this, or I shoot," he growled.

Feng jumped in. "Why can't you go back? What's the problem?"

With a flick of his wrist, Dong fired a shot above Feng's head, and snapped the barrel back against mine. The bullet made a neat hole in the ceiling. "I said I'm not going back. Do you understand?"

Feng nodded. "Okay, okay."

I had to take a chance. Dong was likely to kill the lot of us in this mood. "Maybe I can help—can I use the computer, Dong?"

He hesitated a moment, but backed the gun off a few inches. "Slowly...move slowly," he said.

I scrolled below his picture which was still up on the screen, and scanned a couple of lines below. I found what I needed.

"I think I understand the problem. You were Russian Army. And now you recruit clients for Sebastian. You deserted?"

Dong didn't answer.

"If you did, you can't go back, can you? Siberia? Or worse?"

"I'm *not* going back." Dong's wrist flicked the pistol back onto my temple. "I will take *everyone* out here, before that."

That was a real possibility. The next word on his resume, after Army, said 'Sniper'. He knew what he was doing. He knew what his fate back in Russia would be if he was deported. Either that, or a hell-hole Chinese prison. Dong had nothing left to lose. The bullets would come at us in that boardroom, one-by-one, until someone agreed to his demand. One roll of the dice left, I figured, before the shooting resumed.

"There's only one person here who can guarantee you won't be sent back," I said. "It's not me. I don't have that power."

"Who? Feng?" Dong demanded. He flicked his pistol at Feng again. Feng ducked.

I shook my head. "Wang."

Wang didn't react. Dong snapped the barrel into me again. "What is this? A joke?"

"How can Wang guarantee that?" asked Feng.

"The whale," I said, "the biggest deal in the People's Liberation Army. Remember? The man who founded this club, and the whole money-moving operation. I told you Mr Cho here had established some background on him. Well, he was universally known only as CD. But his real name was CD Wang."

Nobody moved. The information didn't seem to register with either Feng or Dong. And I needed them to work it out, fast.

I looked across the table and nodded at the figure on the end. "And *that* is his son."

Wang looked at me. A cold, impassive stare. He made no move to help.

"Y...y...you mean," said Feng, "Wang here is PLA?"

I nodded. "Right at the top. The business continues. He can start, or stop, anything he wants."

"A three count, and I shoot." The anger had gone from Dong's voice. Calm. Back under control. A bad sign. Execution countdown. And the barrel was still hard at my head.

"One...two...th—"

"Feng," I said, "the book...pass it to Wang. He may need it."

Dong waved the gun in the direction of the board table, and back to me. Feng slid it across. Wang grabbed the book and clasped it under his arm. I could feel my breathing. Harder, faster. This *had* to work.

"No. More. Time." Dong spat each word. "One...two..."

Two breaths for each count. This was it. I screwed my bruised, swollen right eye. That would take the shot. I could see Sally... and little Jack. For the last time.

"...thr—"

"Stop!"

The room held still.

All looked at Wang.

Silence. I counted the seconds in my head. One...two... three...four...five...

Dong shoved the pistol back on my temple.

"I can't help you, Dong," I said. "Only Wang can."

Dong finally registered. He turned, aimed the pistol at Wang's head, and took slow, deliberate steps toward him. Two paces short, he stopped, braced and took dead-aim. The hammer-cock echoed across the room.

Wang's eyes widened. His arm and book trembled. He gulped a breath. The first hint of emotion I'd seen in him…maybe the first for everyone. I strained to hear his voice. It was almost a whisper. "Whatever you have seen, or heard, in here today…all of it."

Wang stared at each person. Feng, CH, Zhou, Ma, me. One at a time.

"Everything."

And last at Dong. "You understand?"

Dong nodded.

"Never happened."

73

Our courtesy limo, a black Rolls Phantom owned by The Golden Mountain Club, pulled up at PSP headquarters at 1:15 p.m. The meeting had taken an hour. It felt like half a lifetime. I farewelled Bynow and Johnny, who were to be transported on to the ferry terminal for their return to Hong Kong.

Johnny said, "I told you at the beginning you were working in exalted company, Ash. Who knew it would be near the top of the Chinese political regime? Different world, eh? And like I said *bīng bù yàn zha*, which means…"

"I know, I know…*nothing is too deceitful in war*. Anyway, you get a copy of *Animal Farm*—you'll enjoy it."

Bynow said, "You sure you want to go home? I thought a little trip here would do you good, but Toddy…I didn't mean it to end like this. I'll find something else for you. Safer…you know?"

I said, "Thanks…but I think I need to go back…get back on the horse, as they say."

Johnny gave me a quizzical look. "What horse? You police… you ride horses…in Australia?"

"No, Johnny…it's just a saying…"

Bynow came to the rescue. "Well, if you want a permanent change, and can stand living here—let me know. I reckon we'd make a damn dazzler of a team. There's a truckload of work, Toddy. You can see that…"

I grabbed my duffel from the boot and sent them off, saying I'd think about it and with a promise to transfer their part of the bounty when it hit my account.

I still didn't like being called 'Toddy'.

The receptionist at PSP was waiting for me. Obviously, someone had worded her up. Probably Feng. I was ushered into a small interview room with another officer.

The paperwork I signed stated that Patrick John Hogan and Wilson Donald Wallis were released from protective custody, and that all their personal belongings were intact. These consisted of money—fifty-three US dollars and some local coins—one mobile phone and two Australian passports. I had no idea if that was all they were carrying, but I signed anyway.

After about seven or eight minutes, they were brought to the small room, first Wallis and then Hogan. The officer left us. They cast nervous, twitchy glances at each other, and at me.

Wallis screwed his eyes at the sight of Hogan. "You look terrible."

Hogan shrugged at him. "Yeah, thanks. Anyway, what's this about? Why are we alone?" The young cop had obviously given him a shower and new clothes. He peered at my face. "Hell, what happened to your head?"

Wallis also gave me a good look-over. "Holy mother…"

I turned to Hogan. "So, Skip, they stop belting you?"

He shuddered a little, and nodded.

"And you, Wallis, they give you some smokes?"

Wallis pulled a pack from his pocket and held it up. "Full pack," he grinned. "And a lighter." A major triumph, it seemed.

"Well, this little nightmare is over. You're free to go."

They both looked at each other again. "You're fucking kidding?" said Wallis. "Who did they arrest instead?"

"Nobody…yet. They're watching the guests. But my guess is in the end, it will still be nobody."

"Ha," Hogan said, his old belligerence returning, "I told you. See, we did nothing. And no-one believed us. No-one."

I placed the money, phone, and passports on the small table. "Cops say this belongs to you two—is this all? I signed for it, but I figured you'd want to get away without another argument."

Wallis looked it over, and scooped up the pile. "That'll do." Then he looked at me and made the strange sucking sound on his teeth. "The Mikes, eh? They must have had some argument with him. Do you think they really did slice him up like that?"

I shrugged. "Oh, they're involved all right. You know, the autopsy was a bit strange—it said there wasn't as much blood as could be expected. I guess like he was on his way out already, before he was knifed. So, the cause of death they put down to the knife, but said it was inconclusive."

"Weird," said Wallis.

"But we'll never know. The Mikes have money, connections, and control. Of the casino, the cops, and us. That's how the system here works. You know they have a saying—*bīng bù yàn zha*—which means 'nothing is too deceitful in war'? Like everywhere else, the spoils go to those at the top. Even though, here, they pretend to share it with the whole country. So whatever war they're running, it is deceitful. What the Mikes say…goes. And right now, they say you are off the hook. That could change any time."

"Then I'm out of here," said Hogan. He looked at me. "What are your plans?"

"Got myself on a flight at 4:30 today. Back to Sydney." I glanced at the wall clock. "Got to get going. What will you two do?"

Hogan pursed his lips. "I need a holiday after this. Caribbean will do me. Had enough of this place."

Wallis said, "But first we have a little task—some money and another passport to collect. Under a mattress." He gave me a quick wink.

"Yeah come on, Wallis, let's go," said Hogan. He was getting impatient again.

Wallis moved over to me. "Don't worry about him—and hey, thanks for getting us out of this shit." He gave me a little dummy punch to the stomach.

"Whoa, careful," I said, "a bit tender."

Hogan looked a bit embarrassed. Sheepish. He held out his hand. "Yeah, thanks, Ash."

I shook his hand, moved to the door and turned back to him. "I've asked you this before, I know, but are you sure we haven't met somewhere?"

Hogan looked away. "And I've told you before…never!"

74

China Eastern flight 2008 idled at Macau airport awaiting clearance to taxi. In seat 23A Ding Jei De sat nervously, wishing the plane would just get moving. He fingered the in-flight magazine, but not reading, and peered out the window at the Philippine Airlines jet alongside. Five minutes after its scheduled departure for San Francisco, the big jet finally moved away from the terminal.

Ding let out an audible sigh of relief. The passenger next to him, a hefty fifty-something American heading home, had his earphones on and heard nothing. Ding looked out the window again and checked the tarmac, just to make sure they really were in motion. He wanted out of there, fast.

The plane taxied out to the island runway, and then came the familiar push as they gained speed and lifted off to the north. Ding could see the big Wynn and MGM casinos off to his left. Next to them lay the Nam Van Lake, and on the other side of it, The Golden Mountain Club. As they climbed, he could just make out the building which housed it. And almost underneath, lay the *Golden Empress*, still stuck in her harbour mooring.

He smiled. Probably for the first time in months, Ding actually felt happy enough to smile a proper smile. It was a feeling he'd almost forgotten. It made him feel good. He leant back and closed his eyes. He felt the vibration of the plane, and allowed it to run right through his body. Then his mind began to wander back.

He thought of his father, beavering away in his medical practice in Hong Kong. And Winston, his boyfriend from long ago. Winston was in the US. He wondered if they would run into each other. Part of him wanted to, and another part didn't. Still, it would be nice to give Winston a little payback for the trauma he'd caused when he left.

He thought of his time in Macau. With his new boobs, gentle face and trim body, he'd become a successful lady-boy. He thought of some of the clients. Many he couldn't remember, particularly from the early days. A rushing swirl of faces, dicks and bodies ran through his brain. Like a giant vegetable soup of human flesh.

All those jobs. Hotel rooms, seedy apartments, flash apartments, lavish casino suites, rear seats of limos, and the occasional local park. Hell there was even one in a lift. He thought of his latest job. And now it was his last...on the *Empress.* His heart jumped a beat as he recalled the sensation of Sebastian Lam with his hands around his neck, entering him from behind. That terrible choking sensation. He could stand the smell of some clients, of whisky and cigarettes on their breath, of stale sweat from too many hours sitting at a card game. He could stand the strange 'other games' some of them liked to play. But he couldn't stand the claustrophobic feeling of being choked.

He thought of his latest, new lover. Mr Grekov. "Call me Vadim, call me Vadim," he would say in his thick Russian accent. But to Ding he was way too old for that. Ding called him Mr Grekov. After a while they struck a deal, and he began to call him 'uncle'. Grekov liked that. "Better—not so formal," he said. Another funny little game, thought Ding.

He thought how much Grekov despised Sebastian. Grekov was rough around the edges, swore a lot and drank much, particularly vodka. But he never hurt anyone physically, as far as Ding could tell. And he hated the sight of Ding after a Sebastian encounter. All that belting—and the bruises it left. It was pure coincidence that the three of them should end up on the same cruise. He would never have taken the job, had he known Grekov would be there too. Bound to cause trouble of some sort.

He thought about the night Sebastian died. Ah, yes. That night. How Grekov had sought him out, and found him up on the sundeck. In the jacuzzi. Right after the security guy, Ash Todd, had been speaking to him and suggested he go back to Sebastian. To cheer him up, for God's sake.

"Look what he does to you," Grekov had said. "This is criminal, and you can't get away from him. While you are in Macau, he will own you. Or most of you. I know him…and his business. He might even kill you. There's only one way out—you'll have to kill him."

"I couldn't kill anyone," Ding said.

"You can, and you will. I will help you, and no-one will ever know," said Grekov.

He remembered how he went back down to Sebastian's suite. Sebastian was sitting on the edge of the bed, naked and in a foul mood. "Damn those clients," he had snapped. "Bastards the lot of them. And Hogan, the drunk—even he wants my money. I need some relief." Sebastian had then dropped to the floor, on his back, and demanded, "Get the leather and screw me."

He recalled how he'd found a knife earlier in the evening, sitting on top of a low cupboard. It appeared to be a big, black hunting knife of some sort. He'd never seen it before. Ding had moved to place it in the cupboard, and Sebastian had said, "No, don't put it there, put it here," indicating the bedside drawer. He even wondered if Sebastian might use it to kill *him*.

He then opened the bedside drawer to fetch the leather, the noose which Sebastian liked around his own neck. And now the knife lay beside it. He had taken both out. Sebastian had his eyes closed, in blissful anticipation, so didn't see a thing. He remembered how he gradually tightened the noose, with Sebastian repeating over and over, "Yeah baby, yeah baby. Tighter, tighter."

He thought how easy this little ritual had become. How smoothly the leather slipped tighter, and how much Sebastian liked it. No. Loved it. How he had slipped it tight, really tight, and then started entering Sebastian. Just as he liked. No. Loved. And he twisted that leather tighter, and tighter. Sebastian had said something, but it was just a gurgle, and he remembered how he couldn't understand what it was. Perhaps Sebastian was saying how much he loved it.

He recalled how Sebastian then went quiet, and stopped moving. Sensing an opportunity Ding reached over, picked up the knife, and plunged it into Sebastian's stomach. And his chest. Again and again. Then he'd heard a knock at the door. He stopped, and listened. He heard a voice, a hoarse Russian whisper.

Grekov was outside calling him. He opened the door. Grekov wobbled in, carrying a large cleaver.

He remembered Grekov saying, "See, I knew it…you can kill. Excellent shit." And Grekov dragged Sebastian into the bathroom. Grekov called out, "Anything else you want to do to him?" Ding remembered he'd taken the hunting knife, and slit Sebastian down through his belly. Then he'd sliced off his dick, and thrown it into the bath. Grekov then said, "You go outside. Clean up."

He recalled hearing some loud thumps as he got dressed. Grekov had appeared holding Sebastian's head. He remembered thinking he would throw up, but Grekov said, "You go, you go…back to the jacuzzi. I'll fix this." That's the last thing he could remember of that night. And the police had hardly questioned him. But he did have something on the cops. On one of them.

One face stood out from the 'vegetable soup'. Not for any particular reason, except that for the most part you'd never see a face a second time. But this one turned up on the *Empress*. Chief Feng. And maybe Feng recognised him. Feng would be desperate to avoid any connection to Miss Jay-Dee. Maybe that's why he went easy. So, 'uncle' did fix it—somehow. He wondered if he might see 'uncle' again one day. It all seemed a bit of a dream.

Ding heard the sound of a bell. A soft tone, two rings. He opened his eyes, and looked up. He thought he was dreaming, and then realised the sign saying seatbelts could be removed had come on. He wasn't dreaming. No, sir, he was on his way to the US. And then to Rio. A new life awaited.

No more was he Miss Jay-Dee. The breast implants had

flattened against his shirt—they'd have to come out—long eyelashes peeled off, hair cut short to almost a buzz-cut. No makeup. Heck, he even had a tiny stubble shoot appearing. Yes, he still liked men, but as a man, not in drag. Miss Jay-Dee was gone—consigned to history. And in his bank account, the sum of three million United States dollars. A present from 'uncle'. To help him start his new life.

It made Ding Jei De smile.

75

The taxi delivered me to the front door of my apartment block about eight in the morning. My plane was an early arrival, dropping in a little after six—the second or third flight touching down after the end of the night curfew. I slid the key into the lock, and pushed open the door.

The last time I was here, I'd felt like I was on another planet. I couldn't get the thought of Sally or little Jack out of my head. Every conversation, every noise, for some reason seemed to bring them to front of mind. I didn't know whether I wanted that feeling, that memory, to stay or leave. If it left, would I be betraying them?

The apartment was dark, warm and smelled a little musty. I pulled apart the curtains, and opened the door onto the little balcony. The familiar salty breeze wafted up from the harbour below. That felt better. Cooler.

I sat on the sofa, and listened for sounds. Before I'd left there was an accident outside. I remembered how the sound of it brought back the sound of my own crash. And the sickening feeling that went with it. But now I couldn't bring up the sound of either. Maybe that was a good thing. But I didn't want to forget Sally or little Jack.

I checked the fridge. No food much. What there was would be stale. I needed milk. And eggs. And bread. There was a small convenience store a couple of doors up the street. I threw my duffel on the bed, and strolled up. The owner greeted me with, "Hey, Ash, been up to anything? Haven't seen you for a few days."

"Not much, Mr Strong, just a little trip away."

"Work or holiday? Where'd you go?"

"Oh, just up to Asia—you know? Get away for a bit."

"Good idea, what with your troubles. Nice relaxing place, that Asia, eh?"

I gave him a weak smile, collected my bag of food, and headed for home, but decided to continue down the hill to Vince Lombardi's mechanic shop.

"Heyyyy, Ash," said Vince, "where you been? You bought a new car yet? Not a bloody convertible, eh? You better drop her in before you do…so I can check her over. Jesus, Mary and Joseph…what happened to your face…?"

"But you haven't got any room here, Vince. Place is full."

"Not you worry—I'll fit her in." He threw his arms round in a big circle. "Look, so many cars…all the time…and no money. The business she's no good. I'm gonna give her away, y'know?"

"I know, I know…okay, I'll drop her in before I buy."

I retraced my steps back up the hill. The place seemed happy. Normal. People just doing their thing. Quite the opposite to the *Golden Empress.* I needed to go back to work, I decided. Give it another whirl. If it was no good, I had options. Bruce Bynow and Johnny Cho for starters. That might be an interesting move. And

Venus was there. I could still smell her shampoo. And her Jo Malone. But one thought nagged—was she part of Sebastian's Russian troupe?

I made myself breakfast, showered and changed, and rang in to the AFP office. McPherson thundered, "Ash, welcome back, glad to hear you're so well…but is this a bit too soon? You can take longer."

"No Mac…I need to come back."

"Well, your desk is ready—nothing's been moved—and there's work to start on, right now, if you're up to it."

I put a call in to Fothers. It went to voicemail, so I left a message…*How's the second most beautiful woman in the world? I'm back from my exotic trip to Asia, and I thought you might like lunch. Call me when you can.*

By eleven o'clock I was firmly seated in my old chair, at AFP headquarters in Goulburn Street. I booted up the computer. Dozens of emails flooded in. Most were of the 'so sorry for your loss' variety. People were kind, but I didn't want to read them. Plenty of time for that later.

The notifier on the computer went off with a 'ping', and a message appeared in the bottom right corner. Sally's birthday. Tomorrow. A little reminder I'd set up months ago. My heart sank—I'd completely forgotten. I sat for a moment, head in hands. Tears welled up and I blinked hard to clear them. I had to get past this.

Dick Mayvers sauntered in and put an arm across my shoulder. "Heyyy, mate—you sure you should be here? It's barely been a week, and a tough one according to Bynow. You really okay?"

I looked up, gave him a weak smile and pointed at my head. "What do *you* think?"

He looked at my face and poked a finger at my half-closed eye. I snapped my head back—defence on auto-pilot.

"Hell…I think Bynow's right," he said.

"Catch any crooks while I was away?"

"No," grumbled Dick, "geez they're slippery, some of them. Cunning. Anyway, if you're up for it, this is one they want us to get on to—we got a tip-off the prime suspect may have resurfaced. You did some work on it a while back, and the fraud guys reckon if we look hard enough, we might be able to find him."

Dick clicked a couple of files on my computer, and a case opened up. Dick continued, "This investment banker bloke—pissed off with eleven mill a couple of years ago. Name's Brendan O'Hara. You remember him?"

"Brendan O'Hara? Hmm, vaguely. Wasn't he some cold case I looked at after Sally, you know…had died?"

"Yeah, well I'll refresh your memory. This might help—here's an updated picture of him." He brought up a photo.

I looked at the snap now taking up the full screen. My mind went blank. I looked at it again.

I said, "You are *kidding*? Is this for real?" I stabbed the monitor. "This is O'Hara?"

Dick gave me a look of 'who else would it be'? He said, "From Ireland they say…that's him. Why?"

I slammed my fist on the desk. Everything jumped. I bellowed, "Unbelievable." Dick looked nervous.

Staring back at me, from my own computer, was a clear-as-day mug-shot, of Patrick John Hogan.

And I knew where he was headed.

Also by Ross Crothers

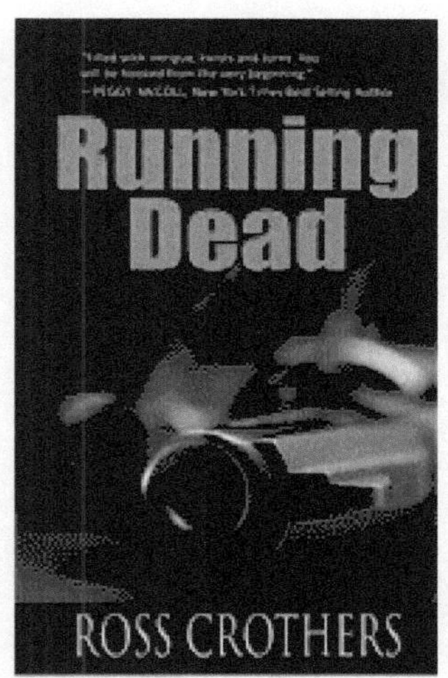

"Filled with intrigue, twists and turns, you'll be captivated from the very start. Very rarely a book comes along that hooks you from the beginning, and holds you to the very end."

Peggy McColl
New York Times Best-Selling Author

"For those who love a good mystery and intrigue – this is the book for you, it is an adventurous, nail-biting read, full of action, danger and conspiracy."

—Nicua Shamira - Terraverum - Blog

ABOUT THE AUTHOR

Before turning to writing, ROSS CROTHERS spent much of his working life in the world of international trade and finance.

Characters and events from these years inspired his first Ash Todd thriller, Running Dead. Dead Man's Cut is the second.

He and his wife live in rural Australia.

Visit

www.rosscrothers.com

www.facebook.com/rosscrothersauthor

www.twitter.com/RossCrothers

www.ingramcontent.com/pod-product-compliance
Lightning Source LLC
Chambersburg PA
CBHW021403110726
47901CB00008B/2038

* 9 7 8 0 6 4 8 1 7 7 1 0 4 *